CW01619916

KARMA CLUB

HARBINDER MATHADU

Copyrighted Material

First published in 2021

Copyright © Harbinder Mathadu, 2021

The right of Harbinder Mathadu to be identified as the author of this work has been asserted by him in accordance with the Copyright, Design and Patents Act 1988

ISBN: 978-1-5272-9096-9

ALSO AVAILABLE BY HARBINDER MATHADU

The Stolen Soul of Somita

'Hope not ever to see heaven.

I have come to lead you to the other shore;

Into eternal darkness;

Into fire and into ice'

Dante Alighieri, Inferno

PROLOGUE

The village lay still and peaceful in the darkness that shrouded its streets and alleyways. A serene quietness caressed the flat roofed homes as families lay in their beds snug and safe. The slight chill in the air had kept the villagers huddled up in their homes away from the roof tops that would become their bedrooms in the sweltering summer heat. Even the stray dogs had settled down for the night after a tiring day of scavenging. They lay together in groups under the banyan trees close by to the dozing cows that occasionally opened their drooping eyes to swish a fly with their tails.

The market stalls all stood crooked, resting after a long day of being hustled and trampled on by the haggling villagers. The main street, which during the day was friendly and popular, now lay lonely with only rubbish and scraps of food for company. Even the police station, with its empty cell had given up trying to find a tenant for the night.

With no street lights, the darkness swallowed the North Indian village within its belly and awaited first light. Nothing stirred, even the serpent lay silent and still in the tall grass of the sugarcane field. It rested in the shadow of a tractor, enjoying the quietness and cool breeze until her senses caught a smell of movement in the air. She emerged from her hiding place and slithered through the tall grass and headed towards the sleeping village. She passed the homes on the outskirts and then moved deeper, searching for the disturbance that so rudely awoke her. She moved softly into the market square, passed the bakery, through the iron mongers alley and headed towards the school playground.

It was here that she found the reason for her broken sleep. Three boys were huddled together in the corner of the playground. They were sitting under a wooden bike hut whispering conversations that the serpent misunderstood for hissing. She crept closer until she could see the whites of one of the boy's eyes. The serpent brushed against the foot of the boy who sat with his back to her and then slithered to a position where they could all see her.

Raj was fumbling in the pocket of his hooded fleece top looking for the pack of cigarettes he had concealed there when he looked up and met the round yellow eyes of the snake. He stopped fumbling and froze. The night suddenly felt darker and colder, he wanted to run but he knew from the stories his father had told him that running would be the worst thing to do. After a few seconds he regained his composure and sent a warning to his friends.

'Manoj, Vijay don't move a muscle, there is a snake sitting behind you,'

The two boys also froze, uncertain whether to believe their friend or not. To not believe was too high a risk and Raj wouldn't lie to them, so they both sat still. They sat in silence for a few heartbeats.

'What shall we do?' whispered Manoj.

'My father says that snakes don't like loud noises,' whispered Vijay.

'Why are we whispering then,' commented Manoj.

Vijay thought about the question and shrugged his shoulders.

'I don't know anything about snakes so let's try to scare it like Vijay said. On the count of three we should all

stamp our feet and clap as loud as possible,' suggested Raj.
'Are you sure Raj? We don't want to annoy it,' replied Manoj, sweat dripping from his forehead.
'We don't have a choice,' Raj replied.
Raj started counting down and as soon as he reached one, all three boys stomped their feet and clapped their hands as loud as they could. The snake hissed but quickly decided that the terrible noise was not worth the effort, so she slithered away to find another cool shadow to sleep in.
The three boys sat frozen for a few more moments until they were sure the snake was gone and then with a huge sigh of relief burst into laughter and patted each other on the back. Raj once again started his search for the pack of cigarettes and this time found them. He pulled them from his pocket and put them on the hard mud floor between the three of them. Vijay looked around sheepishly making sure no one was around and placed a box of matches next to the pack. The three boys looked at each other, their eyes daring one another to be the first to pick up the pack of cigarettes. They sat in silence for over a minute until Manoj snatched up the packet and removed the only cigarette within it. He rolled it around his fingers, feeling the texture and placed it into his mouth. He then removed it from his mouth, enjoying the grown up feeling it was giving him. Raj lifted the match box; removing a match, he set it alight and held it up as an offering to the cigarette. The soft glow of the match covered the three boys in an ethereal light pushing back the oppressive darkness in the hut.
Raj moved the match slowly towards the cigarette in Manoj's hand, all the while holding his breath for fear of blowing it out. There was only one more match in the

box. The young boy held the flame to the tobacco until a faint red glow appeared and the tobacco caught light. All three boys looked in wonder as the smoke danced upwards and disappeared into the night. Manoj lifted the cigarette into his mouth and took a long drag; he erupted into a coughing fit and immediately shoved it towards Raj.

Raj took hold of the cigarette and without hesitation also took a long drag; he blew out smoke like an eighty a day smoker. He lifted the cigarette and prepared to take another puff but stopped when he heard raised voices coming from somewhere in the village. He looked at the other boys with concern written over his face. Had they discovered that they were not in their beds?

'We need to get back home, quickly!' said Raj urgently. Jumping up, he threw the cigarette to the floor and put it out with his sandal.

'If we can get back without anyone seeing us, we can sneak back into our homes.'

The other two boys nodded and also jumped up and turned towards home. That's when they noticed the huge plume of smoke that was floating into the night sky like the shadow of a demon rising from a furnace of red flames. The boys stood staring into the vision of hell for what seemed like forever and then slowly, as the paralysis freed them, they started to run franticly toward the blaze. As they ran through the alleyways and streets, the shouts and screams of the villagers grew louder. Approaching the village square, they saw a line of men forming a human chain carrying buckets of water from the village well. The boys ran past them and onwards towards the fire. The oppressive heat from the flames started to wrap its warm arms around the boys. Sweat dripped from their foreheads and their lungs burned but

they ran on as panic filled their hearts.
Whose house was burning?
As the boys turned the corner of Parijan Road, they came to a sudden stop and looked upon the inferno that was engulfing the home directly in front of them. Men and women were running back and forth with buckets of water that were being swallowed up greedily by the angry fire. A large crowd stood staring in disbelief a safe distance away. Raj looked into the crowd and spotted his neighbour and ran to him in dread. He reached the man and pulled on his white tunic.
'Where is my family!' he shouted, looking at the burning house with tears already filling his eyes.
The elderly man looked down at the boy in disbelief and grabbed hold of his shoulders.
'Raj, what are you doing here?' he shouted.
'I was in the school yard with Manoj and Vijay,' Raj shouted, 'they all got out right?' Raj asked in hope.
The man fell silent and pulled him close in a tight hug. Floods of tears swelled up in Raj's eyes and his body started to shake uncontrollably. He looked towards his burning home and thoughts of his mother, father, two brothers and sister engulfed in flames overcame him. His body went limp as he slipped into an unconsciousness filled with terror and deep sadness, a sadness that would stay with him and torture him for the rest of his life.

CHAPTER ONE

The darkness consumed the chilled air of the tiny one-bedroom flat that sat looking embarrassed above the kebab shop on South Ealing Road. The confined kitchen lay silent and empty in the corner of the flat, unused and unloved. The cupboards lay bare; a gallon of milk and a couple of bottles of Stella Artois were the only company the fridge kept. The threadbare living room with its one armchair, coffee table and television bore the weight of a dozen takeaway meals. Foil cartons, pizza boxes, cans of fizzy drink and fragments of unfinished food decorated the floor and table. The walls held no memories; they held no love, no photos of family, girlfriends, friends or holiday snaps. The room spoke of sadness, of neglect, of loneliness, of pain and of suffering.

In the bedroom, a haunted figure sat up wide awake staring into the darkness. The single bed lay against one wall and a wardrobe against another. Again, the walls were bare and nothing else filled the room. Raj lifted his mobile phone and checked the time. There were still a few minutes left. He lay still, his breathing shallow but he could feel the anxiety beginning to rise in the pit of his stomach. He recognised the feelings but had no control over them. They had overcome him, they had possessed him and he had been living with them every night for the past fourteen years. He checked the time again: one minute left. He lifted the pack of cigarettes and matches from the floor next to his bed. He waited until exactly one fifty-two in the morning and then lit the match. He stared intensely into the small flame for a few moments and then held it to the cigarette. The tobacco caught alight and sent smoke spiralling into the darkness. Raj held the cigarette between his lips and took a deep drag, allowing the nicotine time to make its way into his lungs. He breathed out. He repeated the ritual until the cigarette grew smaller and smaller and all the while his thoughts were four thousand miles and fourteen years away. He felt again the heat of the fire as it swallowed his home and engulfed his family. He felt again his soul being ripped from him as a spark of fear touched his mind and became his constant nemesis. That fear had stayed and festered within him, controlling him, growing inside him, talking to him, sending him into despair.

He pushed the stub of the cigarette into the ash tray that lay next to the bed and climbed out. He felt a shiver as the cold air ran over his body penetrating him to the bone. He walked over to the wardrobe, picked out some warm clothes and got dressed. In the bathroom, he splashed cold water over his face and ran a hand over his stubble. He decided against a shave and instead brushed his teeth and then picked up his coat from by the front door and left the flat. The January freeze was in full effect and he lifted the collars of his coat and tucked his hands into his pockets. The streets were deserted and peaceful; it was his favourite part of the day as it took him back to a moment before the fire, when everything was as it should be. Those minutes before the fire with his friends smoking in the bike shelter were his last memories of happiness.

He walked for twenty minutes down St Mary's Road and entered the Karma Club. He gave a nod to Sam at the door, who let him straight in. The thumping bass and strobing lights hit his senses, but he paid no attention to them. He had no desire for dancing or listening to the horrid music, but he also didn't want to be alone with his thoughts at home and this was the only place open in Ealing at this time. He ordered a Jack Daniels at the bar and went over to the furthest corner of the club and sat down in the shadows. There was another reason that drew him to this club time and again and he scanned the club looking for her. She worked as a bartender and it was always a gamble whether he picked the right night for her shift. So far it looked as though he had picked wrong again. He sipped his drink as he looked out over the dance floor and felt a mixture of pity and envy for all the clubbers. Pity because he knew the majority of them were there to fill some kind of emptiness in their lives, a dull job, no meaningful relationship, no future and no hope. Envy because he wished he could be as carefree as them. Even though their lives had no meaning, they still laughed, danced and pretended everything was perfect. They all wore masks that would come off in the loneliness of their homes when the sadness returned.

As he stared through the crowded dance floor, he saw the girl walking towards the bar. His eyes followed her as she took her position behind the bar and poured a drink for a guy who could barely stand. He tried focusing on her expression but she was too far away and the flashing lights disguised her face. He took hold of his glass, emptied it in one go and then started to walk towards the bar, but he froze. His legs no longer functioned and the panic started to rise within him. He looked deep into the empty glass hoping for an answer but none came. Eventually he sat back down and placed his head in his hands. He had been through this motion a dozen times and the result was always the same. He couldn't pluck up the courage to talk to the girl and the night would always end with him skulking out of the club, hoping that she didn't see him.

He decided it was that time again and stood to leave but as he turned towards the exit, he was met with her hazel eyes. She looked at him and smiled. She was saying something, but he couldn't make out the words. His ears felt muffled, not because of the music but because his head had started spinning. He felt as if a cloud had come over him and it threatened to engulf him. She was still talking and now she was pointing towards his glass. He took a couple of deep breaths, slowed his heart rate down and slowly her words began to form and make sense.

'Do you want a re-fill?' she was asking.

Raj looked at the glass and all he could do was nod his head like an idiot. She smiled again, picked up his glass and walked away. He was confused. Should he follow or wait there? He decided to follow because she wouldn't know what drink he wanted. He followed her through the crowd, hypnotised by her movements. He watched her as she went around the bar and started pouring him a Jack Daniels. He sat on one of the stools as she placed the drink in front of him.

'How did you know?'

'It's my job,' she replied.

Raj got out his wallet to pay.

'This one's on the house.'

'I don't understand.'

'I've seen you come in here for months and you always order the same drink and sit on the same table way out there in the corner. I wanted to get you out here in front.'

'Why?'

'Why not? No one should be alone.'

The girl paused and looked at the man in front her. She had noticed the way he always looked at her but also that he couldn't look her straight in the eyes, if she was anywhere close. He wore sadness like a heavy cloak and over the last few weeks she had started looking out for him. Through his despair, she saw a person whose soul was good but that soul was being controlled by

demons. She wanted to help.
'Listen, I finish my shift in half an hour. Why don't we walk round the corner and grab something to eat?' the girl suggested.
Raj hesitated for a split second as the anxiety threatened to force him to flee but he knew that he couldn't blow his chance of getting to know her.
'Ok, sounds good,'
The girl smiled and put out her hand, 'Names Gabby.'
'Raj,' he replied.
Raj grabbed hold of her hand and felt a sudden spark of light somewhere in the depths of his being. A place which he thought had been lost and that he would never feel again and for the first time in a very long time he smiled.

*****

Deepak Chopra had been in the UK police force for fourteen years and was feeling apprehensive about his impending retirement. His health was declining and the long hours and the physical strain of the job were beginning to take their toll but being a detective constable in London had its upside. He had built up a network of lowlifes from the city he patrolled. He always volunteered for the night shifts because that was when all the misfits and scum would creep out of their hiding places like cockroaches. The drug dealers, the hookers, addicts, drunks, pimps and the desperate who could be manipulated and were willing to do anything for the next fix. He would miss the power of the position he held and the control that he possessed over these pitiful creatures. His sombre thoughts were dragged back down to earth by the trainee constable sat next to him in the car.

‘What are your plans after you retire, Sir, if you don’t mind me asking?’

Deepak paused for a moment as he mulled over the question in his head. He had given this a great deal of thought over the past few months but hadn’t decided on which path to take.

‘I was thinking of going back home,’ he answered.

‘Back to Birmingham?’

‘To India, you idiot!’ snapped the detective.

The constable didn’t seem to notice the annoyance in the detective’s voice. ‘I’ve always wanted to go to India; Bombay would be my first choice and then Delhi. Which part of India are you from then?’

Deepak ignored the constable’s question and instead instructed him to turn at the next left. They drove halfway down the road and then Deepak motioned for him to pull up. The constable parked up on Rectory Road and both men climbed out of the police car. The lights on top of the Ford Focus flashed silently turning the darkness into a disco of blue light. The two men walked towards a lonely figure that lurked in the shadow of a building, his hood covering the top half of his face. The man shifted nervously from foot to foot and dug his hands deep inside his tracksuit bottoms. Deepak approached the shadowy figure, who averted his eyes and stared down at a piece of chewing gum stuck on the concrete floor.

‘What are you doing here, Carl?’ asked Deepak.

Carl looked nervously at the detective and shrugged his shoulders. ‘Waiting for a friend, boss,’ he said, again averting his eyes not wanting to meet the stern gaze of the detective.

‘Really, at two-thirty in the morning, that must be a damn good friend of yours. What’s your friend’s name Carl?’

‘Name’s Jack boss. He’s not from round here so you won’t know him so don’t worry about it. I don’t think he’s

gonna turn up anyhow so I'm gonna be on my way.' He shrugged and shuffled his feet again.
'Mark, go back to the car and wait there. I won't be long, just want to have a quiet chat with my old buddy here.'
It had been a long night and Mark couldn't be bothered to argue so he walked back to the car, climbed into the driver's seat, put the radio on and closed his eyes.
Carl shifted his feet again and started to move away from the detective trying to avoid the putrid smell coming from his mouth. Deepak moved closer in, blocking his path.
'We both know that you are not telling the truth, Carl. There's no friend coming to meet you, is there? Do you know how I know that? I know because you haven't got any friends, Carl. You see, people like you are worthless and don't deserve friends. You don't deserve any love. Even your mother abandoned you when you were a child because she knew you would amount to nothing. Drifting through life like a bum high on whatever shit comes your way.'
Deepak paused and from his trouser pocket produced a packet of cigarettes. He took out a lighter from his coat pocket and lit the cigarette. He silently took a couple of drags, blowing the smoke into Carl's face.
'I've told you this before Carl, I am your only friend on the streets. I've always looked after you and made sure that you haven't ended up in a prison cell with a bunch of perverts. Haven't I?'
'Yes boss,' replied Carl despondently still looking at the chewing gum on the floor.
'Let me see your arm, Carl,' demanded the detective.
'I haven't done anything wrong!' replied Carl in a more forceful tone than he had intended. The fear of what was about to happen had made him panic.
'Just lift your sleeve please, Carl. Don't make me ask

you again!'
Carl reluctantly lifted his jacket sleeve and revealed his forearm to the detective. He closed his fist tight and looked away from him.
Deepak shook his head. 'Fresh needle marks, Carl, that's not good.'
'Listen, I just needed it this one time. I've been feeling low and its cold sleeping out on the streets. You got to believe me.'
'If you do bad things, Carl, then bad things will happen to you. It's called karma.'
The detective brought up the hand that held the cigarette and slowly lowered it down towards Carl's arm, pressing the burning end onto his forearm. Carl clenched his teeth but refused to scream or cry. Deepak pushed the cigarette deeper into his skin until he could smell burning flesh and then slowly released it. As he released it, the detective closed his eyes and felt the usual flow of arousal course through his body. He held onto the feeling for a few moments and then opened his eyes.
'Now show me what you have,' asked the detective holding out his hand.
Carl reached into his pocket and removed a small packet of white powder and handed it to the detective. Deepak took the packet, patting Carl on the shoulder, walked back to the car and climbed into the passenger seat.
They drove further on to Horne Lane and then left into Steyne Road in the direction of the police station. It had been a long night and Deepak knew that he still had a couple of hours of paperwork to complete before he could go home. He looked out of the window and stared into the darkness of a town that was ridden with crime and poverty. He looked at the tall foreboding tower blocks that silhouetted the shadowy skyline and thought of all the miserable people who lived their meek lives

within its walls. He had lost count of how many times he had made their lives a little more miserable. He felt a pang of sadness, not for the people he had abused with his authority but for himself. He would miss this life and that was one reason he was being drawn back towards India. Back home, there were limitless downtrodden lives that he could prey on and thus continue to satisfy the hunger inside of him. As they drove past the tower blocks, the detective looked into the deserted car park of a Morrisons supermarket and saw the outline of a man crawling towards the main road.

Deepak instructed the constable to pull up. He climbed out of the car and walked towards the car park with Mark following close behind. He could see the figure was now lying still with his face buried into the concrete. He quickened his pace and as he grew closer, he noticed a dark pool of blood slowly seeping from underneath the body.

'Mark, phone for an ambulance!' the detective shouted. Deepak approached the body and bending down, he grabbed hold of the man and turned him around. He staggered back and stared at the horror in front of him. The man lying on the floor had a face that had been beaten so badly, his features were barely recognisable. His lips were swollen and teeth were missing from the front of his mouth. His eyes were bruised and covered in blood and a jagged cut started from the middle of his forehead and finished at the bottom of his chin. A cut had been made on both sides of his lips giving him a false smile. The detective looked at his face and then looked at the man's torso. He noticed that his buttons were undone and so squatting down, he opened up the man's blood-soaked white shirt. Blood dripped from several knife cuts on the man's torso and as Deepak looked at the cuts, a number started to reveal itself. He

stood up and looked at the man's chest from above. There in the middle of his chest was carved a large number seven, which appeared to have a circle drawn around it.
Mark came and stood next to the detective and upon seeing the body covered his mouth and turning around he threw up. The sound of an ambulance and more police cars could be heard approaching in the distance. The detective looked at the body in fascination and felt the familiar sense of excitement as he always did when faced with the suffering and pain of others. His dark and solemn mood had suddenly lifted as he sensed that the last few weeks of his police career would at least bring a fresh challenge.

*****

The fast-food restaurant sat empty and silent as a young man swept the floor pausing every few moments to enjoy a great yawn. Outside, the occasional person walked by, hands tucked deep inside their pockets to ward off the bitter wind. Inside, Raj wringed his hands trying to suppress the nervousness he was feeling but he also felt as though he was caught in some sort of illusion, an alternate reality where he was a different person with a better life. He was sat opposite the most beautiful girl he had ever seen. She radiated a serenity that washed over him, cleansing the pain within him. He watched her as she attacked a vegetable burger with great zeal; even with a mouth full of food, she looked radiant.
'So how come you always sit by yourself in that favourite corner of yours? Like some baddie from a James Bond film hiding in the shadows. I half expected you to be stroking a cat when I came up to you today,' said Gabby.

'Just prefer my own company, I suppose,' Raj replied.
'I'll get my coat then,' replied Gabby with a smile.
'No sorry, I didn't mean...,' said Raj hastily. He hadn't seen her smile as he was too busy trying to avoid looking directly at her.
'I was only yanking your chain,' she interrupted.
'Sorry.'
'And stop apologising!'
Raj was about to apologise again but stopped himself at the last moment and then stared into his chips feeling embarrassed.
'It's fine to enjoy your own company, but it's also nice to share things with others. I don't have many friends but working at the club means I get to meet all sorts of people and that's fun.'
'I get uncomfortable around new people and always come across a bit awkward, so I find it hard to make friends.'
'Why do you feel awkward?'
'I feel they are judging me.'
'Why?'
'Everything really, the way I look, my clothes, my strange accent.'
'There's nothing wrong with the way you look, dress and that accent of yours is rather interesting,' reassured Gabby.
'Thanks, you're very generous but being bullied for years at school for the way you look, dress and talk does leave its mark. I could hardly talk English when I first arrived and I've never been able to shake off this slight Indian accent. That's why I chose a career in software development so I wouldn't have to talk to anyone.' replied Raj.
'Children can be very mean,' replied Gabby.
'Sorry Gabby, I don't want to burden you with my

problems. Let's talk about something far more interesting.'
'What?'
'You,'
'Not that interesting then.'
'So how long have you worked at the club?' asked Raj.
'About three months.'
'What were you doing before that?'
'I travel a lot, so I was in Australia.'
'That's a big place to be, all at once.'
'Have you ever been to Australia?' asked Gabby deflecting Raj's question.
'No, I was born in India and have only lived in London since I was thirteen. Apart from that I haven't seen any other part of the world.'
'Why did you leave India?'
Raj sat in silence for a few moments trying to gather his thoughts. He didn't want to say anything that would frighten her away. He liked her and felt drawn towards her, but his past was full of hurt and he didn't want her taking on his pain. He knew he could be distant and was prone to mood swings that could last for days. There was so much that he couldn't tell her, but he needed to explain why he preferred his own company and found it hard to make friends. At school he struggled in English so was naturally drawn to computers. He had chosen to work freelance so he could work from home whenever he needed the money and that way he could avoid having to meet his clients face to face. He looked up from his chips and met Gabby's gaze. Suddenly he felt as though he could tell her anything.
'My village, Sufipind was like a small piece of paradise in the heart of Jalandhar. There was a harmonious mix of cultures that thrived there, Hindus, Sikhs and Muslims all living together peacefully. It was covered with lush green

fields growing wheat, corn and sugarcane. I remember spending countless summer days with my friends playing Lagori in the sugarcane fields and eating the curries and chapatis that mother had packed for us.
'What's Lagori?' asked Gabby.
'It's a game where you have to try and knock over a stack of stones with a rubber ball and then try to build it up again while being hit by the opposing team with the ball. It's a lot more fun than it sounds, trust me.'
'I trust you,' replied Gabby sincerely.
'I was a bit of a mischievous boy and was always getting into trouble. Not serious trouble but silly little things like stealing milk from Mr Chatteerjee's house or bunking off from school to go wondering around the markets. I'd always get caught and be dragged in front of my mother by my captor. My mother would apologise profoundly, tell me off, but then give me the biggest hug. There's nothing quite like a mother's hug to make everything better.' Raj paused as images of his smiling mother floated around his head. He could still feel the tightness of her hug and the smell of frying on her clothes. She would always cover for him when their father arrived home and everything in the world had seemed good.
'Sounds like a very happy childhood,' said Gabby.
'It was, but everything changed one April night when as usual I was being mischievous and I had persuaded my best friends to sneak out in the middle of the night. I had stolen a packet of cigarettes from my English teacher, Mr Joseph, earlier that day. It was way past midnight when we sneaked out and ran to the school yard and there under the bike hut, we lit the cigarette and dared each other to smoke it and that's when my life changed for ever. I was thirteen years old and my entire family died that night in a fire that possessed my home.'
'I'm so sorry Raj; I can't imagine what that must have felt

like.'
Raj looked into Gabby's eyes and looked for the pity he thought would be there but all he saw was a genuine concern. That night had shaped the rest of his life up to that point. He had never spoken to anyone, let alone a stranger, about that night and hearing himself say the words out loud felt liberating. It felt like an out of body experience, where he was floating above two strangers, talking about the lives of someone else.
'That night, I lay in my friend's home terrified about what would happen to me with my parents dead. I started thinking that the fire and the death of my family must be my fault. I had been punished as everyone had said I would be, for being mischievous. God had made something bad happen to teach me a lesson. It was me who stole the cigarettes, not my friends but me. I've carried that guilt with me for the past fourteen years and every minute of every day I feel a hollow pain in my chest that just wants to be fed with sorrow.'
Gabby instinctively took hold of Raj's hands and held them gently. The touch of her hands seemed to pull his floating body back down into him. He felt a huge wave of relief at sharing his guilt with another person and not being judged.
'Raj, I know one thing for sure! God would not punish a small boy for smoking by killing his entire family in a fire. God is gracious and righteous; he is full of compassion. What happened to your family was an accident. There was nothing you could have done about it. You must not feel guilty about it and you should not abandon your faith and your belief in God.'
'I have abandoned my faith but my belief in God is as strong as it has ever been.'
'I don't understand, Raj; you can't have one without the other?'

‘My belief is strong because you can’t believe in God without believing in the devil and I’m certain that Satan lives here on Earth.’
‘How so?’ asked Gabby holding tighter onto Raj’s hands.
‘There is so much pain and grief in this world and God does nothing to stop it. I ask you, which compassionate God would allow a small child’s family to die? So that is why I believe in Him but have no faith in Him,’
Gabby got out from her seat and walked around the table to sit next to Raj. She put a comforting arm around him and for a while the mad chattering voice of Satan fell silent.

CHAPTER TWO

The boy crouched in the corner of the wardrobe and tried to stop the shivering that had taken control of his body. It wasn't the cold that was causing his shivers but fear. He held a hand to his mouth in the hope that the man would not hear the sobs. For the last few weeks, he had tried his best to stay out of his way but even so there were times when the man got so drunk that nothing would stop him. Every evening, he would sit in his room and hear the key turn in the front door and pray that his uncle hadn't been drinking. When sober, he would not even acknowledge him and made cold remarks about him to the rest of his family.

Those were the good days.

He could tell within a few heartbeats of the man coming home whether he was drunk or not. If he was, then his wife would get it first. He would look for any excuse to start an argument and then the shouting would begin. The argument would always end the same way with blood and bruises for the wife and the night's dinner over the kitchen floor. He would then stagger up the stairs shouting obscenities. He would stumble into little Kiran's room and yell incoherent instructions to her, but she always escaped a beating, perhaps because she was a girl and his child. Then it was the scrounging boy's turn and the man would first stop outside his door allowing a brief calm before the storm. Within a few heartbeats, the door would be kicked open and a volley of abuse would be hurled his way. Finally, when he had worked himself into a rage, he would lash out at the boy. He never attacked the face as that would alert teachers at school so he always went for the body. There was never any

remorse in the man's eyes or any guilt, even when the alcohol had worn off.
The boy heard the footsteps coming up the stairs and held his breath. He heard his uncle's muffled shouts and then the silence. He dared not breathe and prayed to God that he had walked past his room. The silence grew and hope filled the boy's heart and for a split second the shivers stopped, but then the door was flung open with the man's boot. For a few heartbeats there was again silence. Then slowly the wardrobe door opened and a hand grabbed hold of his arm and dragged him out. The boy stood pathetically in his undersized soiled pyjamas in front of the man. The shivering grew more intense and the boy clenched his fists as he shouted at him. The shouting went on for what seemed hours and then with no warning a fist flew out and caught the boy in the chest. The boy screamed and curled into a ball waiting for the next strike. The man lifted his boot and was about to strike, when Raj was jerked from his sleep. Sweat dripped from his forehead and the shivers he had felt as a child returned, as they did most nights. He took deep breaths to calm himself down and once he had regained his composure, he noticed that daylight was streaming into his bedroom through the gaps in the curtains. He grabbed hold of his mobile phone from the floor beside his bed and jumped frantically out of bed. It was already nine o'clock and he had promised Gabby that he would meet her at quarter to ten. He jumped in the shower and after brushing his teeth went back into his bedroom and opened the wardrobe. He had no idea what the dress code for going to church was. After staring blankly at his clothes for a few moments, he decided on the only smart clothes he had: a pair of black trousers and a white shirt. Putting on his warm coat he rushed out of the door and made his way towards the church.

As he approached the church gate, he saw Gabby waiting for him and the sight of her lifted his spirits in a heartbeat. He walked a little faster to reach her. As he got closer, she beamed a smile towards him and gave him a little wave. She was dressed in a long-sleeved white dress that stopped above her knees with long brown leather boots protecting the rest of her legs. Her jet black hair fell onto her shoulders like a beautiful waterfall. He wondered how she was not shivering to the bone without a coat, as it was a chilly Sunday morning although the sun was shining brightly.

'Morning Raj,' greeted Gabby, 'I hope I didn't wake you up too early?'

'No, I was up for a while,' lied Raj, 'you haven't been waiting long have you? Only its freezing out here and you haven't got a coat on.'

'Only about an hour and thinking about it, I can't feel my legs anymore,' Gabby replied putting on a concerned look but when she saw Raj's face drop, she placed a consoling hand on his shoulder and reassured him that she was only joking. Without thinking, she placed her arm through his and led him through the church gate and towards the front arched wooden doors. Raj looked up at the magnificent gothic building and felt nervous at entering another religion's holy ground. He hadn't been to a temple in years and feelings of guilt were rising within him

As they entered the nave, he was surprised at how light and spacious it felt. A beautiful ethereal light shone through the large windows onto the pews pouring warm winter sun onto the congregation. Gabby led him down the aisle until they found a couple of empty seats about halfway down. Raj immediately sat down, while Gabby knelt on one knee and bowed her head towards the altar before sitting. Raj sat there conscious of the closeness of Gabby next to him; her intoxicating perfume was making him feel dizzy. To take his mind off the feelings that were rising within him he looked around the church and took in the various depictions and figures from the Bible. On the east wall was a large painting of the archangel Michael wielding his spear and carrying the scales of justice that he would use to weigh the souls on judgement day. On the opposite side was a painting of the Virgin Mary standing with her arms open wearing a white robe with a halo surrounding her head. As he looked around, he was surprised to see only one large stained-glass window in the entire church. Upon it was a nativity scene showing the gathering of the wise men and shepherds around the manger of baby Jesus. The last painting in the room was that of Jesus and Pilate. The image showed Jesus standing before Pilate with hands bound in ropes behind his back. Pontius Pilate sat on his throne in his regal white robes handing out the judgement of crucifixion to Jesus. Raj's attention was dragged away from the painting by the loud sound of an organ playing by the side of the altar. The sounds of the organ continued for a few minutes before the priest stood up and started his sermon. For the next hour and a half, the priest took the congregation on a journey through the gospel stories, all the while relating them to modern life. He talked about absolution, sin, confessions, forgiveness, scripture and countless other themes that all religions banged on about, but very rarely practised. Although not religious, Raj had studied religion in depth and knew the gospels and the other books from the Bible. He had been searching for years for an answer to why life had treated him with such animosity. He was hoping to find the truth in the pages of the Bible, the Vidas and any other religious text. But in the end, he found only emptiness and lies that led him to believe that religion had only been created by men to control the lives of other people. Like he had told Gabby, he did believe in a God but only because he believed in the power of the devil to manipulate humans into carrying out acts of depravity. After his fruitless search for comfort in religion, he had decided that he would never step foot on holy ground again. That was until he met Gabby and somehow his tortured mind began to see some light.

*****

Deepak stood emotionless with a smoking cigarette in his right hand as he stared at the corpse lying on the table in front of him. Mark the trainee constable, stood a few steps away from him to avoid the stench that was coming from the detective's crumpled, stained suit. Mark nervously looked around the room trying his best to avoid looking at the dead man. The body lay on a table in the centre of the post-mortem examination room, which lay in the bowels of Ealing Hospital. The small room looked somewhat like a modern restaurant kitchen with its stainless-steel walls and tools that resembled utensils. As the young constable looked around, he grew even more disturbed at the sight of the chisels, forceps, clamps, scissors, saws, knives, needles and countless other devices that resembled a macabre torture scene. As the detective took another drag of his cigarette, in walked a plump blonde lady wearing a pristine white lab coat. She approached the two men and shook a disappointed head towards Deepak.
'How many times do I need to tell you that this is a non-smoking area? In fact, the entire hospital is a non-smoking area, so put it out, detective, or get out!' she said in her strong Scottish accent. Having scolded the

detective, the pathologist walked over to a table where she retrieved a brown paper file. She opened the file and looked up at the two men, pleased to see that Deepak had extinguished his cigarette.

'So, who's the stiff?' asked Deepak before the doctor could open her mouth.

'His identity is your problem, detective. My job is to tell you the cause of death,' she replied. 'He is a white male in his early fifties. He is five foot six and overweight at one hundred and eighty pounds. Cause of death is extreme blood loss.'

'What do you call extreme?' asked Mark.

'After a twenty percent blood loss, the body goes into haemorrhagic shock, which this man has all the symptoms of. But normally death doesn't happen until fifty percent of the body's blood has been lost. So, from the examination of the wounds, I would say that it would have taken anything from twenty-four to thirty-six hours for this man to bleed to death.'

'So, the wounds were not what killed him?' asked the detective.

'No, this man has been tortured over several hours. All the cuts and wounds are fairly shallow and have not penetrated any of the vital organs. I suspect the intention was not to kill the man quickly, but to make him suffer for as long as possible.'

The doctor walked around the table and pointed at the man's wrists. 'You can see from the ligature marks that he was bound and you can also see evidence of gagging around his mouth.' She led them to a light box that hung on one of the walls. 'From the x-ray, you can see he also has a broken left shoulder and a crack in his right tibia. So along with the missing teeth, several bruises and cut wounds, I can clearly say that this man was tortured for some time before being dumped and left to die. He was

beaten with both fists and a weapon like a baseball bat. The weapon would have been used to break the bones. Wherever he was kept will have a lot of blood on the floor and probably some stray teeth too.'
'You say there would have been weapons and fists used so do you think that there could be more than one assailant?' asked Mark.
'Good question, yes that's a strong possibility. This is a big guy and to kidnap him, move him, torture him and then dump his body would be difficult for one person. Also, the different type of wounds on his body would make more sense, if there were more than one person hurting him.'
'Any idea what the number seven may signify on his chest and this cut along the length of his face seems very deliberate,' asked Deepak.
'I've been racking my brain over this but haven't come up with any answers I'm afraid,' replied the doctor.
'Any sexual abuse?' asked the detective.
'No,' was the conclusive answer.
The detective thanked the doctor and walked out of the lab into the corridor towards the lifts.
'So, what do you think, Sir?' asked the young constable.
'I think we are looking for a pair or more of psychopathic killers who like the taste of blood,' replied the detective hoping to place a sense of fear into the trainee.

*****

The bright winter sun that had beamed into the church during the Sunday sermon now shone through the large glass windows of the Pear Tree Café. The small but elegantly decorated café was completely full and the glorious smell of breakfast filled the air. Gabby and Raj had managed to claim a small round table by the window. The warmth from the sun created the illusion of a hot summer day, which gave the café an exotic feel of being in a faraway place. The sense of being in another place and maybe another time made Raj feel almost content. If he could, he would have captured the moment and held onto it forever so he could relive it again and again. They both sat in comfortable silence while waiting for their food to arrive. Gabby took a sip from her orange juice and looked over at Raj and smiled.

'Penny for your thoughts?' she asked.

Raj hesitated as he did not want to tell her what he was really thinking. He did not want to come across as some kind of weirdo by telling her that he wished he could bottle the moment forever. He looked towards her while thinking about a response but had to avert his eyes. Looking at her was like looking into a bright star, beautiful and mesmerising, but ultimately unreachable.

'So, you are Church of England?' asked Raj eventually, still looking down into his apple juice.

'Wow, it took you that long to come up with that! Wouldn't it have been easier to tell me what you were really thinking?'

Raj again hesitated and then smiled a rare smile, 'probably not,' he replied.

'Ok then, no I'm not C of E.'

'Catholic?'

'No.'

'Protestant?'

'No, one more guess left.'

'Kimbanguism?'

Gabby looked at Raj in amazement. 'You really are a man of mystery! How do you even know about Kimbanguism, which I am not by the way?'

'More to the point, how do you know about it? Come to think about it, I don't know anything about you at all,'

replied Raj.
'I live a very boring and normal life, so not much to tell really.'
'I wouldn't say you were boring.'
'What would you call me then?'
'Elusive is a better word.'
Gabby let out an infectious laugh and picking up her glass clinked it against Raj's; 'I like that, thank you. It makes me sound all mysterious and exciting.'
As Gabby was about to speak, a waiter appeared and placed two plates on the table. Gabby licked her lips and dived into her full vegetarian English breakfast with ferocity. Raj took a calmer approach with his cheese and ham omelette by first analysing the smell and presentation as if a judge on *MasterChef*. He looked at Gabby as she shovelled a mouth full of hash brown into her mouth. He was amazed at how elegant she still looked even with a face full of food. He carefully cut a piece of the omelette and tasted it before adding a little ketchup. He looked over at Gabby again and noted that even with food the differences between them were evident. She was carefree, with a 'suck it and see' attitude whereas he was always nervous and hesitant about everything he did. He wished he was more like her and hoped that her influence would rub off on him.
Gabby placed the knife and fork on the table and took a gulp of her orange juice, 'Wow that is sublime; I could eat two of these.'
'Really, after all that bread and wine at the church, you're still hungry?'
'I don't believe in that stuff; it's only symbolism, but I do it so the priest doesn't tell me off,' Gabby laughed.
'But you seem very religious,' said Raj.
'The ritualistic elements are just there as an outward show of faith, but what's important is the message.'

'Which is?'
'If you strip away all the pomp and layers of Christianity, the message is simple. The crucifixion and the resurrection of Jesus symbolise salvation and redemption as he died for our sins. He died on the cross so that people who believe in him can be forgiven for all their sins. For me, forgiveness is the most powerful message that can bring redemption and salvation.'
'Would you forgive Hitler?'
'The key to forgiveness is repentance. You must show remorse and true repentance before the Lord to receive forgiveness. Someone like Hitler would only repent because he wanted to enter the gates of heaven and not because he was actually sorry.'
Gabby picked up her cutlery again and scooped up a fork full of beans while Raj prodded his fork into his omelette unaware Gabby was peering at him intensely.
'Omelette no good?' asked Gabby.
'It's fine, just not that hungry,' replied Raj.
'You know you can talk to me about anything,' offered Gabby.
She paused and then continued when Raj didn't reply.
'I've been thinking about what you told me about your family and the way they died. That was an incredible trauma for a small boy to experience and something you need to talk more about to release some of the pain you are holding inside.'
Raj continued to play with his food and thought back to that life changing moment and the immediate days after it. His entire world had collapsed and the pain had never left him. Day after day, he suffered the same nightmares, the same feelings of guilt and grief. He knew that no matter what he did, those memories would forever remain and haunt him.
'The day after the fire, I was taken back to the house by

my neighbour. It was early in the day but the sun was already pouring its heat over everything and a cool breeze swept through the village providing some relief. As we approached the house, I saw a row of white shrouds that had been laid before the burned out house. I knew exactly what was under all those cloths but still I couldn't take my eyes off them. As I got closer, my heart started beating faster and I could feel panic rising within me. Suddenly the breeze caught hold of one of the shrouds. The white cloth slowly floated ghost-like from the body and flew away into the air. I stared at the body in complete horror as a couple of policemen ran to cover it back up. That image has stayed with me throughout my life. The black charred body lay there emotionless, lifeless, featureless, a shadow of the person I loved. The neighbour tried to pull me away but I pushed his arm away and walked closer to the bodies. That's when I noticed something strange. There were six bodies lying there on the floor but there should have been only five. My father, mother, two brothers and sister, but whose was the sixth body? For weeks after, I asked the question to anyone I could find that was interested, but I never got an answer. I was told there was no one missing from the village and I knew that no one was staying at the house. It saddens me to think that someone else died in that fire that day. I always think that the grim reaper came for six bodies that night, but when he found only five, he went hunting for another. I believe I cheated death that day but caused the death of another innocent person. I shouldn't be alive and I am certain that death waits for me in the shadows for his chance to finally possess the soul he should have taken on that dark day.'

CHAPTER THREE

Vijay leaned back in his seat and closing his eyes, took in a deep breath. Getting out of the big city always made him feel more relaxed but this time it felt even more welcome. The last few weeks had been the most traumatic of his life and all he wanted to do was see his family and try to forget about what he had been through. He pictured his family in his mind and the thought of them made him smile. He had not seen them for over six months and he could not wait to give them the presents that he had bought. His thoughts were dragged away by the train's waiter, who was standing above him with a silver tray. Placing the items from the tray onto the table in front of him, the waiter asked him if there was anything else he needed and then left. Vijay took hold of the spoon, tried the lentil soup and then dipped a bread stick into it. After he had finished the starter, he poured himself a hot cup of tea from the teapot into a paper cup. Sipping the tea, he looked out of the window at the beautiful green fields that disappeared into the distance. He felt at peace in the countryside and had only moved to Delhi to progress his career in the police force and earn more money. The big city was noisy, exciting and full of adventure but he was at his happiest when spending time in his childhood village. As he turned to pour more tea, he felt a sharp pain in his left leg. He gently rubbed at his thigh but as the pain increased, he slowly lifted himself from his seat and grabbed hold of his walking stick. Moving out into the corridor, he limped slowly with the stick and made his way into a larger open space, where he stopped and leaned up against a window. He rubbed at his thigh again and tried pushing

away the feelings of anxiety that were rising within him. The pain in his leg was always accompanied with a flashback of the exact moment when the bullet was fired. He remembered it as if it was yesterday although the incident was six weeks old.
It had started as a normal day as he left Geeta Colony police station and headed off in his Maruti Gypsy. The morning shift brought the usual day to day pleasures of crime fighting in a busy city. The petty shop lifter; the domestic argument; the drunk sleeping in the middle of the road and the man who swore that his neighbour had stolen his dog and sacrificed it to the deity Kali. As he was leaving the home of the accused shaman, he received a call from the station to proceed to Punjab National Bank. It took Vijay five minutes to reach the bank and as he approached it, he saw three men carrying black bags running from the bank towards two Hero motorbikes. Two of the men climbed onto a single bike and the third climbed onto another. Instinctively, Vijay knew that the men had just robbed the bank and without thinking, he got out of his car and ran towards them. There had been no way he could have chased them through the narrow alleyway in his car. As the men started their bikes, Vijay neared them and as he reached for his gun, he realised with panic that he had left his Glock 17 in the glovebox of his car. The motorbike carrying one man sped off into the city but the men on the other bike turned towards Vijay and stared directly at him. The man in front shouted out to the second and instructed him to shoot. The second man reached into the inside of his black leather jacket and produced a gun. He lifted the gun and aimed it straight at Vijay's head. He held it there for what seemed like forever as the other man repeated the instruction to shoot. Then he slowly lowered the gun and just when Vijay thought the

robber was going to replace the gun in his jacket, he lowered it further, aimed at Vijay's leg and fired a shot straight into his thigh.

Vijay shook the memory from his head and forced himself to think of the present day. He had spent six weeks in recovery and only in the previous week had he been able to move independently with a walking stick. During the recovery period, he fell into depression and couldn't understand why the man on the motorbike had not killed him. Since then, he had realised his luck; the bullet had not hit the femoral artery, but instead had hit his femur bone. Had it hit the artery, he would have bled to death in minutes.

*****

Vijay's taxi slowly navigated through the crowds in the market square and then stumbled along a narrow dirt road that led to the village school. Vijay instructed the driver to stop and climbing out he paid the fare and thanked him. It was approaching four o'clock in the afternoon so the schoolyard was deserted, as the children had finished for the day. He leaned on his walking stick and drank in all the surroundings. Some of his happiest memories lived and breathed in the school yard and seeing the old place brought back many of them. As he stared at the bike shed, he could still see those delightful times, but there was a shadow forever cast over them. The night of the fire had tainted all his memories and he was forever trapped in a connection with the friends he was with that night. Sadly, he had lost contact with both Raj and Manoj and hadn't seen them in years, but they were always in his thoughts. He often wondered where they had ended up and he had at times searched social media for them, but to no avail. He had decided a while back that sleeping dogs are sometimes better left alone, so he had stopped trying to find them. He unconsciously breathed a deep sigh and slowly hobbled down past the school and towards the shrine. Every time he visited his home, he started his trip with the same route that he and his friends had taken on that fateful night. He walked towards the village square that was teaming with people shopping, eating, hawking their wares at the market or just casually hanging about for a chat. As he hobbled through the crowds, he was greeted many times and each time stopped to catch up and then slowly moved on. By the time he reached the well, he was exhausted and the throbbing in his leg had intensified. He felt like stopping off at one of the dhabbas for a sit down and something to eat, but this journey had become a kind of ritual. It was his own way of honouring the memory of his friend's family, which he thought in his own mind would somehow also aid Raj in his life. So with great determination, he moved on through the alleyways and finally reached the place where Raj and his family had lived. The house was no longer there and in its place stood a shrine that had been built by the local villagers. It stood as a memorial for the family who had lost their lives and also to Vijay's own father who had died three weeks prior to the fire, in a car accident. He held his hands together towards the small statue of Lord Ganesha and sent out a prayer for all the souls who had been lost.

Vijay opened his eyes and with a heavy heart walked the small distance from the shrine to his house. As he approached his home, his mother and young sister opened the front door and greeted him with a long and warm hug. Vijay held onto both of them as his mother stood on her tip toes to stroke his hair. Holding his face in her hands, she looked at him through tears.

'What is this thing you have growing on your face?' she asked smiling.
'Does it not make me look more mature, Ma?' replied Vijay.
'You look like an old man with your walking stick and long beard.'
'I feel like an old man Ma,' replied Vijay looking down at his leg and stick.
'Nonsense, you will be better in no time. You are home now and I have a cupboard full of home remedies that will have you jumping around like a two-year-old.'
Vijay was led into the house by his sister holding onto his hand and once inside they were greeted by other members of his family. His elderly Uncle Dev sat on a low wicker bed and his grandma was lying on a bed in the corner of the room, fast asleep. A couple of aunties were clattering away in the kitchen, preparing a feast for the returning hero. Vijay spent the next hour catching up with all the guests and re-telling the story of his shooting. They all listened intently and gasped and shook their heads in all the right places. Throughout the story a variety of foods were brought out from the kitchen and handed around. First came the vegetable samosas and pakoras; then chickpeas cooked in a curry sauce were poured over the samosas. This was followed by large pieces of paneer tikka covered in coriander and green chilli. The round coffee table in the middle of the room was swamped with food and the guests sat rubbing their tummies with glee. Once Vijay had come to the end of his tale, his mother brought out tea and cake.
'Vijay, did you visit the shrine?' asked Uncle Dev.
Vijay nodded and sighed, 'Yes Uncle, but it was very sad to see that it has become quite overgrown and dirty. Is no one maintaining it?'
'We are all growing too old and these youngsters don't

really bother, I'm afraid. I keep it clear of rubbish but I am too old to be pulling out weeds and scrubbing. I have asked the locals for donations so we can hire a regular caretaker, but no one seems to care. Many of the people who lived here and remembered the fire and your father's accident have since left. I was telling Mr Anand the other day that it is a shame that people don't care anymore.'

'Mr Anand?' asked Vijay, slightly surprised.

'Yes, yes, Mr Anand, you know Manoj's father.'

The look of surprise on Vijay's face widened further.

'Uncle Anand was in the village?'

The old man looked around the room and lifted his shoulders and shook his head. 'Am I talking in Sanskrit or Chinese?' he asked the room. 'This boy doesn't seem to understand what I am saying. Yes Vijay, Mr Anand, Manoj's father was in the village the other day and I met him as he was leaving the police station. As usual he was a little drunk.'

'What was he doing at the police station?' asked Vijay.

'Do I look like his mother?' replied the old man as he twisted his white moustache and stroked his long white beard.

Vijay ignored the comment and asked another question, hoping this time not to receive a sarcastic reply.

'Is Manoj here as well?'

'I don't know if he was here with his father. I didn't see him but anyway, Mr Anand has left already, so if Manoj was here, then he would also have left with him. Mr Anand comes back to the village every year at the same time and he always visits the police station, but I have never seen Manoj with him.'

Vijay's slim hope of seeing his old friend evaporated into thin air and he was left with a touch of sadness. He fell silent and let the rest of the guests mutter and gossip on about other members of the village and their private lives. He lifted his tea and took a sip and thought again of his childhood friends. As far back as he could remember, the three of them had been as close as brothers and inseparable. Over the last few weeks, while he recuperated from his injury, he had thought about them constantly and had a desperate longing to see them again. Maybe it was because of the shooting, which made him think of his own mortality and the shortness of life. At first, he had been worried about how he would spend six weeks out here in the countryside, but now he knew the answer. He would spend the time looking for his two best friends and try to get them all to meet up. He would start his quest in the morning with a visit to the local police station to find out why Mr Anand had been visiting annually, always at the same time of year.

*****

Rahul looked across the city of Mumbai through his panoramic top floor penthouse window. It was seven thirty in the morning and the sun was beginning its ascendance behind the thousands of buildings that dotted the landscape in front of him. He loved this part of the day as it always represented a fresh new start, a new dawn, a resurrection of sorts. Anything was possible with the coming of the day; endless possibilities were there to be enjoyed. He used this part of the day to clear his thoughts and make his decisions for the day. The vast empire that he ran was forever vulnerable and any signs of weakness could cause its downfall within a heartbeat. His attention to detail was what had made him successful, but that meant spending most of his waking hours at work or thinking about work. He looked down at

the City of Dreams below him and thought of the millions of people who lived in its luxury penthouses, its ordinary homes and also in its poverty ridden slums. He thought back to his childhood and the years spent living in the Dharavi area of Mumbai, which was one of its poorest regions. There had been days without food and he wouldn't see his parents for days, while they searched for work. As a ten-year-old, he had to look after his two sisters and protect them from all the vileness of the slums and the big city. He would lie awake all night with a stick held close to his chest just waiting for some depraved soul to enter their metal makeshift shack. He would dream of escaping and made a promise to himself that one day he would be rich enough to never go hungry again. He turned away from the view and headed out of his office into the kitchen; he beamed a smile towards his wife, kissed her on the cheek, grabbed a cup of coffee and turned towards his son's bedroom. He gently opened the bedroom door and walked over to his son's bed. The six-year-old was fast asleep so Rahul placed a kiss on his forehead and quietly left. Outside the Imperial Heights apartment, he climbed into the back of his chauffer driven bullet proof Land Rover. The driver headed off down Road Number 6 towards the Shree Shankar Maharaj Mandir, where he waited outside for fifteen minutes while Rahul performed him morning rituals; they then drove towards Rahul's office.
'Mohan, please go to the warehouse in Shalimar Industrial Estate but drive pass Dharavi,' instructed Rahul from the back of the car.
As the car drove past the slums of Dharavi district, Rahul gazed at the pitiful children who stood glumly with their begging bowls and rag torn clothes like apocalyptic versions of Oliver Twist. The majority of the thousands of children living in the huge complex of alleys and shacks

would never escape. The cycle would continue as they grew up, got married and had their own children, who would then take up the baton of poverty. A few, like him, might drag themselves out of the hell and squalor and make a life for themselves, but the chances were little. He stared at the self-constructed homes made from corrugated metal and material found in rubbish tips. He felt a sense of hopelessness as he thought of all the millions of Rupees he had poured into trying to eradicate the slums, money which had not even made a dent.

The car moved on from Dharavi district, entered the Shalimar Industrial Estate and parked up outside a large warehouse with 'Rahul Industries Ltd' emblazoned on it. Mohan opened the car door for his master and then followed Rahul into the building. A man sitting at a front counter and idly flicking through Facebook on his phone jumped to attention on seeing Rahul walk in.

'Mr Bachchan I wasn't expecting you today,' said the man nervously.

'Is Sanjeev here?' asked Rahul ignoring the man's comment.

'Yes, he came in about half an hour ago with Toni and another man. Sanjeev said he would be waiting in the boardroom but he didn't say who for,' replied the man.

Rahul ignored the man and walked through a door that led to a flight of stairs. Climbing up, he opened the door to the boardroom where Sanjeev and Toni were both waiting. The two men were suited and sitting down, drinking tea, as if waiting for an important meeting to start. Behind the two men suspended upside down by a rope tied to his feet was Manoj. The rope had been tied around an iron girder high above them in the warehouse roof. Manoj's hands were tied behind his back and his chest was bare and dripping with blood from several freshly made cuts. His face was black and blue from the beating he had received at the hands of two of Rahul's right-hand men.

Rahul walked past the two seated men and stood in front of Manoj.

'Take him down,' instructed Rahul.

The two men put down their cups of tea and as one held onto Manoj's legs, the other untied the knot in the rope, allowing the beaten man to slump to the ground. Manoj turned over onto his back and coughed as blood from his battered lips entered his mouth and ran down his throat. He wanted to get up, but with his hands tied behind his back and pain racking his body, he had no strength to do so.

'Remove the ropes from his hands and put him in a chair. This is no way to treat a friend,' said Rahul, taking a seat himself.

The two men did as they were told and picking Manoj up, placed him onto a chair across the table from Rahul. Manoj wiped blood from his lips and looked across the table with fear at the Mumbai crime lord for whom he had been working over the past two years.

Rahul leaned back in his chair and fiddled with the diamond ring on his finger and then brushed his hand through his silver mane. His focused his stare on Manoj for a few moments letting the tension in the air build. Finally he gave his navy blue suit jacket a brush with his palm and adjusted his white tie to ensure he looked pristine. 'My business is run on some basic principles, Manoj: bravery, honesty, transparency and above all loyalty. I need to trust everyone who works for me and I need to know that they will carry out the tasks I set them, without any small detail missed. So how do you think I felt, when I heard that a bank robbery had been botched? Did you think I would be happy, welcome you back with open arms and give you another chance? I am not where I am today because of second chances, Manoj. There is no way I am ever going back to where I started, and if that means setting an example with an idiot like you, then so be it.'

'I am sorry, Mr Bachchan but I don't understand what this is about. We got the bonds that you were after and we didn't get caught,' replied Manoj, wiping blood from his mouth.

'What happened with the cop?' asked Rahul.

Manoj hesitated. If Rahul discovered that Manoj knew the cop, it would be all over for him.

'The few seconds you took to decide whether to shoot the cop could have resulted very differently. Added to that, you left him alive. That is unacceptable. He is a police officer, who now has a personal vendetta against the bank robbers and will be passionate about solving the case. He should be dead.'

'I thought if I killed a cop, the entire police force would come after us, so I shot him in the leg.'

Rahul seemed to ignore Manoj's plea.

'You are a very lucky man Manoj, because today is my birthday and on my birthday, I like to dish out a little kindness. So instead of skinning you alive in this very room, I will tell you what you are going to do. You are going to find this cop and you are going to complete what you should have done in the first place. Sanjeev has found out that he has gone home to Punjab to recuperate and will give you his address. You have seven days or Toni over there will find you and not only kill you, but he will kill your entire family as a message to all in my organisation that failure is not an option.'

*****

Vijay picked up the last of the leaves from around the

shrine and with a wince stood upright. He rubbed at his leg as he hobbled over to a bucket that was full of leaves, wrappers, cigarette butts and dead flowers. He placed the last few leaves into the bucket and then lifted it with his left hand while grabbing hold of his walking stick with the other. He slowly made his way back to his house, tipping the rubbish into a larger dustbin along the way. He then took the empty bucket, half filled it with water and soap and threw a scouring pad into it. He hobbled back to the shrine and spent the next couple of hours scrubbing the stone arch that framed the statue of Lord Genesha. He also wiped down the statue until all the grit and grime had been removed. Once he had finished, he stood back and leaning on his stick, admired his handy work. The shrine was almost back to its original state and even though he felt exhausted and his leg was throbbing violently, he was pleased. He looked down at his watch and decided that he had earned himself a good lunch and a lie down. He already had plans for the afternoon, but that was going to have to wait until he was fed and rested.

As Vijay entered his home, he could smell the smoky aroma of fried chapatis cooking in the kitchen. He followed his nose into the small kitchen and found his mother there squatting on a stool over a hot stove. As he entered, he was greeted by a warm smile. He walked over to his mother and gave her a distracting hug while he stole a piece of chapati from the tin container that sat next to the stove. His mother feigned anger and sent him away while she finished her cooking. After a filling lunch of the potato-stuffed fried chapatis and yogurt, Vijay had a nap. He awoke a couple of hours later refreshed and made his way into the village square and towards the local police station.

The station was a small flat roofed building that was

crammed between a pottery shop and fresh butchers. As Vijay approached the station, he was taunted by a number of live chickens that were caged in confined wooden boxes. Vijay ignored the trapped birds and walked into the building, where he had started his career in the police force. As he entered, he was greeted fondly by an officer sitting at the front desk.
'Hey brother, how are you?' asked the officer as he stood and walked around the desk to give Vijay a huge hug. 'We all heard about your heroics in Delhi. You have become quite the legend around here.'
'Really, a legend for what? Getting shot and letting a gang of robbers escape,' laughed Vijay.
Kirit laughed too and shook his head. 'Who cares about the detail. All we know is that you took a bullet, my friend, and lived to tell the tale. That's enough for us. Trust me! In a few years, your story will become so outlandish that you will be made into a God and we shall have to put a photo of you on the wall and pray to you as the God of luck.'
The two men embraced again. Kirit led Vijay into a larger room that held three desks, but with only one of them manned. Behind the largest of the desks in the corner of the room sat a large, bearded man wearing a bright red turban. As he saw the two men enter the room, he leaned back into his seat and his face took on a sour expression.
'So, you have decided to come back,' he started. 'I said that one day you would come back with your tail between your legs. I told you the big city was a dangerous place, but would you listen? No, you were too eager to leave and become a big shot and look where it got you!' The man paused. 'Ok, no problem, you can have your job back, but you will need to start at the bottom by cleaning my boots.' He lifted his leg onto to

his desk to reveal a foot that wore no shoe. All three men stared at the inspector's bare foot and burst into laughter.

Inspector Singh lifted his large torso out of the chair, walked over to Vijay and gave him a tight hug. The inspector instructed the younger officer to bring tea and food from the village square and before Vijay could protest, Kirit had already run off. Over the next hour, the three men sat and caught up with all that had happened over the time that Vijay had been in Delhi. They sat eating samosas, pakoras and sweets until they were fit to burst. After they had exhausted all the food, the inspector opened the drawer of his desk and pulled out a bottle of Royal Stag whisky and three plastic glasses.

'No, no, sorry Sir, but I have stopped drinking,' protested Vijay.

The inspector ignored him, poured the drink and placed the glass in front of Vijay.

'Having one drink is not drinking; that's just called tasting. Don't worry! I won't tell your mother, if that's what you're worried about.'

The inspector knew just how to get under Vijay's skin and the trick worked.

'Ok, but only the one. Just for old times' sake; besides it may help with the pain,' replied Vijay as he lifted the glass and took a sip.

The three men sat in comfortable silence sipping on their whisky until Vijay broke the peacefulness and turned the air from friendly to frosty.

'My uncle was telling me that he saw Mr Anand coming out of the police station the other day,' stated Vijay.

The inspector immediately put his whisky glass down on the desk, leaned back in his chair and crossed his arms over his round stomach.

'Yes, that's right. He just popped in to say hello, as he

was passing through the village.'
'Do you know if Manoj was with him?' asked Vijay.
'No,' was the inspector's brief answer.
'I am trying to contact Manoj and was hoping that you would have his address,' said Vijay.
The inspector moved in his chair from side to side and Vijay recognised this as a sign he was concealing something.
'I don't know where Manoj and his family live now. As you know, they moved out of the village some years ago and we very rarely see them.'
'That's strange, because Uncle Dev said that Mr Anand comes to visit the police station every year around the same time. So, in all that time, you didn't ask him where he had moved to?'
'I was never that friendly with the man; we are merely acquaintances.'
'Yet he visits you every year?'
'What are you trying to say, Vijay?' enquired the inspector.
There was an uncomfortable pause before Vijay toned down the interrogation and changed the subject.
'Like I said, I'm just trying to contact my old friends, Manoj and Raj and thought you might be able to help.'
At the mention of Raj, the inspector tensed further and now sweat started to run down his forehead.
'Sometimes it is best to leave old friends in the past, Vijay. People move on and are rarely how you remember them. It was lovely to see you again, but I really must be getting back to my work now,' said the inspector, standing up and formally shaking Vijay's hand.
The young officer led Vijay outside and they shook hands warmly.
'Sorry, but the inspector gets a bit grumpy when he's had a drink,' offered Kirit as an apology for the

inspector's behaviour.
'It's not a problem, brother, I hardly noticed,' replied Vijay with a smile. 'Do you know why Mr Anand was here?' asked Vijay, hoping to catch the young officer off guard. The officer looked nervously at the entrance to the police station and then down at his shoes. 'Listen, all I heard was the two of them talking about the night of the fire,' whispered the man.
'What were they saying about the fire?' asked Vijay.
The officer was about to reply when the inspector appeared at the entrance.
'Kirit, you need to complete the paperwork for the stolen jewel case.'
The young officer scampered back into the station.
'Goodbye Vijay,' ordered the inspector.
As Vijay walked past the chickens, he felt uneasy about how the meeting had ended. The inspector was hiding something, something that involved Manoj, Raj and the fire. He was determined to know what it was and the best way to uncover the truth was to treat it like a case. For that, he would need to build up an investigation that started from as far back as the night of the infamous village fire.

CHAPTER FOUR

Gabby walked around Raj's living room and lit the twelve candles that she had placed in various places. Once they were all alight and the flames had started their dance, she turned off the main light. From her bag, she took out a small bottle containing a liquid, poured some into an oil burner and lit the little tea light that started heating the oil. The rich earthy smell of sandalwood filled the room and combined with the flickering shadows from the candles created a relaxing and calm aura. She took hold of Raj's hand and led him to an open area that they had created by moving the sofa and coffee table against the wall. She sat down cross legged on the floor and instructed Raj to do the same. Gabby sat easily with her legs crossed while Raj struggled to bend his legs into position. Gabby waited patiently until he found a position that was comfortable for him and then pressed play on her phone that was connected to a small speaker. The sound of a stream trickling in the distance filled the room and was joined by the soft chirping of birds and crickets. 'Meditation doesn't need to be some kind of path to enlightenment and self-realisation,' started Gabby. 'It can simply be a way of taking away anxiety and bringing about peace. What we are going to practice is a form of meditation that focuses on mindfulness. It will bring you fully into the present and allow the struggles of this world to fade into the background and then disappear totally. During the meditation, I want you to put aside any prejudice you have about the past and forget about the future. If any judgement from your past arises in your head while meditating, make a mental note of it and put it away. It is natural for your mind to wander but this practice teaches you to keep bringing your mind back to the present.

Now straighten your upper body but make sure it is not tight or stiff. Rest your hands on your laps and keep your arms relaxed. You can either close your eyes or softly gaze at a spot on the floor in front of you. Next, focus on your breath and pay attention to the physical sensation of the air moving through your nose and mouth. Feel how your chest and belly rise and fall to the rhythm of your breath. When you feel your thoughts wandering, just let them enter your mind and watch them as an observer, but then return to your breathing and come back to the present.'

Gabby went silent and watched Raj as he sat uncomfortably on the floor with his eyes closed. He was trying really hard to focus, but he also kept fidgeting and opening his eyes and looking around the room. She was pleased that he had agreed to try meditation, but also knew that the journey for him would be long and tough. His thoughts were trapped in the past and they kept dragging him back to that place where he felt comfortable in his misery. He was suffering from low self-esteem and self-worth because he blamed himself for the death of his family. He wore the guilt like an iron suit that was weighing him down and preventing him from living in the present.

After a few minutes, Gabby told Raj to open his eyes and she turned off the sounds of the forest. She offered Raj a hand, which he accepted gratefully, but as he stood up, he felt the rise of pins and needles spreading through his thighs. He limped towards the sofa that had been pushed against the wall and slumped down on to it rubbing at the numbness in his leg. Gabby followed him and sitting herself next to him, she smiled at his obvious discomfort.

'Not funny,' protested Raj when he noticed the cheeky grin on her face.

'From where I'm sitting, it's very funny. When was the last time you sat on the floor like that?' replied Gabby.

'Not since I was a kid.'

Gabby noticed Raj's face change from relaxed to tense as soon as he mentioned his childhood. This was the trigger that affected his mood and set off his depression. He was trying to shut out the happy life that he had enjoyed as a kid in India because of his guilt. He didn't want to remember that he was once happy; he felt he didn't deserve it. It was a subconscious trigger that he was not aware of and he had no control over. The only way that he was going to get better was to disconnect his thoughts from the feelings of guilt every time he thought of his childhood.

'How was that for you?' asked Gabby.

'Honest answer?' replied Raj.

Gabby nodded.

'I struggled with both the physical and mental parts of that. I couldn't sit comfortably, which meant my thoughts were not focused enough. I tried to stay in the present moment and kept taking in the smell from the oils and the sounds of the stream but other thoughts and memories kept pushing the calmness away. Feelings from the past are too strong for me and I can't keep them away. With your help and maybe with a bit more practice, I will learn how to control them.'

'Have you heard of the "Precious Present" story by a guy called Spencer Johnson?' asked Gabby.

Raj shook his head.

'It's a story about a child who loved to talk to an old man, who just sat listening in his home. The old man always seemed happy and content with life. One day the old man told the child about a Precious Present and that when he found this, he would be happy forever. The child believed this to be the gift of a toy and hoped that he would receive it for Christmas. But when the boy thought about this deeply, he soon realised that a toy would not bring him joy forever. So, over the years, as the boy grew older, he returned to the old man again and again to ask him what the Precious Present was. The old man simply told him that when he found it, he would know happiness for ever. The grown man became more and more frustrated and angry and travelled the world in search of the Precious Present. After many years, he returned to see the old man, but he had passed on. As he sat thinking of everything the old man had told him about the Precious Present, he suddenly realised that it was not a physical thing, but a thing of the mind. The Precious Present meant living in the moment. Being fully present in the moment; not worrying about the past or the future brings real happiness.'

Raj listened to the story intently and understood what Gabby was trying to tell him, but he found it almost impossible to stay in the present moment, as the dark memories kept creeping into his mind and destroyed any thoughts of joy. He was desperate to show Gabby that he could change and become a free spirit like her. He needed to change so that she could trust him and in turn, maybe they could become more than just friends.

*****

Deepak sat at his desk in the police station and looked over the pathologist's report again trying to decipher some sort of clue that would give him a lead in the case. As his retirement date approached, he was keen to leave the force on a high by solving one of the most brutal crimes he had been involved with. It had been another long night and his fifth black coffee sat cold next to him. Opposite his desk sat the young constable who Deepak had been forced to take on as a trainee. Deepak preferred to work alone, but over the last few months his workload had been reduced by his boss so that he could ease into retirement. The trainee was given to him to keep him a little occupied up until the fateful day when he would leave the force. He got up out of his chair, walked outside and breathed in the chill early morning air.

Although approaching five o'clock in the morning, it was still pitch dark and deadly quiet out in the streets; even the prostitutes and drug pushers had given up for the night and crawled back under the rocks they had come from. Removing a cigarette from its pack, he lit it and took a deep drag. The nicotine rushed through him and he felt a sense of momentary calm. He had been feeling uneasy for the last couple of days. The appearance of the dead body had interrupted his daily routine of harassing all the deadbeats on the streets. His sanity relied on the daily fix of abuse that he inflicted and when he went a few days without it, he became unsettled and his mind became clouded. This was when he was at his most dangerous. He then needed a bigger fix, someone would get seriously hurt and the abuse would be long and painful. He threw the cigarette onto the floor, walked back to the station and headed to the toilets. He opened the tap and leaning over the basin, splashed water onto his face. He pulled out some paper hand towels and wiped his face. He looked at his image reflected in the mirror in front of him.

His mood darkened further.

Staring back at him was a face that showed no warmth or compassion, a skinny face with narrow eyes and a pencil thin mouth told the story of years of cruelty. His

head was almost completely devoid of hair and the bags under his eyes were a gift from the endless nights that he chose to work. He continued to stare at the image and thought back to when he was younger and more handsome. As a young man on the force, he had been recognised and targeted for development and promotion. He never had any trouble finding partners but there was always one problem. His impotency meant that his relationships never lasted. With the help of medication, he had enjoyed a few good years, but when he discovered he couldn't have children, the problems returned. He felt ashamed and worthless as a man and the abuse he carried out was a substitute release. His current frustration meant that he couldn't think straight, which was why the case was so far eluding him. He walked out of the washroom, through the office and back outside into the cold morning. He walked the short distance to Rufford Tower block and entered with a key. He climbed the stairs to the second floor and knocked on a door. The door was opened by an Eastern European man who immediately took on a worried look. The detective pushed past him and entered the room.
'What do you want Mr DI?' asked the man.
'I haven't seen my old buddy, Marcin, in a while so here I am,' replied Deepak.
'Listen, the last time you came here, it cost me hundreds of pounds. Nadia couldn't work for six months, six fucking months!' spat out Marcin in a strong Polish accent.
Deepak casually walked deeper into the room and looked around the small space. He eyed up all the objects that decorated the flat, though decorated was a far too polite term for the junk and squalor cluttering the floor. He was looking for something that looked valuable and heavy to pick up and throw at the pimp. After a few

seconds, he realised that he would never find anything valuable as the only things of any value to Marcin were his whores.

'You do realise that if I had you raided, you would lose a lot more than a few hundred pounds. I know every room you occupy in this filthy place and I could shut you down in a heartbeat.'

'That is true my friend, but you would find that very difficult with your fucking head in a bag and your body at the bottom of a canal,' replied Marcin with a sly grin.

The two men stared at each other for a few heartbeats, neither one wanting to back down but in the end Deepak conceded as his need was the greater.

'How about I promise not to damage the goods…,' there was a slight pause, '…too much,' he added. 'Half an hour is all I need and then I'll leave you in peace.'

Marcin considered the offer and knew that keeping the detective sweet was also in his interest.

'Ok, room thirty three, third floor, but if you break your promise, your friend Marcin will not be happy and will need some payback, understand?'

Deepak nodded and walked past the man as he opened the door. He made his way up to the third floor where he knocked on door thirty three. A woman who looked middle-aged opened the door. When she saw the man standing in front of her, she gasped in horror. She tried slamming the door shut, but the detective jammed the door open with his foot, which he then pushed open violently. He walked into the room and shut the door behind him.

'Hello, Nadia,' started the detective.

*****

Back in the station, Deepak felt energy flow through him

and the fog in his mind slowly cleared to reveal his thoughts. He walked over to the investigation board he had set up and looked at all the evidence. A photo of fifty-three-year-old Richard Evans, the victim, took centre stage. Pinned next to that was a photo of the crime scene including the corpse and next to that a close-up of the man's chest and face. The board, apart from that, lay bare and pathetic.

'Mark, get your arse over here,' the detective shouted.

Mark ambled over and as usual stood away from the detective giving out a huge yawn. He rubbed his eyes and then also stared at the board. They both stood looking at the evidence, as if some magical clue was going to jump out and slap them in the face.

'So, tell me what we know so far,' asked Deepak.

'The victim is Richard Evans and he was a fifty-three-year-old man from Acton. Married to his wife, Julia, for twenty-five years and had two children, a daughter, Karen, who is twenty-one years old and a son, John, who is seventeen years old. He worked as a sales rep at Furniture World and has a degree in electronic engineering and that's pretty much it.'

'So far, looking at the evidence has given us nothing; the crime scene, the pathologist report and CCTV cameras have revealed nothing. So, we are going to look at victimology and hopefully that will give us a lead,' said Deepak.

'What's that?'

'What do you mean, what's that. Are you some kind of an idiot?'

'Victimology?'

'Don't they teach you anything at college?'

'It's my first year, so we haven't done that module yet,' replied Mark, looking a little offended.

'Well, it's a little self-explanatory; it's the study of the

victim. We need to know everything there is to know about this guy.' He tapped his finger on the photo of the corpse. 'We need to interview his family, his friends, his work colleagues. I want to know what he had for breakfast on the day he died, what car he drove, where he got his hair cut, how often he had sex with his wife, did he have sex with his wife or some other poor cow? I want to know where he went to school, did he go to the gym, or to church. Around here nobody gets brutally murdered with cryptic messages carved on their chest for no reason. Whoever did this knew the victim or paid to have this done to him. Also, get a blown-up map of the area and stick it on the board. We need to look at any buildings that are within a one-mile radius of that supermarket where he was found. Whoever did this could not have travelled far from the torture site. So, go home and get some rest. We can meet at twelve noon to start interviews.'
'But its eight o'clock now!' protested the young man.
'I don't give a shit! Be back here at twelve or they'll be investigating another corpse,' replied Deepak with a snarl.

*****

Raj slowed his pace until he came to a stop by a wooden bench and then used it to prop himself up while trying to catch his breath. He took in deep breaths as he tried to force his heart rate to slow down, but with little success. It was the first time in many months that he had performed any kind of exercise and he was feeling pain all over his body. His legs were shaking and his lungs felt as though they were on fire. His head felt light and the park started slowly spinning around him. With trembling hands, he moved around to the front of the

bench and sitting down, he closed his eyes. He kept taking deep breaths until he felt his heart rate slow and the dizziness ebb away. He opened one eye and when content that the park had stopped spinning, he opened the other one and took a long gulp from his electrolyte drink. He looked down the path and saw Gabby in the distance running towards him. She had lapped him three times but looked as though she hadn't even broken a sweat. As she came close, she slowed down and beamed a smile towards him and then sat down next to him. She unclipped a bottle from her sports belt, took a small sip and then stood up to perform some leg stretches. Raj watched how easily she moved and how graceful she appeared when stretching her body. She looked over to him and gestured for him to join her but he politely declined as his body ached from the run. When Gabby had finished stretching, she sat back down next to him and offered him a high five.
'Thanks, but why do I deserve a high five?' asked Raj.
'You did amazing considering you've been sitting on your arse for months,' replied Gabby.
'I thought I was going to have a heart attack for a minute. That would have solved a few of my issues,' laughed Raj.
Gabby gave him a stern look and slapped him on the arm. 'Stop being so morbid; haven't you learnt anything from me at all? Stay positive at all times and live in the moment. I'm sure your muscles are aching but enjoy the feeling of being alive. The pain means that you have just done something fantastic and that your body can take it. You're beginning to get into really good habits and soon it will become a routine and you won't even think about it. "We are what we repeatedly do. Excellence, then, is not an act, but a habit."'
'That's easy for you to say, you don't seem to have a

pain barrier.'
'It's easy for me to say because I stole the quote from Aristotle.'
'You know what I mean.'
They sat in silence as the mid-morning sun beat down on them creating an illusion of a summer's day in the midst of winter. Raj had been following a routine that Gabby had devised for him and although his body was racked with pain, he felt emotionally richer. Every morning he tried to wake up early and after a shower, he spent some time trying to perfect his meditation technique. He had traded missing breakfast with having a healthy meal of nuts, fruits and bran flakes. He had even reduced his alcohol consumption and not touched any drugs. He had been going on a daily run for the past few days but today he had pushed himself hard in an attempt to impress Gabby.
'How's the meditation going?' asked Gabby.
Raj paused and thought about the question deeply. He didn't want to give Gabby a quick and shallow answer as he didn't want to appear blasé, but he also didn't want to be too negative. He took another sip from his bottle and thought back to his experience that morning. He had tried really hard to keep any negative feelings from entering his mind, but as always, after a few minutes, the usual dark thoughts started to creep into his mind. He used the techniques that Gabby had taught him to push them away, but they were far too strong for him. It would start with a single voice whispering in his ear, telling him that he was a bad person and then another voice hissed and laughed at him. Soon many voices joined them and he could no longer make sense of what they were saying.
'So?' said Gabby breaking into Raj's thoughts.
'I'm finding it really difficult, but there is one thing I have

learnt about myself that I think will be useful.'
'Well, that's fantastic Raj. That's a real breakthrough because learning about one's own feelings and observing them as a third person is a step closer to resolving issues. So, what did you learn?'
'I am consumed with guilt,' answered Raj.
'Go on.'
'As you know, after the fire I was sent to England to live with my uncle and aunt. They had also just left India a few weeks before and had settled in London. My uncle collected me from the airport and didn't say a word to me all the way home. As soon as we got inside, he started drinking and after a couple of hours, he was stumbling around the house swearing in Hindi. I remember sitting in the kitchen at a small dining table trying not to cry. I wanted to be brave and not show any signs of weakness. My aunt was trying her best to keep the drunkard from the kitchen, but she knew if she tried too hard, she would be punished. My aunt gave me a cheese sandwich to eat. I didn't even know what a cheese sandwich was. I was so used to my mother's cooking, but I was so hungry I would have eaten a block of cheese on its own. I lifted the sandwich and took a bite. My uncle came into the kitchen and slapped the sandwich from my hand. My aunt just cowered in the corner of the kitchen and couldn't even look at me. I couldn't comprehend in my mind what was happening. I looked at him and all I saw in his twisted face was hatred and rage. He stared at me for a few moments and then told me that my family dying was entirely my fault. He told me that I had committed mahapataka, mortal sin. Imagine being thirteen years old and told that you were the cause of your family's death. I already felt guilty, but when my uncle reinforced it, then I really believed it.'
Raj paused, letting the silence fill the gap until Gabby

reached out and took hold of his hand. She moved closer to him so that he could feel the warmth of her body. That feeling of calmness and oneness with the world that he always felt when Gabby was close took over his body and he no longer felt frightened of talking about his past.
'Tell me more about your aunt. She seemed like a good soul, who was trapped.'
'She was a good woman at heart and she showed me great love and kindness. She would make me sandwiches and hide them under my bed so if my uncle sent me to my room without any dinner, I would have something to eat. The happiest time I can remember was when my uncle was at work and my aunt would sit between me and Kiran on the sofa and watch television. We would sit in a blanket and eat hot pakoras that she had just fried. But I know those memories were the exception and that the actual reality was my uncle and his wickedness.'
'Why would you say that?'
'Because he was the punishment for my sin.'
'Your uncle is not God so he cannot punish anyone for what he thinks they have done. Besides, the fire that killed your family was not your fault and you have to start believing that.'
'My aunt was the only person who showed me any kind of love after my family died and what did I do to repay her? I walked out on her and left her to live with the evillest person I had ever known. I think about her every day and wonder what she is doing and if she ever had the strength to walk out as I did. Guilt and regret have eaten away at me ever since I walked out on her. I can never forgive myself for leaving without even telling her, but I just couldn't take it anymore.'
'Raj, you were just a boy.'

'I made a promise to myself that one day I would go back and stand up to that monster and protect my aunt, but I haven't even had the courage to do that.'

'It took amazing courage to walk out from your uncle's house without anywhere to go and with no money. To save someone else, you must save yourself first.'

CHAPTER FIVE

Vijay's bedroom was simple with a wooden single bed in one corner, a crooked drawer cabinet against a cracked plastered wall and the only other piece of furniture was a large metal trunk that sat forlorn in a corner of the room. Vijay stared at the trunk with fondness but also trepidation as it contained both joyous memories and those that were filled with sadness. It had been a while since he had looked at the contents of the trunk and he didn't even know what was in there anymore as his mother had recently used it to store things that she thought Vijay would want to keep. He walked towards the trunk silently as if approaching an ancient beast that had been asleep for eternity. With great difficulty, he knelt down in front of the trunk and carefully lifted the lid upwards releasing a cloud of dust that drifted through the air causing Vijay to cough and place the lid back down. After catching his breath and wiping the dust from his eyes, he swung the lid back open fully, letting it rest against the wall. Straight away he could tell that his mother had re-arranged the contents of the trunk. The things that he had expected to be on top were not there; instead, the first thing he saw was some of his baby clothes. He lifted a tiny white vest from the trunk followed by an assortment of outfits that made him chuckle. His first baby blanket was also on top and within it was wrapped his first toy. He opened the blanket and took hold of the small rattle and gave it a little shake before placing it carefully back into the blanket. Underneath the baby clothes were more souvenirs from his childhood; school uniforms mixed with exercise books and a few school reports, which he quickly flicked through. They reminded him that he had been quite a clever kid. He then lifted out a small bundle of photographs held together with a rubber band. He removed the band and looked at the first photo. He felt a wave of sadness wash over him. The photograph showed three boys huddled together in a warm embrace, smiling at the camera. They were dressed in their school uniforms, with white short-sleeved shirts, black shorts, black socks, black plimsolls and a colourful yellow and green tie. He remembered that day clearly; it was the last day of the school term and they had just made plans for the summer. It was one of the happiest memories that he held and that summer was full of fun and mischief. Manoj, Raj and he had met up every single day to go off in search of adventure. He looked back in the trunk and there he saw the rubber ball that had bought them hours of joy. He remembered those days affectionately and recalled a time when they would spend their evenings in the field playing Lagori and eating the curries and chapatis that their mothers had packed for them. As the sun set low across the sugarcane field, the three young friends would gather their tiffin pots and ball and walk slowly back towards the village. He thought back to the many conversations they had had while sitting in the midst of the tall cornstalks.

Vijay closed his eyes and held the rubber ball tight within his hand and took his mind back to the day when during a hot summer afternoon, they had made a pact. The boys had found shade under a large banyan tree and were cooling themselves by splashing water over their faces. They had sat in silence, simply enjoying each other's company.

'I wish this summer would last forever,' said Vijay as he chewed on a blade of grass. 'It will be over in a few weeks and then we will be back at school.'

'So, what! We can still go on adventures at the weekends and after school,' replied Manoj.
Vijay fell silent and looked away from his friends trying to hide his face. Raj crawled over to where he was sitting and grabbing hold of his shoulder, he turned him around to face him. Vijay covered his face in embarrassment as tears flowed from his eyes.
'What's the matter, Vijay?' asked Manoj, who had come over to where the other boys sat.
Vijay wiped away the tears with the back of his hands and looked at his best friends.
'My mother and father are sending me away to boarding school after the summer holidays,' said Vijay, trying to fight back tears.
Manoj and Raj looked at Vijay with unbelieving eyes and shook their heads in disapproval.
'They can't do that, Vijay. You are already halfway through school. You must have done something wrong and they are scaring you as a punishment,' suggested Raj.
'No, it's true, Raj. We went to visit the school last week and I start in three weeks' time,' replied Vijay.
Manoj, who had been sitting quietly looking into the distance, stood up, picked up the rubber ball and threw it aggressively against a tree trunk. He turned to Vijay and looked at him angrily.
'It's your bloody fault, Vijay,' he shouted. 'I warned you that being too clever would bring you nothing but trouble. Now look at what you've done. You've broken our friendship by being too smart. I suppose we're not good enough to be your friends now.'
Raj stood up and put an arm around Manoj, who shook himself free and walked over to where he had thrown the ball; he sat down with his back against the tree. Manoj always had a quick temper, but also became calm just

as quickly.
'He's only saying those things because he's upset,' said Raj, 'Give him a few minutes and he'll be fine.'
'But he's right isn't he? We can't be friends anymore with me being miles away. You will make new friends and soon forget about me.'
Raj looked at the sadness in his friend's eyes. He walked over to where Manoj sat and put out a hand, which after a few seconds Manoj accepted. Raj pulled him up from the ground and with an arm around his shoulders, led him back to where Vijay sat. He offered the same hand to Vijay, who immediately grasped it and jumped up. The three boys stood together in a circle and each one put a hand on the shoulder of the boy next to him.
'We will make a pact,' declared Raj, 'we will promise always to be friends and never to forget about each other. We will finish school, go to college, get jobs and be successful. Then we will marry beautiful girls and have smart kids like Vijay.' The three boys all smiled. 'We will grow old together and sit in the village square when our beards are long and grey. We will teach our grandchildren how to play Lagori and tell them stories of our adventures. Until our dying breath, we will not be torn apart and anyone who tries to separate us will get a punch in the eye,' finished Raj.
The three boys huddled together and gave each other a huge hug. Then, filled with melancholy, they slowly made their way back to the village and back to their homes. Within months of having made their pact, a fire drove a wedge between them and the promise they had made was broken.
Vijay let the memory wash over him and then he slowly let go of the ball and placed it lovingly back into the trunk. He lifted out a package that had been carefully

wrapped in brown paper and string. He placed it on the floor, untied the knot and unfolded the parcel wrapping. From within, he lifted his old police uniform that he had worn when he worked here in the village. He unrolled the shirt and there in the middle he found the two things he was looking for. He picked up both the police station key and the Glock 17 pistol and looked at them with both fear and excitement.

The feelings of guilt about breaking the pact that he had made with his friends had been subconsciously eating away at him for years. Over the last few weeks, a powerful desire within him was compelling him to find his friends no matter the cost. While he was recuperating in hospital and under heavy medication, he had experienced many strange dreams, haunting images of fearsome beasts breathing fire and people drowning in burning hot sand. Amongst these frightful nightmares, there were moments of pure joy as he dreamt of sitting under a banyan tree with his two best friends, eating fresh watermelon in beautiful sunshine. No matter what the dream, he always felt a watchful presence in the edge of his mind. He would turn to see who it was, but he would only ever catch a tiny glimpse of a shining light and then it was gone. He felt he was being driven towards something and that journey would start that night when he broke into the police station and searched for clues that may lead him to Manoj and Raj.

*****

Manoj sat by the side of the road, where he had been dropped off by Toni and Sanjeev. His body ached and the breeze stung his face as it sailed over his cuts and bruises. His white shirt was covered in blood stains and his head pounded with intense pain. He was aware of the stares he was receiving from the crowds of people passing him on the street, but no one cared enough to stop. He had been driven to the outskirts of Dharavi and told to jump out as the car slowed. As he jumped out of the car, he had cut open his knee and he sat there rubbing at the throbbing bleeding wound. He was desperate to get home so he could clean himself up and rest but he was in such pain he wasn't sure if he could make it. After resting for a while, he heaved himself up and walked into an alley leading into the slums. He half walked and half hobbled his way through the narrow alleys of Dharavi. He felt lightheaded as his head spun, causing him to stumble and almost fall into the open flow of sewage that ran along the alleyway. As he swayed through the rat-infested streets, he bumped into a little boy squatting in the middle of the street to defecate. To any outsider, the smell within the slums would have been horrendous and unbearable, but Manoj and the other million residents were immune to its foul presence. As he walked, he took rests by leaning against the small and cramped shacks that lined each side of the confined alleyways and streets that had become camouflaged with rubbish. Unlike outside the slums, the people inside Dharavi had a sense of community and several times he was stopped and offered help, but he refused every time. He just wanted to get home on his own. Deeper and deeper he travelled into the slums and along the way he passed bare foot children playing on mounds of rubbish and jumping into puddles of water containing chemicals, sewage and disease. An old lady pushed aside one of the children as she foraged through the rubbish in search for plastic that she could sell for recycling. A twelve-hour shift of searching through rubbish containing all manner of horrors such as faeces and needles would earn her a measly dollar. As he walked through the alleys, he passed dozens of open doorways with a multitude of stories held within each room. A two-story shack housing twenty-one members of a family, a pottery workshop, where ladies toiled all day to make pots for the rich of Mumbai, a sick old man laid on his death bed being cared for by his daughter in-law, a distraught widow sitting in white on her doorstep worrying about the fate of her young children and a hundred more stories. Manoj stopped by a bakery and steadied himself before slowly setting off to navigate through the goats and cows as they stood in his way like some obstacle course. A fat man in a white filthy vest in an upper floor room lent out of his window and after gurgling loudly spat the contents of his mouth right in front of Manoj's feet, missing his head by millimetres. Manoj turned left into another narrow alleyway that had become dark from the overhanging buildings and finally reached his tiny home that stood smothered between a row of ramshackle lodgings built with odd bits of metal and thrown away parts. He walked through his front door, took off his sandals and lay on the double mattress on one side of the twelve foot square room. A single flickering light bulb that hung from a low ceiling cast shadows around the dingy room. Upon the walls were paintings of Hindu Gods and Sikh Gurus. Hanuman, the monkey God, hung next to Guru Nanak, the founder of Sikhism, and Ram had been placed between Ganesha, the elephant-headed God, and Krishna. The smell of incense and recently cooked chapattis and dhal filled the room. A gas-fuelled stove sat cooling down in one corner of the room that doubled up as a kitchen and Manoj's bedroom. Shelves around the room held cheap tin cooking pots and pans, jars containing spices and condiments, a gas lantern and other such things that added to the total sum of Manoj's earthly possessions.

Along with every other family in Dharavi, the only luxury item that Manoj possessed was a small colour television that sat perched on a wooden shelf in a cobwebbed corner of the room.

Manoj lay as still as possible; the pain when he moved was excruciating. He could hear the sound of shuffling feet in the room next to where he lay. The sound grew louder and a young woman parted the curtain that acted as the door and entered the room. The woman looked upon the broken man on the mattress and gasped in horror. She hurried towards him and knelt down beside him. She looked Manoj up and down with tears brimming in her eyes.

'Manu! What has happened to you?' asked Manoj's wife, tears streaming freely down her face.

'Where is Navjot?' asked Manoj.

'I just put him to bed.'

'How is he now?'

'The fever is less and the coughing seems to have gone, but he's still weak. He will recover because he is strong like his father,' said Radhika. 'Let me fetch some water and a cloth to clean your wounds and then you must tell me what happened.'

Radhika walked out of the house and lifted the lid from a large blue barrel. In the slums, the water supply was only turned on for two hours a day from five o'clock in the morning. All families had to be awake at that time to fill their barrels or they would have no water for the rest of the day. Radhika took a small bucket, which she filled with water and came back inside the house. Taking a cloth from a shelf, she returned to her husband and gently started to clean the blood from his face. Manoj winced as the cloth rubbed against the cuts and bruises but gritted his teeth. He didn't want to show weakness in front of his wife.

'Did this happen because of me, Manu?' asked Radhika. Manoj shook his head gently and lifting his arm painfully, he took hold of his wife's hand.
'No, it was just some hoodlums looking for money, that's all. This has nothing to do with you,' lied Manoj.
Manoj averted his eyes from his wife's and felt her once again working the cloth over his wounds. She slowly undid the buttons on his blood-stained shirt and opened it up to reveal more bruises and cuts all over his chest. As Radhika cleaned the wounds on his chest, he thought back to the last time he had received a similar beating. It was a few months after his marriage to Radhika and they had set up home in a village on the outskirts of Mumbai. They had tried to keep themselves to themselves, but soon word had got around that a Sikh man was living with a Dalit low caste girl. One night, Manoj was returning home after working in the streets of Mumbai selling clothes that his wife had stitched. As he approached his house, he was blocked by a group of men holding sticks and metal rods. In the darkness, they forced him into an alleyway and beat him with their weapons until he almost passed out. They warned him to leave the village or next time he would not survive. He managed to scramble his way home and when he got there, he found it ransacked and his wife hiding under the bed. All his possessions had been broken and the little money they owned had been stolen. After a few days, they had packed up and headed towards Mumbai, where they had moved into the slum house they were now living in.
'Tomorrow I need to take a trip that will take a few days,' said Manoj.
'How can you go anywhere like this,' replied Radhika in astonishment.
'It is something I need to do, so don't argue,' shouted

Manoj.
Radhika recoiled from her husband and started busying herself with putting away the cloth and water. From a shelf she grabbed some turmeric and started applying it to his wounds.
Manoj straight away regretted shouting at his wife but he knew that she would not take it to heart. He had always been quick to get angry but calmed down just as fast and was never violent. He closed his eyes and felt himself drifting off to sleep, which he did not resist. He let the drowsiness overcome him and fell into a deep sleep filled with memories and disturbing images. As a fever gripped his body, he saw himself as a child again running through the fields with his friends, he saw his father throw his clothes out into the street and he saw Rahul Bachchan offering him a job and the dream of leaving Dharavi. All these images melded into one until he didn't know who he was anymore. Scary shadows of beasts with fangs chased him through rooms filled with evil spirits and fire threatened to engulf him. As he ran, he looked into the distance and saw a shining light beckoning him. His heart soared at the sight of the light; he knew it was pure love that guided him towards it. He could still feel the heat from the fire at his back, but as he got ever closer to the light, the heat was replaced with a cool breeze. He stopped running and looked behind him and saw three boys all in a huddle in the middle of a field under a banyan tree. The sky was clear blue and the sun shone directly on them. He turned so he could head towards the light but it was no longer there. Instead, he caught a glimpse of a beautiful woman dressed all in white holding a shining sword. It was only a fleeting glimpse, but nonetheless he knew he had seen it and knew then what he had to do. He would do anything to protect his wife and child. He had already

sacrificed so much and now he had to seek out his childhood friend and kill him.

*****

With great care not to make any noise, Vijay put on his shoes and gently opened the wooden shutters of the window in his room. He was dressed all in black, which made him feel like some petty thief heading into the night to rob the villagers. He had thought long and hard about taking his gun with him, but in the end decided against it. All he wanted was some information and he didn't want to hurt anyone in the process. He checked his pockets for the third time to make sure he had the two things he needed: the police station keys and his mobile phone. He removed his phone from his pocket and made sure it was on silent and that it had enough battery to complete his mission. He placed a small stool next to his window and with great difficulty climbed out of the window and started hobbling forward into the street with his walking stick. The village was pitch black as even the moon had decided to hide behind a bunch of clouds but he knew the streets like the back of his hand so had no trouble in navigating through the dark alleyways and streets. Over the past few days, he had casually asked around about the usual activity throughout the night. He had discovered that Mr Kohli, the owner of the off-licence in the village square, was the last to go to bed at around eleven o'clock but the village's night watchman patrolled the streets at two in the morning until three. The earliest risers were the villagers who worked in the bakery and they started work at four o'clock. That meant he had two opportunities to get to the police station, between eleven and two or between three and four in the morning. He had decided his best option was to leave his house at twelve o'clock, which would give him plenty of time before the night watchman started his shift. He knew that it would take him longer than normal to reach the police station because of his leg so he had allowed himself two hours.

Mr Kohli made very little profit as most of his takings were withered away either by drinking his own stock or gambling away his money. This caused his wife constant consternation, which would often result in heated arguments and Mr Kohli physically attacking her while in his drunken state. The neighbours were well versed with the events that would unfold, so when the drama reached a certain point, one of them would make their way to the inspector's house and call upon him to arrest Mr Kohli before he killed his long-suffering wife. As Vijay made his way stealthily through the village, Mr Kohli awoke in a stupor and found himself in the all too familiar position of lying on the concrete kitchen floor. His mistress for the night was an empty bottle of whisky, which he had been lovingly holding close to his chest. Once he had gathered his senses, he staggered towards his bedroom and upon reaching his marital bed, he tossed away the blanket that covered his wife and unsuccessfully tried climbing on top of her. Mrs Kohli was a strong woman and had over the years learnt to defend herself and give as good as she got. It was rarely difficult to overpower her husband as in his drunkenness he had barely the strength of a two-year-old child. Mrs Kohli could easily restrain her husband and if required tie him up and leave him out in the street for the night, but she chose to play out the drama for the sake of keeping up appearances. As she pushed him away, she screamed at the top of her voice as a signal to the neighbours that the play had reached the point when they could enter.

As Vijay approached the village square, he heard the distant scream of a woman and cursed to himself. He knew straight away who it was and how the next hour of the night would play out. He leaned into the shadow of the pottery shop door and thought about turning back but if he did, he would be heading back towards Mr Kohli's house and a bunch of nosey neighbours. He started to work out in his head how much time he had before the police station would have a new tenant for the night. The inspector's house was on the other side of the village, so it would take ten minutes for a neighbour to reach him by foot. Then another ten minutes to get back to Mr Kohli's house but the inspector would need to get dressed so that meant another ten minutes. From Mr Kohli's house to the police station was ten minutes but it would take longer as Mr Kohli would be drunk and move slowly. He decided he still had about forty-five minutes to get in and out of the police station before anyone arrived and he was five minutes away now. He decided he would risk it so he pushed on trying to walk as fast as his damaged leg would allow.

As he approached the police station, Vijay looked around to ensure no one was about and then watched the station for a few minutes for any sign of movement within. When he was sure that the coast was clear and that the station was empty, he stepped out from his cover point and made his way to the front door. He removed both his phone and the key from his pocket. Using the light from his phone, he unlocked the door and crept inside. Locking the door from the inside he quickly made his way into the main office where the inspector's desk and filing cabinets were kept. He was interested in gathering information about two things; the investigation report into the fire and the reason why Manoj's father visited the police station every year on the same day. He walked over to the first set of filing cabinets and hoped that there was some kind of organised filing system. He grabbed hold of the handle of the top drawer and pulled it but it was locked. He tried the second drawer and a few others but they were all locked too. He swore under his breath and cursed himself for not having anticipated that the files would be under lock and key. When he worked at the station, they were never locked so he had assumed that they would be open. He looked at his watch and rubbed at his forehead; he only had half an hour left. He shone the torch from his phone around the room trying to think where the key to the cabinets might be kept. As the light passed over everything in the room, it finally fell upon the desk of Inspector Singh and Vijay knew that the key would be in his desk drawer. Mr Singh was a control freak and didn't trust any of his officers with anything of any importance. He walked over to the desk and pulled on the drawer but that too was locked. Vijay was starting to panic and knew he was running out of time. In desperation he grabbed hold of a metal plaque that had the inspector's name and title on it and using it as a lever, he broke open the drawer. There, right on top of some brown files, was a bunch of keys. He grabbed hold of the keys and was about to go over to the cabinets when he read the title of the file that the keys were sitting on, 'Investigation into the Katri's Fire.' Vijay couldn't believe his luck so he quickly removed the file from the drawer and opened it. He took photos of every document. Just as he was taking a snapshot of the last page, he heard the engine of a car approaching the police station. He limped over to the front desk and peered through a window to see a police jeep pulling up to the front door. Again, he couldn't believe how stupid he had been; of course, the inspector would come by car. When Vijay had worked at the station, the only mode of transport the police had were bicycles but the inspector had always been trying to convince the state chief of police that he needed a car and evidently he had been successful. He knew the layout of the police station by heart; there were no exits other than the front door and all the windows had bars. His heart was racing as he heard the engine of the police car stop and the door open. He looked round the room for a place to hide and then suddenly remembered the tiny trap door that led to the flat roof top of the station. He quickly placed all the documents back into the file and then back into the drawer. In the last second, remembered to put the bunch of keys back on top. He closed the drawer and then used the inspector's chair as a step to get on top of his desk so that he could reach the rope to the pull-down the stairs. As he tugged on the rope, he heard the inspector's voice coming from the entrance to the police station. He lowered the stairs and as quick as his legs would carry him, he climbed up and just as the inspector entered the room with the drunken Mr Kohli and young Officer Kirit, he managed to pull the stairs up. He sighed heavily and crouched on the roof top rubbing at the intense throbbing in his leg. He tried pushing himself up so he could stretch his leg but the pain was too intense. He looked around for his walking stick and then realised with horror that he had left it next to the filing cabinets. Inside the police station, Inspector Singh held onto Mr Kohli to prevent the drunkard from falling flat on his face. He led the man through to another room and placed him on a chair that sat next to the only cell in the police station. He fished inside his trouser pocket and then cursed himself for forgetting his cell key at home. He turned to return to the office and bumped straight into Kirit knocking the young man onto his butt. The inspector

shook his head but at the same time gave the officer a hand up from the floor.
'You almost gave me a heart attack,' said the inspector.
'Well, you almost broke every bone in my body with that belly of yours,' replied the officer.
The inspector ignored the comment and from his pocket took out a single key and handed it to the officer. 'Go get the bunch of keys that are in the top drawer of my desk,' he instructed.
Kirit took hold of the keys and walked back into the office and over to the desk. As he was about to unlock the drawer, he noticed the damage to the wood and without using the key, he pulled the drawer open. He scratched his head in confusion and was about to call out to the inspector, when he noticed footprints on top of the desk. He looked up to the ceiling and saw that the rope to the roof ladder had become trapped in the door. At that moment, he knew there was an intruder and that they were hiding on the roof. He didn't want to shout out to the inspector as that might alert the perpetrator, so instead he grabbed hold of the keys and went back towards the cell. He approached the inspector and then whispered to him.
'Sir, I need to show you something back in the other room.'
'Why are you whispering, Kirit, has the fall damaged your brain?'
Kirit put his fingers to his lips in an attempt to silence the booming voice of the inspector and then moved back into the office. As he walked into the room with the inspector close behind him, his heart froze and he suddenly felt all hot and flustered. He stared at the walking stick neatly propped up against one of the filing cabinets and he realised who was on the roof.
'Well, what is it Kirit?' asked the inspector running out of

patience.
Kirit was dumb struck and didn't know whether to tell his superior the truth or cover it up. He ran through his head the different eventualities of each scenario: he heard the fat man behind him sighing heavily and knew he had to make a choice. He quickly walked over to the desk to divert the inspector's attention and pointed to his desk.
'Sorry, Sir, but I think I broke your drawer,' he lied.
The inspector stormed over to the desk and looked at it and sighed even more heavily than before.
'You really are a clumsy fool, Kirit. A simple task I gave you and you couldn't even complete that. You will have to fix this tomorrow or I will dock your wages, understand?' shouted Inspector Singh.
'Yes Sir, of course, Sir,' replied Kirit trying to look as embarrassed and sorry as possible.
The inspector turned and hurried back to the cell room to complete the task at hand. As soon as he was out of sight, Kirit wiped the footprint from the desk with his sleeve, picked up the walking stick and hid it behind one of the filing cabinets. Just as he had finished removing the evidence, the inspector walked back into the room.
'You really are a waste of space, Kirit. I seriously don't know why I bothered bringing you along. You've just been a burden. You go home and I'll wait here until our friend sobers up and then we can swap in the morning,' instructed the inspector.
'There's no way I'm letting you ruin your sleep after I've just broken your desk, Sir. As a punishment I will stay up and look after Mr Kohli. It will make me feel better for being so stupid, Sir,' pleaded the young officer.
The inspector thought about it for a split second and decided that he'd rather sleep in his own bed than on his desk chair so he nodded in agreement. Grabbing hold of the file from his drawer, he hurriedly left before Kirit

could change his mind. Kirit ran to the barred window by the door and waited until the inspector's car had disappeared. He then went back to the office and climbing onto the inspector's desk, he pulled down the staircase.
'It's ok, the inspector has gone so you can come down Vijay,' said Kirit in a low voice.
Vijay appeared above him. He slowly made his way down the stairs and assisted by Kirit, he stepped down from the desk. Kirit retrieved the walking stick from behind the cabinet and handed it back to Vijay.
'Thank you, Kirit, for covering for me. That was very much appreciated. I understand how bad it would be if the inspector discovered that you were lying,' said Vijay sincerely.
'You are a good friend, Vijay, and you helped me a lot when I first joined the force so I will be forever grateful but you need to be careful. The inspector is not a forgiving man and if he finds out that you have been snooping around then he will make sure that you either end up in prison or never work in the police force again. He has friends in high places. How do you think he got that car for a village that you can walk around in an hour?' replied Kirit. 'Anyway, why are you so obsessed with finding Manoj now? You haven't seen each other in years. What's going on?'
'Some things just don't add up about the fire that killed Raj's family and that has been bothering me for years. There was never any conclusion on how the fire started and then there was that sixth body. There was never any investigation into who it was or what they were doing there. Add that to the mysterious appearance of Manoj's father every year to visit the police station and it all gives me an uneasy feeling.'
The two men fell silent. Kirit offered Vijay a seat and sat

down opposite him. Vijay rubbed at his leg and pulled up the images of the file that he had on his phone and flicked through them. They contained photographs of the house and the burnt bodies. The file also contained reports of the limited investigation that had been carried out at the time. Vijay wanted to know who the investigating officer was at the time so he could try and get more information but before he got that far, Kirit interrupted him.

'There was one other thing that I didn't tell you about the last time Mr Anand visited,' started Kirit hesitantly. 'The inspector thought I was in the cell cleaning it out but I'd already finished and was heading back to the office when I saw the inspector hand Mr Anand a large brown envelope. He took it and then opened it and took out bundles of money. They shook hands and then Manoj's father left without another word.'

'How much money was in the envelope?' asked Vijay.

'It must have been a few hundred thousand Rupees,' answered Kirit.

Vijay took in the information and all kind of thoughts started to circulate through his head. The money could have been for a number of reasons: it could all be very innocent and maybe the inspector was just paying back some debt or it could be more sinister. Was there some kind of shady deal the two were involved in such as drugs? Could Mr Anand be blackmailing the inspector or was it some kind of extortion racketeering? This latest information added to the uneasy feelings he already had. He must pick up the pace of his search for the truth and his next step was to find the officer in charge of the investigation into the fire all those years ago. He pulled up the files again and scrolled down to where the officer in charge had signed his name. He zoomed into the name and read it out aloud.

‘Deepak Chopra.’

CHAPTER SIX

The houses on Layer Gardens stood upright and proud looking down on all the poorer parts of Acton. The night lay silent and the folks went about their business knowing that crime in their pretty area was low. The lawyers, accountants and doctors ensured that the streets were regularly patrolled and that the neighbourhood watch was in full effect. The Kables in number twenty-four were getting ready for bed after their nightly Ovaltine. Mr Kable had brushed his teeth and sat in his bed reading *Dentistry Today* while waiting for his wife. In number forty-three, Mrs Andrews put the finishing touches to her oil painting of the local vicar while her husband was supposedly working late. In number twelve, the Rahmani's entertained a bunch of people they neither liked nor wanted to entertain but life in Layer Gardens had to be maintained somehow. The Martans in number thirty-six sat watching the last five minutes of *Titanic* for the fourteenth time and low and behold, Mr Martan cried for the fourteenth time. In number twenty-eight, Mr Anton sat in his office chair in his study surrounded by accountancy books and framed certificates. The leather buttoned burgundy chair had been pulled away from the mahogany desk and placed in the middle of the room. The door had been locked from the inside and the curtains shut tight. The only light in the office came from the desk lamp, which created haunting shadows across the room. Two of the walls were covered with bookshelves. The large, curtained window decorated most of the third wall and the fourth wall was mostly bare apart from two family photographs. The first photograph showed an idyllic family, all smiles sitting casually in a park with their Labrador. The second photograph was of an elderly couple, presumably Mr Anton's parents. The only other thing on the wall was a low shelf that held his stereo system.

Mr Anton was a proud family man who had built his business up from scratch and had finally fulfilled his dream of moving to a rich neighbourhood. More than ever now he enjoyed entertaining his clients in his large, landscaped garden and showing off his expensive taste in whiskies. Although he loved being around people and socialising, his favourite part of the day was when he could enjoy a glass of single malt whisky on his own and listen to some music. Today he had chosen a Glenmorangie signet whisky that had been distilled twice through Glenmorangie's copper-pot stills by a team of sixteen distillers known as the 'Sixteen Men of Tain.' The half empty glass sat on the desk neglected; even the ice had lost the will to live. The 'Sound of Silence' filled the room with its soft and melodic tones, the two voices creating perfect harmonies. Mr Anton tried hard to focus on the song but the sound was being replaced by a ringing in his ears as the blood began to flow from them. He tried to keep his eyes wide open and focused on the family photographs but the lids felt heavy and slowly he lost sight of them. The cut across his neck seeped blood onto his Paul Smith shirt turning it from pink to red. A sudden coughing fit forced his eyes open again and from his mouth blood splattered across the room. He tried to cover his mouth with his hands but remembered that they had been bound with ropes to the chair. He knew that he had lost the battle with death so he sat back into his chair and looked at the man standing before him. The tall man dressed all in black stood motionless as the knife in his left gloved hand dripped droplets of blood onto the carpet. He wanted to turn away from the accountant's suffering but was somehow frozen to the spot. As he had drawn the knife across the man's throat, he had hesitated and almost given in to his weakness and fled. He had never hurt anyone in his life before but he knew that this was the right thing to do. He would never forgive himself if he allowed weakness and doubt to enter his mind and let the man get away with his sins. As the man in the chair gasped his last breaths, the tall man lifted the Spock mask. Mr Anton looked upon his killer's face and knew then why this day had come. With all his remaining strength, he silently mouthed the word 'sorry' and with that final rasp of breath, he died. Spock stared at the dead man and felt his eyes fill with water. All the years of pain and suffering came flooding back; everything he had lost and all he had become was down to this man in front of him. He felt deep in his heart that what he had done was right but still doubt gnawed away at him. He looked away from the dead man and towards Chekov who stood behind the chair. Chekov raised a thumb at Spock and then walked over to the wall that held the photographs. With a red paint can, he sprayed a vertical line from high up on the wall down to where it intersected the low shelf. Chekov then sprayed a large number four with a circle around it on the wall. Chekov turned towards Spock and then to Kirk, who was stood by the door, and motioned for them to leave. Kirk picked up a laptop from the desk and unlocked the office door. Together the three of them walked out into the darkness of Layer Gardens.

*****

Deepak Chopra lit a cigarette and took a deep drag while he stared at the red markings on the wall in front of him. He was the first to arrive at the scene of the crime

and had been met by a distraught and hysterical wife, who he gave no emotional support. He was only interested in the crime and had no time or patience for grieving wives. He would wait for his apprentice, Mark, to arrive and ask him to interview the family members. He walked closer to the wall and reaching out touched a section of the red paint with his fingertip. It was still sticky, which meant that it must have been sprayed within the last couple of hours. Deepak looked at his watch and noted the time down in his notebook. He also made a note of the number four that had been sprayed on the wall. He flicked back through his notes to check what number had been carved into the first victim's chest. He found the page and stared at the number seven. He tried to find a connection between the two numbers but came up blank. He ran his eyes down the thick red vertical line that ran the entire length of the wall and intersected a low shelf that held an amplifier. The line was similar in style to the cut that had been made down the entire length of the first victim's face. The killers were definitely leaving cryptic clues but as of yet, he had no idea what they meant. He looked up at the wall again but there, directly in front of him, was Mark.
'One thing's for sure. These killers don't like murdering during the day,' said Mark yawning. 'Maybe they are vampires.'
The detective pushed the young man aside and sent him off to talk to the murdered man's wife. He then walked around the room looking for any other evidence that the killers may have left behind. He walked past the dead man and put out his cigarette in an ash tray that lay on the desk. He immediately took out another and lighting it, sucked in a drag. He noticed that there was a wireless mouse and laptop charger but no laptop on the desk. He looked around the room and checked in all the desk

drawers but could not find a laptop anywhere. After looking around the room, he went back over to the dead man and lifted his head to reveal the jagged cut across his throat. Blood covered the man's clothes and had also soaked into the white carpet leaving a large red stain. He knelt down and looked closely at the blood-soaked carpet and could just make out the imprint of a shoe. He took out his phone and captured a photo of the imprint and then also one of the sprayed wall. Just as he had finished, a group of people rushed into the room. Two paramedics wheeling a stretcher were followed by three forensic officers wearing white overalls and gloves.
'You shouldn't be smoking in here,' said one of the paramedics pushing past him. Deepak ignored him and walked out of the room to find Mark.
Deepak looked around the living room and could literally smell the money. A large gold framed mirror hung over an elegant fireplace. A grand piano stood in one corner of the room and a huge chandelier hung from the pristine white ceiling. The furniture was white, elegant and exclusive and the room seemed barely lived in. Nothing was out of place or broken so the motive for the break in and murder did not seem to be money related. The only item that appeared to be missing was the accountant's laptop. He had checked all the outside doors and windows and there was no sign of a break in so whoever the murderer or murderers were, they had found a way to get inside without using force. The detective was just about to go looking for Mark when he appeared from a doorway that led to the kitchen.
'Poor Mrs Anton; she's in absolute bits. Must be horrific to come home and find…,' started Mark but was then interrupted by Deepak.
'Did you get anything useful out of her?'
'She was out with the children most of the day visiting

her sister so she has an alibi but apart from that she was too upset to answer more questions. Were there any clues from the murder room?'

'It could be someone that Mr Anton knew as there are no signs of a break in, so get me a list of all his current clients. What are your IT skills like?'

'Pretty good,' replied Mark.

'Could you locate a stolen laptop?'

'There's a "Find my Device" feature on Windows but it would need to be enabled first. Plus, you would need the log in details to his Microsoft account. I'll talk to Mrs Anton and ask her if she has his log in details,' suggested Mark.

'Have you set up an interview with the other victim's wife yet? Mrs Evans?' asked Deepak.

'Yes, it's tomorrow. I mean today?' replied Mark looking at his watch.

'These crimes are definitely personal so we need to find the connection between the two dead people. Once we find that link, we will find the killer or killers.'

*****

Mark sat nervously on the sofa with a china teacup in his hand and a Jack Russell sniffing around his boots. He took a sip from the cup and then picked up a chocolate hobnob from a round china plate on the coffee table in front of him. He checked that the coast was clear and then gave the dog a little shove with his foot. The dog gave him a low rumbling growl and then disappeared off to file a complaint with his master. The living room was perfectly positioned in a small bungalow that sat in the middle of a quaint cul-de-sac in suburban Acton. The room was perfectly decorated with tailored pleat curtains, a velvet patterned carpet and smiling family photos on the mantel piece over a fireplace. In one corner of the room on the wall was a wooden figure of Christ on a cross. Deepak had insisted that Mark interview Mrs Evan's by himself and chose to wait in the car. He hadn't asked why but he suspected it had something to do with the smell of alcohol that reeked from the detective's breath. As Mark finished the biscuit and wiped away the crumbs from his trousers a woman walked into the room with the dog skulking behind her. Mark immediately got up and waited for the woman to sit on an armchair opposite him and then he sat back down and placed his cup on the coffee table. He reached into his jacket pocket and produced a notebook and pencil.

'Firstly, I'd like to say I'm so sorry for your loss, Mrs Evans,' said the trainee constable.

The lady looked at him and nodded her approval of his comment.

'As you know, we are investigating the death of your husband and wanted to ask you a few questions.'

'Of course, anything to help,' replied the woman casually.

'Do you know if your husband had any enemies, maybe at work or around the neighbourhood?'

'I don't think so; he was always very civil and nice to people on the outside.'

'Did you notice anything that wasn't quite normal recently, like nuisance calls, your husband coming home late or anything like that?'

'My husband worked at Furniture World so he worked all kinds of shifts. He went to work and when he came home, he would sit in front of the telly and drink. That was his life.'

'Did your husband drink a lot?'

'If you call a bottle of whisky a night a lot, then I guess yes.'

'Any particular reason for the drinking, for example did he have money problems, gambling perhaps? Did he owe anybody money?'
'Money was always tight just like most families around here, but we don't owe money to anyone apart from the bank.'
'Could you tell me what you do for a living Mrs Evans?'
'I'm a mother and a housewife, constable. Well I was a housewife, I should say.'
'Was that your son who opened the door?'
'Yes, he's studying A levels.'
'I must say, he makes a lovely cup of tea.'
The woman nodded.
'You also have a daughter,' Mark consulted his notebook, 'Karen?'
Mrs Evans shifted in her seat and nodded again.
'Does she also live at home?'
'Karen moved out a few years ago and we don't see her much.'
'Any particular reason she moved out?'
'She was twenty-one and wanted her freedom perhaps?'
'You don't seem so sure?'
Mrs Evans averted her eyes from the constable's, picked up the dog that had been watching Mark suspiciously from behind her legs and placed him on her lap. She stroked the soft fur and looked as though she was deep in thought.
'You will have to ask her why she left, constable.'
'Do you have an address for her?'
Mrs Evans shook her head and then placed the dog back on the floor.
'Unless there's anything else I can help with constable, I really need to be getting on.'
'Of course, I've taken up enough of your time.'
The constable rose from the sofa and as Mrs Evans

stood up from her armchair, she gave a little wince and rubbed at her left knee.
'Are you alright?' asked Mark as he stepped forward towards her.
Mrs Evans stepped away from the constable and in some agony forced herself to stand upright.
'I'm quite alright, just some pain from a fall I had the other week. It was entirely my own fault, shouldn't have stood on a chair as I was dusting.' Again, the woman averted her eyes and then slowly walked the constable to the front door and escorted him out. Mark walked back down the road towards the car and climbed into the passenger seat.
As he climbed into the driver's seat he noticed that the detective was asleep so intentionally slammed shut the door.
Deepak jerked awake and rubbing at his temples shot Mark a viscous look.
'So?' asked Deepak abruptly.
'She wasn't very forthcoming and definitely hiding something. She got very defensive when I asked about a knee injury and I'm sure she was lying about how she got it.'
'Check hospital and doctor records for all the family. I want to know if there's a regular pattern of mysterious injuries and accidents,' instructed Deepak as he took a swig from a water bottle.
'Oh yes, her daughter Karen seems a bit estranged, so that's probably worth pursuing.'
'Get me her address and I'll pay her a surprise visit tonight.'

*****

Deepak drove up Baird Avenue and parked outside St

Andrews Tower in the Golf Links Estate. He climbed out of the car and into the darkness of a chilly West London evening. He walked up to the main entrance, pressed the intercom to Flat fifteen and waited for an answer. After a minute, he pressed it again and this time a voice spoke from the other side.
'Yes,' said a woman's voice.
'My name is Detective Deepak Chopra and I would like to speak to you about your father.'
The intercom fell silent for a few seconds before the door buzzed and the woman instructed him to enter and come up to the second floor. The detective climbed the stairs to the tower block and knocked on the door, which was immediately opened by a young woman. She led Deepak to a worn-out green fabric sofa and sat down opposite him on a wooden chair. The small living area was sparsely furnished and the walls were in desperate need of a lick of paint but the flat appeared clean and well looked after. Deepak stared at the tall skinny girl sitting in front of him and could sense her nervousness.
'Would you like a cup of tea, Sir?' asked Karen Evans.
'No, I just need to ask a few questions,' replied Deepak abruptly.
Karen started biting at her nails and nervously tugged at a lock of her shoulder length bleached blonde hair. She avoided looking into the detective's eyes.
Deepak stared intensely at the girl sitting opposite him and knew that she was scared. He enjoyed the power that her fear was giving him and arousal stirred in him. He removed a pack of cigarettes from his coat pocket and lit one. He slowly blew smoke towards the girl, who tried not to show her annoyance at his bad manners.
'You've been in trouble with the police before,' stated the detective.
'What's that got to do with my dad?' asked Karen.

'Drug possession, shop lifting and even GBH. That's quite a collection,' continued Deepak, ignoring her question.
'Like I said, that has nothing to do with my dad.'
'On the contrary, it has everything to do with your dad. Children don't just become bad on their own. It takes years of neglect and bad parenting to turn a good, church going girl into to a pathetic, skinny, substance abusing wretch.' Deepak let his words float in the air and got the reaction that he desired.
Karen pulled at the lock of hair harder with one hand and started fiddling with her crucifix necklace with the other.
'So, tell me about this GBH charge. I can't imagine a weak and cowardly girl like you beating anyone up.'
'That was a long time ago and I've cleaned myself up. I've not abused in ages and I'm getting help…' She suddenly stopped mid-sentence.
'Who are you getting help from Karen?'
'Just a friend,' replied Karen nervously.
'Friend got a name?'
'It's not important.'
Deepak took a slow drag from his cigarette, thought about her response and decided that he didn't want to push her too hard. She obviously didn't want him to know who had been helping her, but he let it go for now.
'Why aren't you living at home, Karen?'
'I'm over eighteen so I can live wherever I want.'
'So, you'd rather live in a flea-bitten council flat with not enough money to put some flesh on your bones than live in a nice home with your mother and have cooked meals?'
Karen didn't answer and instead looked out of the window into the darkness and continued fiddling with her necklace.
'Why didn't you go to your father's funeral, Karen?'

'Because I would have got too teary and that would have messed up my mascara and besides, my only black dress is at the cleaners,' replied Karen sarcastically.
'Do you know what I think?' asked Deepak, as he stubbed his cigarette out on the carpet and then rubbed the ash in with his foot. He removed another cigarette from the pack and lit it up, letting the question hang in the air.
'I think your father was some sort of abuser and your mother was too weak to protect you, so you decided to kill him. We know about all the hospital visits that you and your mother had over the years: bruised legs, broken bones and black eyes. What do you think about my theory?'
'I think you're fucking crazy,' replied Karen, as she got up from the chair and disappeared into the kitchen.
Karen stood by the kitchen sink, filled herself a glass of water and downed it in one go and then re-filled it. The detective had made her feel very uneasy and she had to get away from him to gather her thoughts. She re-filled the glass and turning around came face to face with him. She let out a muffled scream and dropped the glass of water onto the floor. The glass shattered and water splashed all over the floor and onto both Deepak and Karen.
Deepak looked down at his wet clothes and gave Karen a slap across her face, sending her stumbling sideways. She managed to grab hold of the kitchen counter and steadying herself, she gave Deepak a menacing look. The detective leaned right into her until she could smell his tepid breath and feel his chest pressing against hers. He lifted his cigarette and taking a drag blew smoke straight into her face. Karen turned her face sideways, let out a cough and then turned back to face him.
'I've known men like you my entire life, Detective

Chopra, you don't scare me,' she said.
'Men like your father, what did he do to you? Did he touch you where he shouldn't have?' he snarled.
'You're disgusting and if you don't back off now, I swear I'll slice off your bollocks,' shouted Karen.
Deepak looked down at the kitchen knife that Karen was holding against his groin. As she stumbled from the slap he gave her, she had grabbed hold of a sharp carving knife from the kitchen top. Deepak smiled directly at her while simultaneously snatching hold of the wrist in which she held the knife. Karen struggled to get free, but his grip was too strong. Deepak forced Karen's hand onto the kitchen counter and stabbed the burning end of his cigarette onto the back of her hand. She screamed and let go of the knife, which fell to the floor next to Deepak's feet. He lifted the cigarette from her hand and grabbed Karen's necklace, pulling it off. Placing the necklace in his pocket, he left the young woman crying on the floor and let himself out of the flat.

CHAPTER SEVEN

The district line train trundled to a stop at Stamford Brook station and welcomed aboard a freezing blast of air and off-loaded a couple of passengers. The doors swished shut and the train begrudgingly moved on to its next destination. The lights on the train flickered and both Raj and Gabby swayed in their seats as the train rocked from side to side. The cabin they were sat in was totally empty, the only other occupants being crumpled up copies of the *Metro*. The two passengers sat in comfortable silence enjoying the peacefulness of an empty train that was normally packed like sardines. Raj wrapped his coat around himself tightly and stuffed his hands in his pockets. He wondered how Gabby wasn't cold only wearing a thin jacket. He looked at her as she sat next to him with her eyes closed and felt his heart lurch. Even asleep she wore a warm smile that gave her serenity and a look of complete calm. The only time he felt any kind of happiness was when he was with her and he wanted that to last forever.

As the train passed Turnham Green, Raj also closed his eyes and leant his head back. He wanted to let Gabby know how he felt but the risk of rejection was too high and the consequences of that were unthinkable. He found himself drifting in and out of sleep as the train softly swayed him like a baby being rocked by its mother. His dreams, as always, were disturbed and filled with images of beasts and tormented souls. He found himself stood before a creature that had the body of a human but the tail of a beast that slithered and lashed towards him. Upon the creature's head were horns and around him demons hissed and spat. The beast ordered

Raj to confess his sins so that he could judge him and sentence him to hell or heaven. Raj wanted to speak but his tongue wouldn't release the words he wanted to say. He wanted to confess his guilt for abandoning his family and causing their deaths by being treacherous. He wanted the beast to tell him that it was entirely his fault and that the depths of hell were waiting for him so he should repent his sins. The beast lashed his tail out and was about to wrap it viciously around him, when he felt a hand on his shoulder and he awoke.

'Hey, sleeping beauty, we've reached the end of the road, literally,' said Gabby.

Raj stared into the darkness as the train doors opened and gradually he came back to his senses after his distressing dream. He looked towards Gabby, who took hold of his arm and together they walked onto the platform of Ealing Broadway station. They exited the station and walked the short distance to McDonald's, ordered food and sat down. Despite the bad dreams, Raj could feel himself thinking more positively and he had started looking forward to life rather than dreading each waking moment. The difference he felt from the first time he had sat in McDonald's with Gabby was slight, but it was more progress than he had made in years.

'Did you enjoy the concert considering you've never heard of the band?' asked Raj.

'The energy in the hall was amazing and the lead singer, what's his name?'

'Tim Booth.'

'His lyrics are very profound.'

'Sometimes, when I look deep into your eyes, I swear I can see your soul,' said Raj.

'Is that one of his lyrics or did you just say that to me?'

'Both.'

They sat in silence, filling up the time by poking pots of

sauce with the salty fries. It had been such a perfect day and Raj had almost allowed himself to feel happy, but now dark clouds were pushing at his mind again; he tried his best to ignore them. He was at a crossroads. He had to know where his relationship with Gabby was going before he could move on.

'This makes a change.' said Gabby, breaking the silence.

Raj gave her a quizzical look.

'My Friday treat is normally fish and chips, very rarely missed one.'

'I thought you were vegetarian?' asked Raj.

'Yes but I eat fish.'

'So, you're one of those pesci.....' trailed off Raj.

'Pescatarians.' finished Gabby.

'Oh.'

Raj poked another chip in the sauce pot and then looked up to meet Gabby's eyes.

'Where are you from Gabby?' asked Raj suddenly.

'From the human race,' answered Gabby as she picked up another chip.

'No seriously, I can't pick up your accent and you rarely talk about yourself. I need to know more about you.'

'Need?' replied Gabby laughing.

'Sorry, I meant want to know more about you.'

'Let's keep talking about my eyes instead,' said Gabby ignoring Raj's question. 'I like the fact that you can actually look me in the eyes now. When we first met, you were always looking down and avoiding looking straight at me.'

Raj stared into Gabby's bright hazel eyes and a feeling of pure joy and serenity rose up within him. As he looked deeper and deeper into her eyes, he felt himself being disconnected from the earthly world and drifting into the air. As he gazed into them, he totally forgot about

wanting to know more about her, as if her eyes had cleared his memory.
'Since my family died, I have not known a day without being afraid. I wake up and my first thought is of fear. Fear of everything in this world and a fear of my own thoughts, my own past and of the future. I live in a world of constant anxiety and most days I can't even face getting out of bed. The first time in many years that I didn't feel fear was when we first met. Most days, my thoughts are confused but when I am with you, everything becomes clearer. Your soul is warm and comforting and offers my life peace, if only for the time I'm with you. I feel hopeful that things will work out fine and that I will no longer be in this constant cycle of doubt and guilt.'
Raj fell silent and saw Gabby's eyes light up and she beamed a wide smile towards him. The moment seemed perfect and he felt the happiest he had ever been. He grabbed hold of her hands and then instinctively leaned forward to kiss her on the lips but as he got closer, she turned her cheek and the kiss gently brushed the side of her cheek. Raj let go of her hands and placed his head in his hands in embarrassment.
He couldn't believe what he had just done.
He had ruined everything.
She would never forgive him for trying to kiss her, if she had no feelings for him. He had been a fool to think that she could love a loser. Raj stood up and started to pack his food onto the tray. Without looking at Gabby, he took the tray and dumped its contents into the bin.
'I think we should just go home now,' he said, not looking towards her.
'Raj, it's ok, let's sit down and talk,' replied Gabby, who had stood to face Raj.
'Look, I just need to be alone!' shouted Raj.

Gabby took a couple of steps back surprised at Raj's raised voice but then moved forward again and took hold of his jacket sleeve. Raj pulled away from her and started walking towards the door, with Gabby following behind.

'Raj, let me walk you home and we can talk over a coffee, please,' pleaded Gabby as they left the restaurant.

'How about I walk you home? But hey, that's not going to happen, because I don't know anything about you!' Raj shouted. 'Listen, just stay away from me and let me get on with my life and you can go try help out some other loser. I don't need your charity. I may be broken but I don't need your pity, just to make you feel good about yourself.'

'Raj, please.'

Raj stood in the darkness with his back to Gabby and looked up towards the sky. He felt his eyes filling with tears as a deep sadness washed over him. He could see no way back from what he had just tried to do. He was trying to convince himself that it was only a kiss but it meant more to him than that. He had gambled everything on that kiss. His future and his salvation.

'Don't waste anymore of your time with me, Gabby. I have a clear picture of what I need to do, so thank you for all your help, but I can carry on by myself.'

Without turning round, Raj crossed the road and started back towards his flat. Dark clouds gathered all around him and feelings of self-pity and hopelessness welcomed him back into their warm embrace. A single misplaced kiss was all it took to destroy the flicker of light that Gabby had ignited in his life. Now, there was nothing that would bring that hope back.

*****

Raj sat alone on the floor in the corner of his living room, shrouded in darkness. Outside in the cold, the sun was beginning to rise, but his curtains were closed tight to keep out the light. Raj needed the darkness to comfort him, to remind him of where he had come from and what he had left behind. The blackness was warming and kept him hidden from the rest of the world, a world that had been judging him and staring at him accusingly for many years. He heard the whisper of their voices in his mind.
'*You killed your family, they burned because of you and that innocent life should have been you.'* Again and again they repeated the words until he could bear it no longer and the only solace he could find was in the darkness, eyes shut and hands over his ears. He sat for hours until the voices slowly drifted further and further away into the distance, like the white shroud that had covered his dead mother. As the voices slowly faded, he heard the sound of his intercom buzzer. He ignored it. It buzzed again but still he ignored it. He had no need of company. It buzzed again but this time it was accompanied by a female voice.
'Raj, it's Gabby. I just want to check that you're ok. You haven't answered any of my messages.' There was a pause. 'Just let me know that you're ok, please.' silence again.
It had been two days since their argument but he still couldn't face seeing Gabby. He felt embarrassed and full of shame for trying to kiss her, but also hurt and distraught at having been rejected. All his life, since losing his family, he had felt like a failure. Gabby had reinforced that by turning her cheek. The night after the argument, he had come home and thought about ending it all, but he lacked the courage even for that.
When Gabby seemed to have left, Raj stood up gingerly

and walked into his bedroom. The curtains were still closed but the sun's brightness gave the room a dull grey hue. From under his bed, he retrieved a pack of cigarette papers, a pack of tobacco and a packet containing a small piece of hash. He took a cigarette paper and added tobacco to it. He then took his lighter from his pocket and held the flame to a corner of the hash allowing it to crumble into the tobacco. After rolling the joint, he lit it and took a deep drag. He closed his eyes as the effect of the drug coursed through his senses and as it did, he leaned back onto his bed and felt time slowing down. As more of the drug entered his body, he felt himself drifting into a sleep of calmness. For a while, his sleep was dreamless but soon the serenity began to fade and he found himself in the middle of a dark wood. He walked blindly through the darkness until he came to a clearing and there in front of a mountain stood three terrifying beasts. As the beasts circled, he waited for the inevitable pain of teeth sinking into his flesh and then the shock of waking up in a cold sweat but this time there was something different. As the beasts prepared to strike, there was a flash of light behind him and when he turned around, there stood Gabby dressed in silver armour wielding a sword that emanated light. She walked towards him and gently placed a hand on his shoulder.

'I will walk with you my friend and together we shall defeat your demons and bring you peace.'

She took hold of Raj's hand and guided him away from the beasts and as she led him through the trees back into the woods, Raj awoke. He sat up in his bed and felt the normal feeling of panic rising up within him but there was something else niggling at the back of his mind. At first, he couldn't quite put his finger on it but then realisation hit him. In his dream, Gabby had called him ‘friend’ but that was not what he wanted. He wanted so much more. He knew it was only a dream but the feeling of hurt grew inside him like a cancer and all he kept hearing in his head was the word ‘friend.’ The only thing that could take away that pain was another high and another trip to hell.

Raj stood at the edge of the woods and stared into the darkness with fear and a longing to return to his sleeping body. He looked behind him, hoping to see Gabby as she had appeared in his previous dream, but behind him were only shadows of creatures that had the body of a bird and the face of a woman floating on the breeze like vultures. He stepped forwards into the wood that had no path and all around him he saw sorrowful trees full of black leaves and entwined branches. As he walked deeper into the wood, he heard the sound of wailing all around him, which caused him to stop by a tree and lean upon one of its branches. As he held onto the branch, it snapped off in his hand and from the tree came a deep cry. Raj stepped back and saw the face of a woman appear in the trunk of the tree. As he looked upon the face, he fell back in horror and for a few moments was paralysed and could not speak.
‘Why do you break my branches?’ said the tree, ‘Do you have no pity?’
In the wilderness of the wood, Raj could not make out the face of the woman but he recognised the voice. As she spoke, he broke down in tears and wept like a child. He cried uncontrollably as he sat in the thorn maze holding his hands over his eyes. He couldn’t understand why his aunt was in such a terrible place, imprisoned within a crooked and weeping tree. He uncovered his eyes and wiped the tears away from them with his sleeve. On his hands and knees, he crawled closer to

the tree to gaze upon the face of his aunt.

'Aunt Vinisha,' cried Raj as he looked upon the blood dripping from the branch that he had accidently broken off. 'I don't understand why you are in this wicked place. Above all, you are the one who deserves to be in heaven and not in the bowels of hell.'

'Raj, is that you my darling boy? Where have you been all this time and why did you leave without saying goodbye?' replied the tree.

'I am so sorry for abandoning you and little Kiran and leaving you alone with that monster. Please forgive me,' cried Raj.

'Don't cry, my beautiful son. It is not your fault. I was too weak to protect you from that monster. I am glad that you escaped and found a life of your own.'

As Raj stood up, he saw a harpy, a half bird, half woman creature, fly towards his aunt and start pecking at her branches. Raj grasped a stick from the ground and attacked the beast.

'Get away from her, you monster!' he shouted as he struck the creature. The harpy flew over to another tree and watched them with hungry eyes.

Raj dropped the stick and once again fell to his knees in front of his aunt. 'But I don't understand why you are here,' he asked.

'After you left, your uncle grew even crazier. He drank every day. Up until your leaving, he had never lifted a finger to Kiran, but soon his anger turned towards her and when that happened, I had had enough. I could see no way out for me, because if I left my husband I would have been disowned by my family and I could not live with the shame.'

'But what about Kiran?'

'There's something I never told you about Kiran,' sighed his aunt, mournfully.

'What?'

'Kiran was not our child. We adopted her because we couldn't have children of our own.'

Raj looked at her in shock. He had always thought of Kiran as their child; his aunt had always treated her with such love.

'The day after your uncle hit her, I took Kiran to a friend's house to look after her for a while. I posted all of Kiran's adoption papers to my friend, so she would receive it the following day. You must understand, Raj, I had reached the lowest point in my life and I couldn't take any more. I grew up in a loving home with parents who treated me like a princess, but then they betrayed me by marrying me off to a callous, cruel man, who took all my dignity from me and left me broken.'

'Don't blame anything on yourself, Auntie. You are the kindest and most loving person I have ever met.'

'I felt nothing on the day I went to the train station. Kiran was safe with my friend. I had posted the adoption papers. My mind was numb and I felt as though I had already died. I stood there thinking that I could have carried on if it was just me who was being beaten but I couldn't live with myself knowing that I hadn't protected you and that I had allowed that monster to attack my little girl.'

Raj couldn't look into his aunt's eyes. He placed his hands over his own eyes and felt his tears again.

'That day I thought I would be freeing myself from the pain of my body but I didn't realise that it would lead me here to the wood of suicide. Here, the pain is endless and the harpies feed upon my branches and there is no escape. The body and the soul are inseparable and those who commit violence against themselves are left to suffer for eternity.' Aunt Vinisha fell silent and closed her eyes.

Raj uncovered his eyes, wiped away the tears and stood up.
'I will rescue you from this wicked place. This is not your fate and I will come back and take you away from here,' promised Raj.
The harpy lunged at Raj and just as its sharp talons gouged at his eyes, he awoke in a sweat in his bed.
Raj climbed from his bed, swayed into the bathroom and splashed cold water in his face. The dream of his aunt had left him disorientated and troubled. When he had woken, he initially felt relieved that it had all been a dream but recently he had been having strange dreams that mixed reality and fantasy so doubt pervaded his thoughts. He realised that his subconscious was playing tricks with him but the dream seemed so real, which left him with an uneasy feeling. He stumbled his way into the living room, picked up a bottle of Jack Daniels, unscrewed the lid and took a huge gulp. Turning around, he walked straight into the coffee table, which he shoved away with his foot and made his way to the sofa. He sat there in the darkness taking gulps from the bottle trying to erase the memory of the dream but the haunting figure of his aunt kept pushing itself into his mind. The thought of her being dead and having committed suicide was too much for him. One of his only motivations for living in the past few months had been the possibility of seeing her again and seeking redemption. He felt as if he was going mad. Voices inside his mind were whispering their evil rhetoric. He placed the bottle on the coffee table, lay down on the sofa and covered his ears with his hands. He rocked back and forth, sending out a prayer for whichever God would listen, asking for some peace. There was no answer.
He finally faded into a dreamless sleep and when he awoke an hour later, he knew what he had to do. He

walked calmly to his laptop and googled for recent suicides involving trains. It didn't take long for Google to give him the answer he dreaded. The most viewed return was the story of an Indian lady who had jumped in front of a train at Acton station. She had died instantly. Raj re-read the story three times before slamming down the lid of his laptop and hurling it across the room. It bounced off the wall and hit the floor with a thud. Raj let out an inhuman scream and started to smash anything he could around him. He hurled the coffee table towards the television. The impact sent his television crashing to the floor, with the coffee table landing on top of it. He lunged towards the television but stumbled and fell to the floor, hitting his head on the corner of the table. Everything went silent and dark.

*****

Raj dragged himself from the floor and rubbed the side of his head, which was dripping in blood. He swayed towards the half-drunk bottle of Jack Daniels and made his way to the front door. He half stumbled down the stairs and fell out into the street with only a thin shirt to protect him against the biting wind that was turning everything to ice. He walked unsteadily down the street, his feet sliding on the frost that had turned the pavement into an ice rink. He stopped by a lamp post and took a gulp from the bottle and then as he walked on, flashes from his childhood appeared like ghosts in front of him. He was a thirteen-year-old boy watching the flames that engulfed his home soaring higher and higher into the night sky. He was a thirteen-year-old boy looking at the charred remains of his mother as the white sheet that had covered her floated into the air. He was a thirteen-year-old boy shivering with cold as he walked to school for the first time in a new country. He was a thirteen-year-old boy being buried in the snow and called a Paki in the playground while kids jeered and laughed.

He was a fourteen-year-old boy watching his aunt being beaten with the buckle of his uncle's belt for putting too much salt in the food. He was a fourteen-year-old boy covering the ears of little Kiran so she wouldn't hear the screams of her mother. He was a fifteen-year-old boy almost suffocating to death as his uncle strangled him because he asked for football boots so he could play in the school team. He was a fifteen-year-old boy trying to revise silently in the corner of his room, all the while fearing that his uncle would come home drunk.

He was a sixteen-year-old boy, who had just completed his last exam and who, with all his belongings packed in his rucksack, had never returned home. He was a sixteen-year-old boy full of guilt for leaving his aunt and Kiran behind.

He was a seventeen-year-old boy, lying in a shop doorway in the middle of the night, holding on to his meagre possessions so no one would steal them. He was a seventeen-year-old boy being beaten up by a dealer for not paying for drugs he had taken.

As much as he had tried exorcising all these ghosts, they would not leave him and still haunted his fragile mind. He had thought that with Gabby's help he could conquer his past but he could no longer even look at her. Now, she was just another reminder of his miserable pathetic failures. He took another mouthful of alcohol and staggered down the steps of Ealing Broadway underground station. He ducked under the barrier and made his way to the platform, where he knew the Reading to Paddington fast train would soon pass by. He looked into the darkness of the tracks and finished off the last drops left in his bottle. He crouched down and placed the empty bottle next to him and then placed his face in his hands. He felt tears well up in his eyes but unlike all the times before when had had wanted to cry but hadn't, he let the tears flow freely. He sobbed into his hands and all he wanted to do at that moment was to hold onto his mother and feel her warmth one more time. He imagined himself hugging her tight as they stood in their kitchen back in his childhood village. He could smell the freshly cooked chapatis that she had made and could hear his sister skipping in the garden. The sun was shining through the open doorway and the heat felt good on his back. He held onto his mother and never wanted to let her go but in the distance, he could hear the faint sound of a train. He gently let go of his mother's embrace and as she gave him a kiss on the cheek, he opened his eyes and saw the lights of the train move towards him. He stood up and sidled to the edge of the platform and waited for the train to come closer. As it approached, his tears dried up and he felt a calmness that he had never felt before. A calmness that assured him that the pain and suffering would soon be at an end and he would be with his family once more. He could hear the noise from the engine growing louder and see the lights growing brighter. He closed his eyes and as he took a step forward, he felt a pair of hands wrap around his chest and slowly pull him backwards. As he moved backwards, he felt a gentle whisper in his ear like a soft breeze telling him to close his eyes and sleep. His eyes felt heavy and his lids began to close as all tension flowed out from his body. He could feel himself falling backwards as if in slow motion but he did not hit the ground. Instead, he felt himself floating on air and moving back through the streets the way he had come. He tried to wake himself up but he was overtaken by some kind of sleep paralysis and could not move a muscle or force his eyes open. He felt himself moving from the cold into warmth and then finally being lowered onto a soft surface. Sleep then overtook him and he dozed for what seemed an eternity and when he awoke, the sun was shining through the window in his bedroom and he was lying on his bed in his night clothes.

CHAPTER EIGHT

Vijay sat in a cybercafé on Jalandhar Road in the town of Nakodar and sipped a cup of tea that contained far too much sugar. He looked at the computer in front him, hoping it would reveal what he wanted to know. He felt confused and didn't know where to start his investigation into the fire that killed Raj's family. The only clue he had was the name of the investigating officer at the time, which was Deepak Chopra. He placed his tea on the table next to the keyboard, typed the name into the Google search bar and browsed the results. He spent the next half hour searching through various webpages and he learnt that at the time of the fire, Deepak Chopra had climbed the ranks to become superintendent of police for Jalandhar district. He had started out as a constable in the village of Rehmanpur, which was near to the village where Vijay grew up. He had quickly graduated to become a police inspector for Nakodar and was then promoted to his last post as superintendent. He mysteriously left the police force a month after the fire but appeared several months later in London, working for the Acton police as a chief inspector.

Vijay leaned back in his chair and wondered if there was a connection between the fire, Deepak leaving the police force in India and suddenly moving to London. He scratched his head and rubbed at the throbbing pain in his leg. He closed his eyes and thought back to his childhood and tried to remember if he had ever seen this Deepak character around. There must have been a connection between Raj's family and the superintendent. A man that high up in the police force would not get personally involved in a case from a village unless there was some connection. He pulled out a notebook and pen from his satchel and going back to the screen, he started to note down all the addresses of the police stations that Deepak had worked at. The only way he was going to gather more information was by talking to the people who had worked with Deepak. He brought up Google Maps and typed in the address of the Nakodar police station. He was only a fifteen-minute walk away so he gathered his notebook and pen and headed off towards the station.

It was approaching midday but there was still a chill in the air despite the sun that sat proud in a cloudless sky. He slowly walked down Jalandhar Road with his walking stick in his hand and his satchel slung over his shoulder. He passed numerous dhabbas along the way, each serving up delicious smells that made his stomach grumble but he ignored the temptations and strode on. The road was teaming with cars, trucks and motorbikes all trying to get past each other with their insistent honking. The odd cow lounged by the side of the road, swishing its tail and grinding its teeth, while passers-by paid them no attention. The pavement was full of raw vegetable sellers and hot food stalls selling everything from tea to omelettes. Vijay side stepped all the obstacles as best he could but inevitably bumped into daydreamers and those paying more attention to their phones than other people. Vijay loved the countryside but also enjoyed the hustle and bustle of a busy main street; it always relaxed him if he felt frustrated. As he passed the Central Bank of India on his right, he knew he was getting close to his destination, so he quickened his pace as best he could. He eventually came to a set of blue metal gates that were open and which led him down a path towards the police station entrance. He opened the door to the station and walked into a large room with a number of desks scattered around the area. Three of the desks were occupied by police officers but not one acknowledged Vijay as he stood leaning on his walking stick. Vijay let out a cough and all three officers looked sloth-like towards him; they then looked at one another before the one nearest to Vijay stood and approached him. He was a tall man with a large belly and an equally large blue turban; he stood in front of Vijay and rubbed at his black beard.

'My name is Vijay and I work for Delhi Police,' started Vijay but received only silence in return.

'I'm investigating a case and would like to talk to your senior officer please.'

The large officer looked around to his colleagues and then back towards Vijay and was just about to speak when another man, who could have been an older brother of the officer standing in front of Vijay, walked in from behind him.

'This man wants to speak to the senior officer.'

'And what might this man want to talk to the senior officer about?' asked the new man.

'My name is Vijay and I am investigating an old case and wanted to discuss it with anyone who was around at the time.'

'What case?'

'There was a fire fourteen years ago in the village of Sufipind that killed an entire family. The investigating officer at the time was a Deepak Chopra,' replied Vijay.

Vijay noticed a shift in the new man's facial expression when he mentioned the name, Deepak Chopra. He had intentionally dropped the name into the conversation early so that he could gauge the man's reaction. There was no doubt that he knew the name and possibly even knew the man personally but Vijay waited to see whether

the man wanted to talk to him.
'You look familiar,' stated the man suspiciously.
'You may have known my father, Bhavesh Kumar,' replied Vijay. 'He also died around the same time as Raj Katri's family,'
The man's face took on a sad look as he extended his hand towards Vijay.
'My name is Inspector Cheema,' he said as he shook Vijay's hand, 'have you had lunch yet, Vijay?'
'No.'
'Well come on then, there's a lovely place just around the corner from here that serves the best lamb chops you've ever tasted,' said the inspector as he marched on, leaving Vijay hobbling behind him, trying to catch up. Inspector Cheema led him through a myriad of small alley ways until they reached a small doorway that if you weren't paying attention you would have missed. The man disappeared into the entrance and Vijay followed him and found himself in a small café that held just two tables with the kitchen in the same area. A skinny bald man in a white vest stood behind a large tandoor and was moulding a ball of minced lamb around a metal skewer ready to deliver it into the inferno. The inspector had already seated himself on a table and given the cook their order of lamb chops, kebabs and tandoori chicken. Vijay sat down sheepishly opposite the inspector and then broke the news that would surely disappoint the man.
'It does smell absolutely delicious in here inspector, but I'm afraid that I am vegetarian,' said Vijay.
The inspector looked with disappointment at Vijay but then turned towards the cook and without consultation ordered some paneer tikka and aloo sholay. He turned towards Vijay and raised his eyebrows, which Vijay interpreted to mean that the inspector wanted to hear his

story.
For the next fifteen minutes, Vijay told the inspector about the fire and his relationship with the family who had died. He also told him about being shot and finding out about Deepak Chopra but he left out the part about how he had acquired the information. Just as he finished his tale, the chef arrived and placed the food on the table. The inspector, without waiting, dived for a lamb chop and took a large bite.
'You don't know what you're missing,' he said, 'sure you won't try a taste?'
Vijay shook his head, stabbed a piece of paneer with his fork and put it on his plate. For the next ten minutes neither man spoke as the large man completely cleaned up all the meat dishes and then eyed the remaining vegetarian food. Vijay pushed the plates towards the man, who smiled at Vijay and then took his spoon and started eating from the serving dishes. Finally, when there was no more food to eat, Inspector Cheema wiped his face and beard with a paper napkin and looked across at Vijay.
'Deepak Chopra was a man who would betray his own mother if he thought it would get him where he wanted to be,' said the inspector.
'And where was that?'
'Right at the top,' replied the inspector.
'In which case it is even more surprising that he would come back to investigate a village fire.'
'Not really; you see Deepak Chopra was childhood friends with Param, Thakur and your father, Bhavesh.'
Vijay took in the information and digested it slowly. He knew that his father was best friends with Raj's father, Param, and Manoj's father, Thakur, but he had never heard of Deepak from their parents' childhood.
'So, you did know my father?' asked Vijay.

'Yes, Deepak took over the investigation, which was a big insult for us because we should really have been the ones to lead it, but there was nothing we could do as he had seniority.' The inspector paused and looked into the distance as if seeing a scene from the past in the corner of the room.

'What is it inspector?'

'I knew Param and your father very well, Vijay. They were good men and they did not deserve to die so young but there were rumours at the time that they had got themselves mixed up with the wrong type of people and that their deaths were not an accident.'

Vijay looked at the inspector in horror. He found it hard to understand what he was saying.

'My father died in a car accident and the fire was ruled to have been an accident, a gas cylinder that exploded.'

'Listen Vijay, what I am about to tell you are just rumours and have never been substantiated and I need your promise that you won't tell anyone I spoke to you about this. I'm only telling you this because of the respect I had for your father.'

Vijay nodded dumbly as a hundred thoughts raced through his mind.

'Your father and Param were very ambitious and clever guys and they wanted to get out of the village and become rich. They were always talking about escaping and becoming members of the high society, where they would rub shoulders with Bollywood stars, cricketers and politicians. If you ask me, they were living in cuckoo land but they had their dreams. Their plan was to become property tycoons so they borrowed a huge sum of money from the bank, bought some land here in Nakodar and started to build huge villas on the land. I said to them at the time that no one would pay for a villa in a shitty town like this, but they didn't listen. They ran into trouble once the cost of building the villas spiralled; they eventually depleted the money the bank had lent them and the bank wanted their money back. They had no choice but to get the money elsewhere to pay back the bank loan and this is where the story gets a bit hazy. I can't tell you for sure what's real and what's fiction.'

'I never knew any of this. As far as I knew, my father and Raj's father both worked as carpenters.'

'They were carpenters but like I said, they were ambitious,' the inspector paused to order two cups of tea and a block of an Indian pistachio sweet. 'Anyway, the rumour is that they went to this gangster fellow called Rahul and borrowed money from him to repay the bank. When Rahul didn't get his money back, he arranged for your father to have an accident. It was supposed to be a warning, but it went wrong and your father was killed. He threatened Param but when he still didn't get his money, he arranged for an accidental fire.'

The inspector leaned back in his chair and looked at Vijay, whose hands were trembling. The chef came over with tea and sweets and placed them on the table.

'Drink some tea, Vijay. It will make you feel better and have some of the sweets.'

Vijay picked up the tea with a shaky hand and took a sip. He wiped the sweat from his forehead with a napkin. He couldn't believe what he was hearing. Was it possible that his father had been murdered? He'd been told it was an accident. Could the fire that killed Raj's family have been started deliberately? He rolled everything around his head and suddenly realised with a shock why Deepak Chopra had investigated the fire.

'Did Deepak also investigate my father's accident?' he asked.

'I think you already know the answer to that,' replied the inspector solemnly.

‘Deepak was in the pocket of this Rahul guy and covered up the murders for him.’
‘Well, like I said, it’s all just rumours, Vijay.’
‘And where is this Rahul guy now?’
‘He started out as a small-time crook here in Nakodar but he quickly expanded his business into Jalandhar and now he is “big-time” and runs his empire from Mumbai,’ replied Inspector Cheema while taking a great bite from the pistachio sweet. ‘So, what do you intend to do now, young man?’ he asked as he picked crumbs out of his grey beard.
‘I need to find out if these rumours are true. It seems there are only two people who can confirm them. Unfortunately one is in England but the other is right here in India.’
‘Rahul?’
‘Yes Rahul.’

*****

The single light bulb that hung from the low ceiling in Manoj’s slum home flickered once and then the light vanished completely. Manoj sat on his stool next to the gas stove with his metal plate in his lap and continued eating as though nothing had happened. He heard tiny footsteps coming towards him and then a frightened little voice call out. He placed the plate on the floor next to him and opened his arms to receive his one-year-old son. He closed his arms around Navjot, kissed him gently on the cheek and spoke to him reassuringly. From the other room Radhika walked in holding a diya that chased away the darkness as the tiny flame danced ahead of her. She walked softly on bare feet towards her husband and son and placed the diya on a shelf next to them. She knelt on the floor beside them, placed an arm around the little boy and smiled at Manoj. The little boy laughed at the flame as it danced and forged shadows all around the tiny room. He jumped up and tried catching the flame but his father pulled him back down and hugged him tight. In that moment, Manoj felt the happiest he had ever been and nothing else mattered apart from protecting his family. He had spent most of his young life trying to please others and never allowed himself to feel any love. He was the middle child between two brothers and had always felt that there was never enough attention or love left for him. He was left to fend for himself; his parents took no notice of his studies so he fell behind in school. He left education with few qualifications and drifted from one manual labourer job to another. The only time he had felt any warmth and affection was when he was with his friends, Raj and Vijay. He had considered them his family and spent more time with them than his real family. He remembered the day when Vijay told them he was leaving for boarding school; it had totally devastated him. Then a few months later, Raj's family died in the fire and Raj was sent to live in London. Within a few months, he had lost the only family that he cared for and for the next few years he had barely made any friends. Vijay returned in the holidays and they spent time together but it was never the same. Vijay had made new friends and talked about them often, not realising how that made Manoj feel.

Slowly as the years drifted by, he spent less and less time with Vijay and wasted away his time either lazing at home or wandering around the fields. It was during one of his lazy days at home that his life changed forever. It was the height of summer and the sun blazed in the sky turning everything into a furnace. He was lounging in the shade of a mandarin tree, when he saw the most beautiful girl he had ever seen. She was sweeping the front entrance to his house and occasionally stopped to take a drink from a water bottle that she had tucked into a belt around her waist. He sat captivated by her beauty and the graceful movements of her legs and body. He wanted to go over and talk to her, but he always felt awkward around girls and couldn't summon the courage. For the next few days, he waited in the same spot for her to return and just when he had given up hope of ever seeing her again, she appeared like a goddess from nowhere. She noticed him this time and a look passed between them that spoke a thousand words. They both knew at that moment that the universe had brought them together and their lives would never be the same. Manoj walked towards her and she lowered her head in shyness and shame because he was of a higher caste.

'What's your name?' asked Manoj.

'Radhika,' the girl replied.

Manoj was about to ask her another question but his mother stepped out from the shadows of the house and looked distastefully at the two of them.

'Why are you talking to this girl?' shouted his mother, 'she has chores to do,' she continued as she pointed an insulting finger towards the girl.

Manoj looked away in embarrassment and did not reply to his mother but instead walked away back to his bench under the tree. He watched as his mother grabbed the girl by the arm and dragged her inside. A huge wave of shame washed over him and he felt anger rise within his belly. He felt ashamed that he had not spoken up for himself and anger at how he had let his mother talk to the girl. To him, she was just another human being and caste had no relevance but he had let his conditioning overcome him. He sat under the shade for a long time with anger building up inside him and finally, when he had nowhere to vent the anger, he strode back into the house and looked around for the girl. He found her squatting in the heat washing dishes out in the back yard. He walked up to her, knelt down next to her and picked up one of the dishes. He started scrubbing it with his hands. She turned towards him in sheer panic, shaking her head and grabbing the dish from his hands. 'You will get into trouble from your mother,' she whispered.

'I don't care,' replied Manoj stubbornly.

'Maybe you don't care but I will lose this job and then I will be in trouble from my mother,' she replied with a smile on her lips.

Manoj looked deep into her round eyes and felt the sincerity with which she spoke enlightening. The last thing he wanted was for her to lose this job as he knew how difficult it was for members of her caste to find work. He reached out, took hold of her hand and smiled back at her. Then he returned to his spot in the shade.

Over the next few months, they stole precious moments to be with each other, when no one was around. Manoj helped with her chores and they talked of their favourite Bollywood movies and shared each other's food. They fantasised about running away together to Mumbai and how they would become big stars and get married in a huge mansion. Little did they know that their Mumbai dream would be a tiny shack in the middle of Mumbai's biggest slum. Manoj was brought back to the present in Dharavi as his son tried to jump up and catch the flame again. He held him tightly against his chest and kissed him on his cheek.

'What time is your train?' asked Radhika.

'It leaves at quarter to twelve so I will head off at ten o'clock,' replied Manoj.

Radhika placed her head on her husband's lap. 'Please

come home safely and quickly,' she said sombrely.
'I will be back in a few days and then I will take you to watch that new Ranveer Singh movie.'
'That will be nice.'
'I think the little one needs his bed now and I need to get ready,' Manoj said as he handed Navjot to his wife. He waited for Radhika to leave the room and then he got up from his stool and walked over to a shelf above his bed. From the shelf, he lifted a jar, took out a bundle of cash and stuffed it into his pocket. Two thousand Rupees was all the money he had in the world and seven hundred and twenty five of this would be spent on the train fair to Sufipind. He walked over to a small, locked trunk behind his bed and removed a key from his pocket to unlock it. He lifted a small bundle from within the trunk and slowly unfolded it. He looked behind him to ensure his wife had not come back into the room. He picked up the gun that lay in the middle of the cloth and checked that it was loaded. He tucked the gun into his trousers and re-locked the trunk. Over the last few years, he had found tremendous joy spending his life with Radhika but there had also been dark days like the day his family disowned him. He didn't know what would happen to him once he had completed his mission or whether he would ever see his wife and son again. He also didn't know whether he would ever see his parents and brothers again so he had decided to take a detour. He would go to Ajit Nagar in Patiala, where his family now lived, and try to reconcile with them. He wanted to clear his conscience and make peace with his family before he left this world and stood in judgement before God.

CHAPTER NINE

Raj stood in the bitter cold with his hands tucked deep into the pockets of his coat. He wore a woolly hat to keep his head and ears warm but still the cold cut through him chilling him to the bone. He had positioned himself carefully so anyone exiting the Karma Club would not see him. A bus stop concealed most of his body and the blackness of the night did the rest. It was five minutes to four in the morning so he knew Gabby would be leaving the club at any moment.

Earlier that evening, Raj had opened his laptop and typed 'Gabby' into Google but his hands had then hovered above the keyboard while he searched the depths of his memory. He suddenly realised that he didn't know her surname. He opened Facebook and searched a multitude of different name combinations but he couldn't find her. He tried Snapchat, Instagram and even LinkedIn but with no success. He had closed the laptop deciding he needed to find out more about the girl who had suddenly appeared in his life but about whom he knew nothing. Even though he had frequently quizzed her, she had somehow always evaded telling him where she lived or anything about her history. Tonight, he would follow her as she left the club and find out where she lived.

The door to the club opened and a number of people scurried out. He moved a few steps closer to get a better view and saw her leave the club and walk down the High Street towards St Mary's Road. He started walking in the same direction, careful not to get too close. He followed her down the road as they passed the University of West

London and Saint Mary's Church. She then walked around the corner onto St Ealing Road and after fifteen minutes, she suddenly turned into a cemetery and walked across its gardens and let herself into a stone lodge that stood on the edge of the graveyard. Raj stood outside the cemetery trying to register what he had just witnessed. Maybe that was why she wouldn't tell him where she lived. Maybe she was embarrassed that she lived next to a cemetery or was it something more sinister like a fetish for dead people? He stared deep into the graveyard and felt a strange presence around him, which made him slowly back away and return to his flat. As he walked in the cold darkness, he decided that he had to confront Gabby about her secrecy. He would make a surprise visit to her graveyard lodgings the next day.

*****

Deepak stared at the evidence board and looked at his watch again for the tenth time. He had told Mark to be at the station at four o'clock but he hadn't arrived yet. He felt the tension within him rise but he was trying hard to keep calm as he couldn't afford to lose it in the middle of the station. He looked at all the evidence they had gathered so far but none of it made much sense. He knew for sure that the killer or killers knew the victims but what did the numbers mean? Also, was there a connection between the red line on the wall of Mr Anton's office and the deep red cut on the face of Richard Evans? It had been verified by Mr Anton's wife that her husband's laptop was missing but the technical team had not managed to track it down. The detective was deep in thought when he felt the presence of Mark standing next to him. He slowed down his breathing to

abate his anger.
'Sorry I'm late but the queue in McDonalds was a killer,' said Mark, staring at the board while slurping on a vanilla milkshake.
The detective could feel the anger within him rise and he had to clench his fists to prevent himself from punching the trainee in the face. After a minute of slow breathing, Deepak pointed to the board and turned to face Mark.
'We need to focus on the evidence and come up with some answers tonight. I retire in a couple of weeks and this must be solved by then. Turning up late is not acceptable. Do it again and I'll make sure that your career in the police force ends before it has even started.'
Mark nodded and then slowly placed the milkshake on the table next to him and tried hard to look focused.
'Well, I've got some more information for you Gov,' he said.
'What?' snapped the detective.
'Mr Anton has a hundred thousand pounds missing from one of his accounts. According to his wife, the missing laptop had details of all his accounts and log in details on it. It was encrypted but the killer may have got him to unlock it before he was killed. Did you get much out of Karen?'
'I used my powers of persuasion on her; she didn't tell me much that was useful, but I did get something from her that may be of interest.'
'Oooh exciting, what is it?'
'It's a necklace.'
'Boring! What's so interesting about a necklace?'
'It has a crucifix on it.'
'Ok, still boring.'
Deepak took the necklace out of his coat pocket and dangled it in front of the young constable.

‘Why is it upside down?’
‘Exactly,’ replied Deepak.
‘The inverted cross in Christianity symbolises the Martyrdom of Peter the Apostle. He was the first leader of the early Church, regarded as the first pope and he was one of the twelve apostles of Jesus Christ.’
‘What are apostles?’
‘The apostles were Jesus’ closest followers. When Peter was sentenced to crucifixion by Emperor Nero, he requested that he be crucified upside down as he felt he was unworthy to be crucified in the same fashion as Jesus.’
‘So, what does that have to do with any of the murders?’
‘Nothing, but the inverted cross has also been adopted by Satanists who believe that by turning the cross upside down, they are degrading and humiliating Jesus.’
‘Wow, you think devil worshipers killed these people?’
‘Karen was wearing the necklace and every time I asked her a difficult question, she fiddled with the necklace, so it must mean something important to her.’
Deepak handed the necklace to Mark and instructed him to tape it on to the evidence board. He then stepped back and looked at all the evidence again.
‘What are you thinking?’ asked Mark.
‘We have two murdered men, one who was brutally murdered and one who was killed with a single cut to the throat but who has had a vast amount of money stolen. What’s the connection and what do the numbers four and seven represent?’
Mark stared at the board hoping that a clue would jump out at him. As he looked at the photos, an idea started to form in his mind. He stepped closer to the photo of Richard Evans and stared at the angry red cut down the middle of his face. He then looked at the photo of the red line sprayed on the wall of Mr Anton’s office and then

finally at the crucifix on the necklace.
'Sir, take a look at these photos,' said Mark pointing to them, 'that cut on Richard Evans' face goes from the top of his forehead down to his chin but it intersects his lips which have also been cut at both ends. What does that look like to you?' he said as he pointed to the necklace.
The detective looked at the photo and sure enough the image of an inverted crucifix jumped from the photo. He then looked at the red line sprayed on Mr Anton's office wall that intersected a shelf at the bottom of the wall, forming another upside down cross.
'Well that really puts Karen right in the middle of these murders. We need to get some more concrete evidence before we bring her in for questioning,' started Deepak, 'I want you to park outside her flat and when she comes out, follow her. She must be getting nervous and that means she will make a mistake and hopefully lead us to her accomplices. I'll look into the numbers four and seven and check if they have any link to Satanism.'
'But don't we need to get permission to do a stake out? And I shouldn't be using my own car,' objected Mark.
The detective leaned close into Mark and gave him a stare that sent a shiver into the young constable's soul.
'Don't ever question my authority or I will make your life a living misery,' he growled.

*****

Gabby stood in the darkness of her bedroom and through a slightly lifted curtain, she saw Raj turn around and walk back down the road. She had sensed him behind her all the way from the Karma Club and wanted to turn around and speak to him but she knew that would lead to more questions. She felt a huge sadness wash over her; she knew that she had lost his trust. All she wanted to do was help heal the pain that was consuming his soul and set him free from his chains. She walked across her bedroom in the darkness, down the wooden stairs and into the kitchen. The night surrounded everything in the house but Gabby did not turn on any of the lights. She found the backdoor key in the cutlery drawer, opened it and made her way outside. She walked with bare feet through the small flower garden that provided refuge from the imposing gravestones just outside the garden walls. The smell of the daphne, winter honeysuckle and viburnum shrubs filled her senses and she started to feel lighter by the time she made it through the garden gate and into the graveyard. She walked softly between the graves and along the way, she stopped to read many of the names. So many souls who had found eternal sleep and who now waited for the second coming of the Lord. Gabby continued through the graves of the dead until she came to a gravestone that had been carved into a cross. She looked at the cross and felt a deep sorrow. She fell to her knees, closed her eyes and began to pray with her palms tightly pressed against each other.

'Dear Father, I seek your guidance and strength to help a man who has been broken by this cruel world. He has suffered much at the hands of man and he has lost all faith in you. I need to guide him towards the light and out of the darkness before it consumes him. I struggle to keep a clear mind as my thoughts are with you always and I long to be with you…'

Gabby's prayer was interrupted as she heard the crunch of leaves behind her. She fell silent but did not open her eyes or stand up from her praying position. The footsteps grew closer and a figure stopped just behind her and looked upon the large stone cross.

'Oh Gabby, which sad loser are you praying for this

time?' asked the figure. 'You spend more time on your bloody knees, for the wrong reasons I may add,' the newcomer said with a chuckle.

Gabby opened her eyes and standing up she turned round to face the woman, who was immaculately clothed in a red dress, black stockings and knee length leather boots. Despite the cold, she wore no coat and the only indication of winter was the red tartan scarf that she always wore around her neck. Her hair was cut short and as black as the night.

Gaby smiled at the woman in front of her and placing her arm in hers walked up the gravel path back towards the house.

'So, what have you been up to tonight, my dear Lucy? Actually don't tell me. I'd rather not know,' said Gabby.

Lucy laughed out loud and squeezed Gabby's hand tight. 'I will kidnap you one of these days and take you along on one of my adventures. Then, you will see there are more ways than one to save a person's soul.'

'I like my methods thank you very much,' replied Gabby.

They walked the rest of the way holding hands and enjoying the peacefulness of the night. As they entered the house, Lucy skipped into the living room, took a box of matches and lit several candles. She poured herself a glass of Merlot and sat down cross legged on a sofa. Gaby poured herself a glass of milk and sat right next to Lucy, enjoying her closeness. The flames from the candles danced excitedly forming shadows across the walls and ceiling. The flickering lights banished the darkness from fragments of paintings that covered the walls. The light skipped across the possessed boy in 'The Transfiguration' and as it floated across the room, it settled for a few seconds on Saint Peter holding the keys to heaven in 'The Last Judgement' and then quickly moved on to the faces of Capocchio and Gianni Schicchi

in 'Dante and Virgil.' The room was filled with antique vases, statues and furniture that spanned centuries of civilisation. The flickering lights made their way around the room and settled on the two women sitting in silence on the Victorian leather Chesterfield sofa.
'I miss father,' said Gabby breaking the silence, 'Why won't he call for us to come back home. It's been years since we have seen him.'
Lucy put her arm around Gabby and stroked her hair gently.
'He might call you back but I'm still not allowed home,' replied Lucy.
'Well, you were bad Lucy and you acted very arrogantly.'
'Wow that was a long time ago. Surely he can't still be mad with me over that. Anyway, I like it here better, so he can go stuff himself, the old tyrant.'
'Don't call him a tyrant Lucy, that's unfair. I just wish I could talk to him or see him for a little while.'
Gabby wiped tears from her eyes and took a sip from her glass of milk. She felt so home sick and desperately wanted to be back home with her family. Her thoughts of being back home had clouded her judgement and she knew that was why she couldn't get through to Raj. She felt as if she had failed and maybe that's why she was being punished by her father.
'So, tell me about this Raj fellow?' Lucy asked trying to distract Gabby, 'What's his story?'
'He lost his family in a tragic fire when he was very young. He's another lost soul that I need to save Lucy. If I can't change the path he has set upon, then it will lead him to more pain and finally his life will be lost. I can't let that happen.
'I have total trust in you, my dear sister,' Lucy replied.
Both women fell silent but within Lucy a tiny thought began to grow. Very quickly she had a plan fully formed

for how she would take over Raj's salvation.

*****

Raj felt his stomach heave and quickly made his way to the bathroom. He leaned over the basin and took in deep breaths. Turning on the cold tap, he splashed water over his face and then stayed in the same position, waiting to feel better. Once the nauseous feelings started to fade, he staggered back into the living room and crashed onto the sofa. He closed his eyes and rubbed at his temples.

After he had returned from following Gabby, he had been so confused and deflated that he had opened a bottle of Jack Daniels and almost drunk the lot. He opened his eyes and squinted at his phone and swore to himself. It was three o'clock in the afternoon and if he didn't get a move on, Gabby would already have left her house for work. He forced himself from the sofa and went back into the bathroom. He looked in the mirror and was horrified by what he saw. He didn't recognise the face staring back at him. The dark sunken rings under his eyes appeared like craters against a pale skin that had almost turned yellow. His hair all greasy and tangled made a good companion for his wild and tramp-like beard. He looked deep into his own eyes and all he saw was emptiness, a deep dark well of blackness and self-loathing. He stepped away from the mirror, collected his coat and walked out of the flat, while shrugging on his coat. At least it covered the stained jumper and jeans that he had been wearing for the last three days.

He walked down South Ealing Road and rehearsed in his head what he would say to Gabby when he surprised her at her house. He would tell her that she needn't be embarrassed about where she lived. He would tell her how he felt about her and that he wanted to be more than friends. He wanted a fresh start with no more secrets and he wanted to tell her everything about his childhood and all the pain he had endured. He was willing to give up everything for her, the alcohol, the drugs, the self-pity and all the rest of the baggage he had been carrying around all his life. As he walked down the road where Gabby lived, his nervousness and anxiety began to creep back and for a few heartbeats, he thought about turning around. He fought the rising panic and with determination made it to the front doorstep of the house which he had seen Gabby enter. He stood staring blankly at the oak panelled door and then slowly lifted the black iron knocker and banged it three times. Almost immediately he heard footsteps from inside the house and his heart started racing. He could feel sweat form on his brow and he clenched his fists so tight that his nails started to cut into his palms. The footsteps stopped and as the door slowly opened a woman appeared in front of Raj, who looked identical to Gabby. Raj stood foolishly stone still, not comprehending what was happening. His mind was so exhausted from all the drink and drugs that he couldn't process the woman in front of him.

'You must be Raj,' said Lucy as she gently took hold of Raj's arm to lead him inside the house.

Raj found himself in a passageway that had a wooden dark oak staircase directly in front of him and walls that were covered in religious and historic paintings. A large chandelier hung from the ceiling that almost touched the top of his head. Under his feet was a red carpet that matched the nail polish on the toes of the bare footed woman who stood in front of him. She wore a red knee length dress and around her neck was a tartan scarf.

'So, I've heard a lot about you from Gabby,' continued

Lucy still holding onto his arm. She led him further into the house and into the living room, where only hours before, Lucy and Gabby had sat huddled together.
Raj walked into the room in an almost hypnotic state and before he could protest, he found himself sitting on the leather sofa. Lucy perched on the armrest with her bare feet on the sofa. Raj looked in astonishment at all the paintings and artefacts that cluttered the room. The space seemed larger inside than from the outside, but the ceilings were low giving it an oppressive and dark feel. All around the room were dozens of candles despite a large chandelier that hung in the middle of the ceiling. The carpet similar to the one in the hallway was blood red but the ceiling in contrast was painted a light blue.
As he looked around at all the paintings, one in particular caught his eye. He lifted himself from the sofa and walked across the room to stare at it. He stood there silently feeling he was suddenly trapped in time, until he heard a voice behind him.
'Seeing my tears, he answered me: "There is another road. And that, if you intend to quit this wilderness, you're bound to take."'
Raj turned from the painting and there was Lucy standing right behind him. He rubbed at his temples and again turned and looked at the painting.
'That's a William Blake painting called, 'Dante running away from the three beasts.' The leopard symbolises worldly pleasures, the lion worldly ambition and the she-wolf avarice,' continued Lucy. 'Virgil has been sent by Beatrice to guide Dante to Paradise.'
'I know this scene,' interrupted Raj. 'I have this recurring dream where I am faced by these exact three beasts and they are always blocking my path to where I need to go. I don't know where that is but I know that I desperately need to get there. I have tried defeating the

beasts many times but every time I get attacked and then wake up,' said Raj still staring at the painting. He wanted to tell Lucy about the last time he had experienced the dream and how Gabby had appeared with a sword but he knew that would sound crazy. He was at a loss to explain how the twins had a painting of the exact scene that he had been dreaming about.

'The painting depicts the start of Dante's journey into hell,' explained Lucy.

'Who is Dante?' asked Raj.

'He was an Italian poet from the fourteenth century who wrote the masterpiece, *The Divine Comedy*. It follows Dante as he journeys from darkness to the revelation of divine light and the Glory of God. He is guided by the poet Virgil through the horrors of hell in Inferno and passes Satan himself along the way. Virgil departs the story when they reach Purgatory where repentant sinners are purged of their sins. His beloved Beatrice then leads him up the ascending levels of heaven into Paradise where Dante is allowed to glimpse for a moment the Glory of God. It is, at heart, a poem of his unrequited love for Beatrice.'

Raj stood staring at the painting, still in shock at how a painting he had never seen or a poem he had never heard of could be haunting his dreams. Even stranger still, the dreams had only started when he met Gabby.

'Would you like a drink?' asked Lucy.

Raj turned away from the painting and looked at Lucy.

'I would offer you a glass of wine but I don't think you need an alcohol top-up. I'll put the kettle on. A nice black coffee will do you good,' said Lucy as she disappeared out of the room.

Raj walked back over to the sofa and sitting down, leaned his head back and closed his eyes. He had hoped that coming to this house would resolve all his issues and he and Gabby could start anew but things had become infinitely worse. Why hadn't Gabby told him she had a twin sister? Seeing the painting of Dante and Virgil had left him in a dreamlike state. He wondered what Gabby had been telling her sister about him.

Lucy re-appeared with two mugs of coffee and, handing one to Raj, once again perched on the end of the sofa. She looked at him intensely as she took a sip from her mug and then playfully poked him in the thigh with her toe.

'So, what's with you and my sister?' she asked.

Raj thought about the question in his own mind and couldn't really answer it. He didn't know anymore what their relationship was or where it was going but he knew that he loved her. He had a deep desire to be with her and to spend the rest of his life with her but then there were all his doubts: doubts about her intentions and her honesty. How could he love someone who was not truthful or trustworthy?

'We are just friends, that's all,' replied Raj unconvincingly. 'She's been helping me out with a few issues, which she may or may not have told you about.'

'Do you want to be just friends?' asked Lucy knowing the answer.

Raj looked away from Lucy and didn't respond.

'I think it would be better for you in the long run if you just forgot about my sister. She has this effect on men but in the end, she always breaks their hearts. She's saving herself you see.'

'Saving herself for what?'

'Jesus,' replied Lucy, enjoying the feeling of power she was having over him.

'I didn't think she was a nun,' replied Raj with a tone of bitterness that he hadn't meant.

Lucy moved to sit close to Raj making him feel

uncomfortable. He shifted in his seat as she put an arm around his shoulder.
'Gabby told me about the fire,' started Lucy trying to sound sincere. 'I know what you must have gone through as a child and how you must still be suffering still.'
'You know how I felt or how I feel now? Really? Have all your family burned to death in a fire recently?' replied Raj angrily. 'Nobody can understand what I've been through unless they have experienced it. I was thirteen and my entire family died and then I was shipped thousands of miles to live with a sadistic uncle.' Raj stopped and stood up. 'I'm sorry. I've said too much. I think I'm just going to go and maybe it's best not to tell Gabby I was here.'
Lucy also stood up and took hold of Raj's hands. 'Listen, I said I understand because I run a support group that helps people just like you. I have helped hundreds of people who were trapped inside their own minds and now they are free. I can help you too, if you let me.' Lucy let go of Raj's hands and walked over to her handbag that lay on the carpet. She retrieved a card from her bag. 'Here take this. The details of where and when we meet is on there and you can come along anytime you like.'
Raj took the card and then without another word, he left the house. As he walked back towards his flat, he felt more lost than ever. The dark clouds in his mind that had been slowly lifting since he had met Gabby were returning and were darker than ever. He looked at the card he was still holding in his hand. Suddenly a thought came into his mind. What if the lady in shining armour in his dream wasn't Gabby, but instead Lucy?
Perhaps Lucy was the one who would save him.

CHAPTER TEN

Manoj stood up from his seat and stretched out his back and his arms. It was past five-thirty in the morning and the train had just left Pachora Junction Station. He had been on the train for almost six hours but still had twenty-nine hours to go. He was crammed into the cheapest cabin the train had to offer and the smell of stale sweat had started to fill its small space. As there wasn't enough room in the cabin to walk around, he continued to stretch for five minutes and then sat back down in his seat. He had managed to get a little sleep but not for too long, which would be dangerous as there was always a risk of being robbed. He leaned his head against the window, stared into the darkness of the early morning and wrapped his shawl tighter around himself. He felt inside his shawl to make sure his gun was still there and then closed his eyes. He had no intention of sleeping again but wanted to shut himself off from all the people around him. It was strange but he felt more apprehensive about meeting his family than his impending confrontation with Vijay. He had replayed in his mind many times the events of the day when he was thrown out of his home. He always wondered if he could have somehow changed the outcome. It was another beautiful summer's day and he was feeling his usual happy self as he knew Radhika would be coming to the house soon. They had managed to keep their relationship secret for almost a complete year and had also started meeting secretly outside. As time passed by, they had started to take more and more risks and had almost been caught many times. Looking back, Manoj wondered if subconsciously they had wanted to be caught so they wouldn't need to sneak around anymore.

The fateful day started with Manoj sitting under his favourite mandarin tree, enjoying a breakfast of aloo paratha. He tore a piece off, dipped it into some homemade yogurt and then stuffed it into his mouth. He took a sip of his masala tea and then searched into the distance to catch Radhika walking elegantly towards the house. She wore her usual Indian dress and sandals. She had her bottle of water tucked into her belt around her waist and carried her lunch in a small metal box. As she came closer, Manoj's heart started to race and he felt butterflies in his stomach, as he always did whenever she was near. He put his plate down and jumped off the bench to walk towards her. He couldn't risk talking to her outside the house with all the gossipy neighbours around so he quickly went into the house before she did. Once they were both inside, he took hold of her hand and gave her a kiss on the cheek.

'What have you cooked for me today?' he whispered as he tapped a finger onto her tiffin pot.

'It's a surprise,' she whispered back.

Manoj heard footsteps from the kitchen so he quickly went back outside. He could hear his mother giving Radhika instructions on what she wanted done that day. As he stood leaning against the front of the house, his mother appeared and shot him her usual look of disappointment.

'I'm going to the market and then to Aunt Kamal's house so I will not be back until three o'clock,' she told him and then walked off.

He should have known straight away that his mother was setting him up for something. She never told him where she was going and definitely never what time she would be back. He was naive and in love, which had clouded his judgement but he was also too trusting. His father had already left the house early that morning and his older brother had joined the army so was rarely at home. His younger brother was at school so Manoj and Radhika thought they had the entire day together. They planned to complete all the chores by lunchtime so that they could then sit and talk until three o'clock. The first part of their plan worked perfectly as together they cleaned the house and washed all the dishes and clothes. At midday, they sat huddled together in the backyard on a low bench and presented their food to each other. Manoj had saved two aloo parathas from his morning breakfast and Radhika opened her tiffin pot and showed the contents to Manoj. They both stared into the pot and laughed out loud as Radhika lifted two aloo parathas from the pot.

'We shall share yours, as I am sure they will taste better than my mother's,' Manoj said and smiled at Radhika but as he looked into her face, he saw a look of horror. He followed her eyes to where she was looking and there behind him in the doorway stood his mother. He jumped up from the bench and saw the look of disgust on his mother's face. Instead of speaking, he decided there was nothing to say. He was finished with hiding his relationship with Radhika.

'Radhika, this is the last time you shall step foot in my house or any other in this village. I will personally see to that. Get your things and get out!' his mother spat.

'You will never see this girl again,' she commanded to Manoj.

Radhika collected her tiffin pot and water bottle and started to walk towards the door when Manoj grabbed hold of her arm and held her there next to him.

'Radhika is the only person in this world who understands me and there is no way that I'm never

seeing her again,' protested Manoj.
His mother laughed and slapped her hand against her forehead. 'You have gone crazy boy, and if you think having a relationship with this scrawny animal will bring you joy, you are deluded. If you don't listen to me, you will spend the rest of your life looking over your shoulder and you will never know peace. Let the girl go and Mummy will find you a nice girl who will gain you respect. Do not dishonour your family, Manoj!'
Manoj felt his anger rising. He grabbed hold of Radhika's hand, stormed past his mother and made his way out to the front of the house. There he tried to convince her that letting the secret out was the best thing that could have happened. They planned to meet the next day and talk to her parents about arranging a meeting between the two families. They were indeed naive and within a few days both families had disowned them. They were left to fend for themselves with little money and few belongings. The following year was hard as they drifted from village to village trying to find work but as soon as the rumours of their inter-caste relationship spread, they had to move on. Their love for each other had kept them going, although many times, Manoj had considered taking his own life, but he knew that would leave Radhika by herself and he could not bear the thought of that.
Manoj was brought back to the present as the train slowed down and approached Jalgaon Junction. It was now half past ten in the morning and the platform was busy with passengers disembarking and others climbing on board. Manoj watched the busyness from his seat; as he had often witnessed at stations, the platform looked utterly chaotic but worked perfectly because everyone knew their role and their place. Maybe that's how the universe works, thought Manoj. Everyone must play their

role whether they like it or not and the universe will be kind and work its magic. But he had broken a rule and his world had been turned upside down. He couldn't see how he could move his family out of the slums, other than to seek out his father and ask for forgiveness. Learning that he had a grandson might convince his father to allow him back into the family.

*****

Manoj stood at the end of the road with a baseball cap pushed down low over his forehead and hands tucked into his pockets. By one o'clock, he'd been waiting for one and a half hours. He looked at the houses that lined both sides of the road and wondered how his father could afford to live in such a rich area. Each detached villa was huge with beautiful greenery lining the pavements. He stood a few houses away from his parents' house because he didn't want his mother to see him. He was hoping that his father or younger brother would come out so he could get their attention. He was stuck in the city for a day as the train to Jalandhar wouldn't leave until the next day. He had rented a small hotel room in the city for three hundred Rupees, so he had plenty of time, but was beginning to get frustrated. He wasn't sure whether his father would be home; he could easily be away on business, which was usual when Manoj lived with his family. Manoj was trying to stay calm but the thought that he had wasted his time with this detour was fuelling the anger inside him. He had also seen the same person walk past him twice and throw him curious glances. If he wasn't careful someone in the neighbourhood would call the police and then he would probably miss his train. He didn't have enough money to buy another ticket. He rubbed at his chin nervously and looked around at the houses. He saw a face in one of the windows stare directly at him. He decided that he had no choice but to go and knock on the front door of his parents' house. He hesitantly walked down the road. When he reached the front gate, he stopped and gathered his thoughts. The gates towered above him and had no gaps so he couldn't see inside the house, which made him more nervous. He had rehearsed his monologue a hundred times during his long train journey, but his thoughts were already beginning to scramble. He took deep breaths and looked at the intercom that hung on the pillar next to the gate. Once his breathing was back in control, he raised his hand to press the buzzer but before he could, the gates started to open. He panicked and stepped away, standing behind a tree that lined the road. He poked his head round the tree to view the opening gate with trepidation. As the gates fully opened, a silver Maruti Suzuki slowly made its way out of the drive and turned into the road. He sneaked a look into the car and saw his younger brother driving with his mother in the passenger seat. As the car sped down the road, he looked towards the gates that were now beginning to close. Instinctively, he ran towards them and slid in sideways just before they closed shut.

He found himself standing in a large driveway looking up at a beautiful white-washed house. He walked up to the large ornate wooden double front door and pressed the doorbell. He felt calmer knowing that there was no risk of his mother opening the door. He waited a while and then pressed the doorbell again but after a couple of minutes and no reply, he turned and started to walk back towards the gate. As he walked down the driveway, he heard a voice behind him call his name. He turned and saw his father standing in the doorway. He was standing there in a suit, he was greyer than Manoj remembered, but he appeared healthy and his clothes were smart and expensive.

'What are you doing here, Manoj?' asked his father.

'I wanted to talk to you,' Manoj replied rather nervously.

'I don't think we have anything to talk about, Manoj, unless you are single now.'

Manoj stared at his father in anguish and wanted so much to turn away and leave, but he had so much to get off his shoulders.

'Ok, if you want to talk, let's talk but you will have to be quick as your mother's due back soon and she won't be as thoughtful as me.'

Manoj walked up to his father who side stepped, let him into the house and closed the door behind them. He led Manoj through a marble-floored hallway and into a large kitchen where he walked to a kettle and turned it on.

'Tea or coffee?' he asked.

'Tea please, no sugar,' replied Manoj as he stood awkwardly in the middle of the kitchen.

His father gestured for Manoj to sit at one of the high stools that lined the breakfast bar and once he had finished making the tea, he placed one cup in front of Manoj. He held the other in his hand and looked at his son with a blank, cold expression.

'You have a grandson,' said Manoj. For a fleeting second, he saw his father's face relax and become warmer but just as quickly, the acceptance disappeared.

'You are right Manoj, I do have a grandson. He is three years old and his name is Daljit and he is your older brother's son. That is the only grandson I have.'

His father's words cut Manoj deep in his soul. He felt as though he would be sick but he didn't want to show weakness in front of his father. He had hoped that the emotional pull of a grandson would melt his father's cold heart but he knew now that all was lost. There was no way for him back into the lives of his family unless he gave up his wife and child. He felt the usual anger rise within him and he tried to control it but the emotions of the last few days were too much for him and he exploded. He placed his cup of tea on the granite worktop and rising from the stool pushed it forcefully to the ground.

'How dare you dismiss my son as if he means nothing? He is your grandson whether you like it or not. My entire life you have treated me like some worthless idiot. My brothers received all the love and attention but I was your son as well,' Manoj shouted losing all his composure. 'You have done nothing for me but you stand there and judge me. I am your creation and the result of your failure as a father. You have no right to treat me with such contempt. You have no idea about my life or what I have to do to support my family, while you live in luxury.'

Thakur Anand looked at his son and placed his cup of tea on the worktop. He turned around and walking over to the glass patio doors that led to the landscaped garden, he stared out into the distance. He knew that he had not given Manoj enough attention and that he had lavished his other sons with more love and for that he felt remorse. Manoj was always the quiet one, who would spend most of his time daydreaming and on his own. He knew that wasn't an excuse but he forgave himself; it was human nature and unfortunately the weak were always left behind, and he could never forgive his son for marrying out of caste.

'I know what you have been through Manoj and I know how you are suffering living in the slums of Mumbai.' He turned around and looked at his son's stunned face. 'I have people providing me with regular updates on where you are and what you are up to. Who do you think paid your medical bills when you were beaten up by that gang and who do you think got you the job working for Rahul?'

Manoj looked at his father in disbelief. He had never understood how he came to be employed by Rahul. Sudden realisation struck him as he looked around him. Now he knew how his father could afford such luxury.

'You work for Rahul,' said Manoj thinking aloud. 'I only agreed to work for him because I didn't know what he was. Once I knew, it was too late and I couldn't leave; I needed the money to look after my family and get them out of the slums. You stand there smugly, but you don't realise how you have condemned me!' Manoj spoke coldly in anger, but then laughed with the irony of his situation. 'Even when you thought you were helping me, you fucked things up.'

'Stick with Rahul and you will be able to get your family out of the slums. Don't screw it up. I have put my neck on the line for you,' his father said sternly.

'I have a job to do in Jalandhar and then I'm done with Rahul and I'm done with you,' spat Manoj.

His father marched over to his son and grabbed him by the shoulders, 'Listen to me son, Rahul is a dangerous man and is not a man to be crossed.'

Manoj took hold of his father's arms and forced them from his shoulders and pushed him away. His father stepped forward and slapped his son across his face. Manoj was thrown off balance and fell to the floor.

'Sorry son but you need to understand that you cannot leave Rahul's service. It will end badly for you and for me.'

Manoj jumped up from the floor and approached his father.

'Still just thinking about yourself then.' Spat Manoj.

'I'm trying to protect you Manoj!' shouted his father

stepping forward again.

Manoj instinctively threw a punch that landed on his father's chin and knocked him onto the floor. Thakur Anand lay on the floor holding his chin and smiled at his son.

'So, you have a little of your father in you after all,' he said.

Manoj didn't reply, instead he turned to leave. When he reached the front door, he heard his father shout out another warning about Rahul. He hesitated for a brief moment before leaving the house and walking out into the street.

CHAPTER ELEVEN

Raj stumbled down St Mary's Road with half a bottle of Jack Daniels in his right hand and a cigarette in the other. His mind was a complete mess with shifting images and visions from all the haunting dreams he had been having. He bumped shoulders with yet another person without apologising but instead ploughed on into the darkness as a chill wind tore through his shirt. Halfway down the road, he stopped by a tree and put down his bottle. While still holding onto the cigarette, he proceeded to urinate against the tree trunk. A passer-by pulled his dog away and shook his head. Raj picked up his bottle and taking a few seconds to steady himself against the tree, continued his ragged walk down the road. A minute later he had reached his destination and managed with great difficulty to sit down on a low wall outside St Mary's Church. He took a swig from the bottle and a drag from his cigarette; he then placed the bottle on the floor next to him. He threw the cigarette onto the floor and tried stamping it out with his foot but failed miserably. He looked around and tried to focus but everything was a blur and his head was starting to spin. He placed his head in his hands and felt an unbearable anguish build up inside of him. All the years of pain overtook him and he broke down. Tears flooded down his face and onto his hands as he wept uncontrollably. He was oblivious of the world around him and consumed by his own misery. His head spun faster and faster and those familiar voices started their low rumble at the back of his mind. He rocked back and forth with his hands covering his ears and with his eyes firmly shut, he tried to practice meditation as Gabby had taught him, but it was no use. Just when he felt his head was about to explode, he felt a pair of warm hands take hold of his arms and pull him upwards. He opened his eyes but the world was still spinning and he couldn't focus on who had taken hold of him. Like the night of his suicide attempt, he felt the presence moving him into a warm space. All around him, he saw blurred images of Jesus and crucifixes and then he was being led up a flight of stairs. He stumbled but was helped from falling by not only one pair of hands but what now felt like many. The shadowy figures led him up another narrower flight of stairs and as they entered a small dimly lit room, he felt himself being lowered into a chair. There were many voices in the room fighting against the voices inside his mind. He felt a hand on his head and then a gentle kiss on his forehead, which made him drowsy and suddenly the room stopped spinning but he still couldn't see the faces of the people around him. He struggled to keep his eyes open and finally surrendered to a deep, dreamless sleep.

Raj awoke to find he was sitting on a chair in the middle of the church attic. The room was devoid of people with the lights turned low and the door shut. A beam of coloured light shone from behind him and when he turned around, he saw the image of Jesus in His mother's arms upon a stained-glass window. The light from a streetlamp illuminated the round window and filled the attic with a soft multi-coloured glow. Raj felt his breathing grow ragged as he looked around the small space with its low ceiling and wooden slanted beams. On his left were placed two chairs and another three chairs to his right. In front of him was a flip chart that had the single word 'karma' written in black pen. After the sleep, his head felt clear, but there was a slight throbbing at his temples and his throat felt dry. Just as he was thinking that he needed a drink, the door to the room swung open and in walked Lucy. She was wearing a red dress, similar to the one she had worn the first time he had met her and around her neck, she wore the same tartan scarf. She walked up to Raj and held out a cup of steaming black coffee.

'This is becoming quite a habit?' said Lucy with a shake of her head.

Raj accepted the coffee and holding the cup with both hands, he took a sip and closed his eyes. The caffeine hit the back of his throat and relaxed his breathing. He opened his eyes to see Lucy had pulled up a chair opposite him and was sat there staring at his face.

'Oh my, what has my sister done to you?' she said shaking her head again.

She reached out with both her hands and ran her fingers through his thick scruffy beard and then through his mottled hair.

'You do realise that you stink?'

Raj looked down at his shoes not wanting to look into Lucy's eyes but he felt hers burning into him making him feel uncomfortable.

'I really should go,' said Raj as he started to rise from his chair.

Lucy pulled her chair closer until their knees were touching and placed both her hands onto his lap preventing him from getting up.

'Life is a bitch and so is karma,' she said staring intensely into his eyes as if that statement would somehow solve all his problems. 'What are you doing here, Raj?' asked Lucy.

'I need help,' he replied.

Lucy looked at Raj and rubbed her hand down his arm. 'Unfortunately, you just slept through today's session. There's another one tomorrow but if you want help, you

need to make me a promise.'
'What promise?'
'You need to do exactly as I say and in exchange you will receive riches and glory,' she replied softly as she took hold of his hands and squeezed them tight.
Raj looked into Lucy's deep black eyes and saw only darkness but he was desperate and felt that he had no other hope so he nodded dumbly at her.
'I need to hear you say it Raj.'
'I promise,' replied Raj.
'Excellent. When was the last time you ate something?'
'Not sure. I think yesterday morning,' replied Raj realising that he had lost an entire day of his life to drunkenness.
'Well then, back to mine and I'll cook you a steak and you can get washed up.'
'I can't face Gabby at the moment,' Raj protested.
'Don't worry. She's working tonight,' Lucy reassured him and leapt up, grabbing hold of his hand. She led him from the room and out of the church.

*****

Raj sat on the leather sofa in the dimly lit living room of Lucy and Gabby's house. A fire blazed in a hearth in the corner of the room, casting deep shadows around the richly decorated room. He tried not to look into the flames which remained a constant reminder of the night his family perished. He felt as though he was sitting in a museum or in a room in the Vatican with its grand religious imagery. From somewhere in the room flowed the sorrowful sound of violins and cellos reflecting the deep pain he was feeling. He closed his eyes and let the music wash over him and his feelings rise from deep within him.

'Do you like it?' asked Lucy as she walked into the room holding two glasses of red wine.
'Like what?'
'The music?' she replied.
'It sounds like all the sadness in the world gathered in one place.'
'It's 'Siegfried's Death and Funeral March' from Wagner's opera, 'The Ring Cycle.'
Raj looked at her blankly as she passed him one of the glasses and sat next to him on the sofa.
'It's an epic story about a ring of power forged by a pissed-off dwarf named Alberich.'
'Why was he pissed off?'
'These Rhine maidens…'
Raj looked at her blankly again.
'Think mermaids, humiliated him so he stole all their gold and forged a magic ring.'
'Makes perfect sense,' Raj commented.
'Anyway the ring passes from a King to a giant who turns himself into a dragon. Move forwards a few years and the King's grandson, Siegfried slays the dragon and the ring is returned to the mermaids but not before Siegfried is killed himself.'
'Are you just re-telling *The Lord of the Rings*?'
'Strangely similar, but Wagner wrote his opera about seventy-five years before Tolkien wrote his story.'
'Quite a story,' commented Raj.
'I thought you might like it.'
'I didn't say I liked it.'
'It doesn't matter whether you liked it or not but the basic message is that life is a cycle and we all return to ash one day; there's nothing we can do about it. What matters is what we do from birth to death.'
Raj took a sip from the dark red wine and then, standing up, walked over to the painting of 'Dante Running from

the three beasts' that he had seen the first time he had visited the house.
'So, what is the purpose of your life Raj?' asked Lucy from behind him.
Raj stood there blankly staring at the painting, not understanding what he was meant to say. He felt that he had no purpose and that he was destined to suffer for his sins for the rest of his life.
'Everyone has a purpose in life and a reason for being,' continued Lucy without waiting for an answer. 'The trick is to find out what that is and fulfil your potential. Once you have done that, you will find peace and an end to all suffering. Do you believe in karma?'
'Do you?'
'Yes.'
'I thought you were a Christian?'
'Why do say that?'
'Your group operates from a church and I know that Gabby is.'
'Why does it matter?'
'Karma is an Eastern philosophy and not believed by Christians.'
'"Do not be deceived, God cannot be mocked. A man reaps what he sows,"' quoted Lucy, 'Galations 6:7, sums up karma quite well I think, but that's a debate for another day.'
Raj fell silent and contemplated the principles of karma and how his belief in it had controlled his life for many years. He truly believed that all his suffering was down to his own actions of disobedience. His family died because of his actions and he had almost learnt to accept that fate until Gabby had come along and tried to persuade him otherwise. Now he was more confused than ever and didn't know what to think anymore. If he wasn't to blame, as Gabby kept telling him, then why did

his family die and why had he suffered so much misery? He thought back to his aunt and how his uncle had treated her so badly; he could never find an answer in karma for what she had gone through. Maybe it was her actions in her previous life that had caused her so much pain in this one.

'I had a dream in which I saw my aunt trapped in this horrible forest and she had become entwined with a tree. I accidently broke a twig and it dripped blood causing my aunt to scream in anguish. She told me that she was there because she had committed suicide and that she would never be able to leave. When I awoke, I searched her name online and found out that she had really committed suicide.' Raj stopped and looked towards Lucy. 'How can that be?' he asked in anguish.

Lucy walked over to where Raj stood and entwined her arm into his and leaned her head onto his shoulder.

'What you are describing is another part from Dante's Inferno, where those who have committed suicide are punished. In the poem, those who discarded their bodies in life are made to suffer without a body. The trees with their black leaves and twisted branches represent someone who is suicidal and has lost the will to live. The beauty of life is all gone and all that is left is a lost soul. Dante believed that committing suicide was offensive to God as it was God who had given the person the gift of a body. Your aunt is suffering because she did not look after God's gift.'

'But surely God should show pity on those who commit suicide. They are not evil people but people who have been driven to the act by their circumstances. I can't understand how karma can exist in a world where bad people are allowed to get away with their deeds without consequences,' pleaded Raj.

'Like your uncle you mean?'

'Yes. My aunt was driven to killing herself because of the torment she suffered at the hands of my uncle. Surely it should be him suffering and not her? It makes no sense. Explain to me how karma works here?'

Lucy released Raj's arm and grabbing hold of his shoulders, she twisted him to face her.

'The problem is that she didn't take control of her own destiny, Raj.'

'The teachings of karma are bullshit!' Raj shouted suddenly.

'Why do you say that?'

'If karma exists then we can't change our destiny. It's pre-ordained. My family were meant to die and my aunt was supposed to suffer and my uncle was meant to be an evil bastard, so what's the point of sitting here discussing something that we can't change. It's crap!'

Raj wriggled from Lucy's embrace and placed his wineglass on a table, before heading towards the door. He stopped at the entrance, realising that he was still wearing Lucy's bathrobe. He stood there for a few moments letting his heartbeat slow and then returned to sit down on the sofa. Lucy picked up his glass of wine and handing it back to him, sat down next to him.

'Only two thirds of your life is pre-ordained, which includes where you are born, what you look like, if you are born into poverty, if you are a genius or an imbecile and other aspects like this. These are controlled by your previous life and actions,' Lucy explained, 'but the other third you can change through your actions in this life. My teachings focus on the one third of karma that can be changed. If we can't change our future, there is no free will and life becomes mechanical. Any act bears its own rewards and punishments and we can create our own karma through our own deeds. So, tell me, if you were sat in heaven next to God and He gave you the power to

control karma and dish it out where you saw fit, what would you do to your uncle?'
Raj thought about the question and knew exactly what he would do to him, if he had that power.
'He would receive the same number of beatings that he gave me and my aunt and then I would ensure he ended up in that forest instead of her. Unfortunately, life doesn't work like that and like you said, karma is a bitch,' replied Raj sombrely.
'We create our own heaven and hell and we create our own happiness or misery. We are the controllers of our own actions. A girl who I've been working with was beaten and abused by her father for years and finally, through me, she has gained peace and resolution. She understands how karma works and that it has the ability to heal. Sitting still on the floor and practicing mindfulness and chanting can only get you so far. You need to turn that energy into effect. You've tried my sister's way but all you managed to do was fall in love with her and have your heart broken. She has that effect on people; she means well but it always ends tragically. Follow me and I promise that peace will come.'
Raj looked into her dark eyes and nodded. Lucy jumped from the sofa and skipped lightly on bare feet towards a chest of drawers, where she pulled out a small delicate velvet pouch. She walked back over to Raj, knelt in front of him and retrieved a silver necklace from the pouch. She reached up and placed the inverted crucifix necklace around Raj's neck.

*****

The slamming of a door awoke Raj and he groggily opened his eyes and rubbed the sleep from them. He looked around the room in confusion expecting to be looking at his own room but instead the imagery of gods, beasts and opulence met his eyes. The disorientation made his head feel light and he had to close his eyes to focus. He slowly opened them again and looked down at the bathrobe he was wearing and then felt around his neck for the necklace that Lucy had given him. He held the crucifix in his hand and slowly the events of the previous night returned to him. After Lucy had given him the necklace, they had talked deep into the night, while drinking countless glasses of wine. At some point they had eaten a meal in the kitchen, which may have been steak, lamb or pork; he couldn't remember. More wine followed and then at some point he must have fallen asleep on the sofa. He rubbed at his eyes again and yawned as a figure appeared in the doorway to the living room. Raj looked up and agony pierced his heart as he looked upon Gabby, standing there as beautiful and elegant as ever. He hadn't realised how much he had missed her and how much he still wanted to be part of her life. He sat there dumb struck and embarrassed to be sitting on her sofa in her sister's bathrobe.

'How have you been?' asked Gabby still standing in the doorway.

'Been better,' replied Raj.

'You seem to be wearing my sister's bathrobe,' stated Gabby.

'Long story.'

'Please be careful with my sister, Raj. She has a habit of controlling people and getting them to do what she wants.'

'She understands what I'm going through, Gabby, and she can help me. I'm lost and I've tried everything but I feel like I am on this downward rollercoaster and there's nothing that can stop it. I tried meditation and thoughtfulness and all of that but look at me! I'm still a

mess.'
'You didn't give me a chance, Raj.'
'You are the kindest and most gentle soul I have ever met. I thought you would be my salvation but I'm more confused than ever.'
'I can still be your guide, Raj, if you let me...,'
Gabby jumped as Lucy came up behind her, grabbed her around the waist and kissed her on the cheek.
'What are you two love birds chatting about?' Lucy asked cheekily.
Both Gabby and Raj fell silent. Lucy, sensing the tense atmosphere, let go of Gabby, entered the room and stood between the two of them.
'Do I sense some weirdness here?' asked Lucy. 'Gabby, you are not jealous of me are you? I can ensure you that nothing happened between the two of us.'
'Why would I be jealous?'
'I thought you and him...' Lucy pointed a finger towards Raj and then Gabby, 'Awkward.'
'Lucy, stop your mischief now and let me talk to Raj.'
'Raj, poached or fried eggs?' asked Lucy
'Not hungry,' replied Raj.
'I'll make poached,' Lucy said as she walked out of the room.
Gabby walked to sit down next to Raj and they both sat in silence. Raj felt his heart beat faster and faster as Gabby's presence overtook his emotions. As he looked at her, he sensed a feeling of peace and light, something he only felt when he was with her. When she wasn't with him, his feelings of dread and grief returned. Raj reached out to take hold of Gabby's hand and held it to his chest. A flood of emotion enveloped him and he could feel a warm glow growing around his heart.
'I need to give Lucy a chance to help me as I don't see any other way at the moment. I hope you understand?'

said Raj.
'As long as you don't let her take advantage of you and make things worse. Don't get too involved with her.'
'Nothing happened between us.'
Gabby reached out and rubbed his cheek.
'Lipstick marks rarely lie Raj,' said Gabby as she stood up. 'I'm here for you,' she said as she walked to the door, where she stopped and looked back at him.
'Worship the Lord your God and serve him only.'

CHAPTER TWELVE

Raj shifted nervously in his chair as specks of floating dust became trapped in the soft beam of light that shone through the stained-glass window of the church's attic. He was all alone and was beginning to wonder if he had come on the wrong date. Unconsciously, he started to bite at his fingernails and his legs shook nervously. He had promised Lucy that he would attend the session but seeing Gabby that morning had seeded a doubt in his mind. He missed Gabby so much but he had to distance himself from her. Being with her was too painful. He looked at the time on his phone for the tenth time and was just about to get up and leave when the door opened and Lucy walked in with her usual red dress and tartan scarf. Behind her came four men who all walked silently and sat on the chairs around Raj. Lucy waited for the four men to settle down and then stood in front of all them.

'These four men are members of my team and you can call them Kirk, Chekov, McCoy and Scotty. We don't use real names, so during your time here, you will be called Spock,' she said looking at Raj. She then walked over to stand behind the first of the four men. She placed her hands on the shoulders of a young man who looked as if he had just left school. 'Chekov is an IT expert and has helped by networking and helping with social media to connect with likeminded people. He's also a great hacker.' She moved over to the next chair and patted the back of a large West Indian man with not a strand of hair on his head but a well-groomed beard upon his face. 'Kirk works for the police and has helped people with a background in crime and drugs.' She walked to the next chair and placed a hand on the shoulder of a short, plump, middle-aged man. 'McCoy is a doctor and has helped people with drugs, alcohol and mental issues.' Finally, she walked past Raj and stood behind the last man, an elderly man with a weathered face and hands that had seen manual work for over forty years. 'Scotty owns a foundry in Acton and has helped many youngsters with work placements. Spock, please tell the team a little about why you are here.'

Raj looked around nervously at the four men, who were all staring at him with blank expressions. He was unsure about opening up his emotions to strangers but with Lucy standing in front of him, he felt a compulsion to open up. He cleared his throat and shuffled in his seat before he started to tell his story. He told the audience about the death of his family and the guilt he had since carried with him. He spoke of living with his uncle who beat and tormented him until he had the courage to leave. He talked lovingly of his aunt and then the sadness of finding out about her suicide. In all these stories, he harboured a deep guilt of not having done anything to protect himself or his loved ones. He went back further into his life and spoke fondly about his two friends, Vijay and Manoj and how losing their friendship had been hard on him. He had tried making friends in his new school in London but because of his accent and ragged clothes, he had spent most of his school life being bullied.

'Thank you,' said Lucy, 'Everything that has happened to you has happened for a reason. The laws of karma state *whatever one puts out into the universe will come back to them* but does this mean that we don't have control of our own destiny?'

Lucy paused as she looked towards Raj but he wasn't sure whether she wanted an answer or was pausing for

effect.
'Karma requires our participation; it doesn't just happen by itself and you have to accept it before you can change it. It is important to take responsibility for your own life. It's all very well sitting on the floor cross legged and asking for the universe to sort it all out, but at some point, you have to take action. The following anecdote sums up this principle perfectly. A man was drowning in the sea when a ship pulled up beside him and the captain told him to jump aboard. The man told the captain to leave him because he believed that God would save him. This happened another three times and each time he told the captain that God would save him. Eventually, he drowned and died. When the man reached the gates of heaven, he sought out God and asked him why he hadn't saved him. God replied that it was He who had sent all the ships.'

Lucy fell silent, allowing the message to sink into Raj's consciousness. She knew that it wouldn't take much to convince him to follow her teachings and carry out her methods. Vulnerable people were always the easiest to seduce and gaining their trust wasn't difficult. The first step was to discover their secrets and then you could exploit them.

'History will keep repeating itself until we learn our lessons and change our paths. You are caught in a loop and can't get out so the same things keep happening to you. The misery of your family dying, the torment of living with your uncle, the bullying at school, losing your friends and even my sister rejecting you; these are all cyclic patterns playing themselves out. We must break that cycle.'

Raj shifted nervously in his chair and looked down embarrassed at the mention of Gabby.

'You only get back from something whatever you put in.

You will only get a result from energy and intent that you exert. Sitting and doing nothing has absolutely no impact on anything.'

'But I don't understand what action to take,' pleaded Raj.

'First you need to understand the truth,' stated Lucy, 'If you know a truth, then at some point in your life you will be called upon to demonstrate that truth. This is when you will be called upon to put into practice what you claim to be the truth. To put this into simple terms, think of a time when you heard that someone talked falsely about you. Is it right to sit back and let karma take care of it? Is karma going to send you a text message when it has dealt with that person and their lie?'

Lucy looked at Raj with intense eyes and this time expected an answer.

'I suppose not,' answered Raj looking around the room nervously.

'So, what would you do?'

'Maybe take matters into my own hands,' replied Raj without much conviction.

Lucy placed her hands on her hips and took a couple of steps forward towards Raj, 'At least say it like you fucking mean it!'

Before Raj could answer, the door to the loft opened and a young girl entered. She stood at the back of the room trying to avoid eye contact with Lucy.

'Right, let's take a break there; be back in five minutes!' Lucy instructed.

The four men all walked from the room silently and Lucy went over to where the girl stood.

'What is it Karen?' asked Lucy.

'That detective came over to the flat yesterday,' said Karen as she looked around at Raj nervously, 'He took my necklace.'

'What did you tell him?'

'Nothing, I swear.'
Lucy placed a hand on the young girl's shoulder, 'There's no need to worry Karen,' she whispered, 'You have done nothing wrong. You must remember that and everything will be fine. Trust me.'
'But what happens now I've left the group?'
'Karen, start your life and don't look back. If you come back here, it means that everything we did was for nothing,' Lucy said, showing her towards the door.
Karen walked towards the door and tears started to well up in her eyes. Her actions had done nothing to ease her suffering. Her painful memories of her past were still there, but now they were joined by the guilt of more recent memories.

*****

Deepak gingerly opened his eyes as his phone buzzed by his bed side. He reached out towards it and looked at the text message. The message was from Mark asking to meet at the station. He lay in the darkness thinking about the case and he could sense that he was getting close to solving the murders. His bedroom was freezing and his entire body ached with old age and arthritis. He often wondered if all the pain he was suffering was payment for his sins. He had always had disturbing thoughts and a tendency towards violence. Many times, he had tried to get psychological help and over the years he had taken many types of medication to stop his urges. As a young man, he had even tried turning towards God, but even He had abandoned him. Deepak once had a wife and a child but now he was alone in a house that was crumbling around him from the years of neglect. His bed sheets smelt of urine and decay and cockroaches and mice were the only company he kept.

He slowly and painfully climbed from his bed and walked from his bedroom to the bathroom. He switched on the light and standing on a sticky lino floor, pissed into a toilet bowl that over the years had turned dark brown. Without washing his hands, he brushed his teeth with cold water and splashed water onto his face. Walking back to his bedroom, he picked up the clothes he had worn the day before and put them on. Without turning on any other light, he went downstairs into the kitchen and put the kettle on. He had very little need for food and relied mainly on cups of coffee to keep him going. He opened the fridge and a waft of rancid air escaped but the pathetic old man didn't notice. Instead, he took out the already past its sell-by-date milk and poured a tiny drop into a mug he found in the sink. On top of the milk, he poured the boiled water and then heaped two spoons of coffee into it and stirred the concoction. He took his cup of coffee into the living room and sat on a sofa in the dark. From a stool next to him, he picked up a pack of cigarettes and lit one. He inhaled the tobacco and let his lungs swell with the poison. He had no television set so instead he stared into the darkness, letting his thoughts focus on the case. Apart from the depraved violence and suffering he bestowed on people, his only other pleasure was solving a case. He had finally figured out what the numbers on the first dead body and the wall of the second victim meant. He also knew that Karen was the key to finding out who the mastermind behind the murders was and he could taste victory in his mouth. He looked at his watch and saw that it had just gone eleven in the evening. His shift wasn't due to start until twelve, so Mark calling him no doubt meant that he had some new information. He finished his coffee, stubbed his cigarette into the mug and then placed it on the small stool. Picking up his car keys, he left his three-bedroom suburban detached house and climbed into his car. Deepak drove the short distance from his home to the station passing Rufford Tower block along the way. He had a strong urge to stop off and pay Nadia a visit but her pimp was still pissed with him so he drove past and decided to go hunting for a victim later that night. He parked up in the police station car park and made his way into the investigation area where Mark was waiting for him.

'Hi, Detective,' said Mark.

Deepak ignored his greeting.

'What have you got?' Deepak asked.

'Well, I was parked outside Karen's tower block from two o'clock this afternoon and basically nothing happened for bloody hours. I had my lunch, finished all my lemonade and an entire bag of pretzels and bugger all happened.'

'You woke me up to tell me that bugger all happened?' asked Deepak angrily.

'I haven't finished,' replied Mark calmly.

Deepak clenched his fists but resisted the urge to punch the trainee in the face.

'Anyway, about six o'clock Karen emerges from the block and gets into her little green Micra and heads off so I follow her, just like you said.'

'Mark, get to the bloody point!'

'Ok, well I followed her to the church of St Mary's and then followed her inside. She went up to the church's attic and was in there for literally a minute and then she was out and back into her car.'

Mark paused and started peeling a banana that he had magically produced from somewhere. He took a big bite from it and stood there eating noisily. Deepak wanted to grab him by the throat and slam him against the evidence board. Mark continued his debrief.

'Once Karen left the church, I sneaked up to the attic

and peeked through a door that was slightly ajar. There were five men all seated and a woman in a red dress and tartan scarf was talking to them. I didn't want to get caught so I went back down and looked on all the notice boards but there was nothing advertised for anything happening in the attic.'

Mark took another bite from the banana and scratched at his chin.

'Anyway, there were a couple of these old dears in a little kitchen, so I went in and asked them what was going on in the attic. They didn't seem to know what the group was about but I did get a useful bit of information,' said Mark as he shoved the last piece of banana in his mouth.

'Mark, I swear I will put a knife through your fucking eyes!' shouted the detective.

Mark looked at the detective and shrugged his shoulders. 'Apparently, the group are meeting again tonight,' he said, 'So, maybe we go along tonight and question that woman in the red dress. She must be the leader?'

'I will go and question her alone,' said the detective, not wanting to spend any more time than he had to with the constable.

Deepak walked over to the board and looked at all the evidence they had gathered and it all began to make sense. The two murders were revenge related attacks and the group that Karen had visited must be behind the killings. It was obvious from hospital and police records that Karen's dad had been abusive. He had been tormenting his family for years. Karen must have joined the group to get some help but was led into killing her dad for revenge. The evidence against Mr Anton, the accountant, showed that he had large amounts of money stolen from his account. A number of court cases had been started against the accountant for embezzlement but he had never been convicted. The last piece of the jigsaw was the numbers that had been carved on the body of Karen's dad and on the wall of Mr Anton's office.

'The numbers seven and four have been puzzling me since the start of the case but when I discovered the inverted cross on Karen's necklace it gave me a clue. For the last couple of days, I have been going crazy searching for combinations on the internet. I've tried searches for 'numbers and the devil,' 'Seven and Satanism, 'four and evil,' and multiple other combinations. All the searches led me to either the sign of the devil, 666 or Brad Pitt.'

'Brad Pitt?' questioned Mark.

'Seven?'

'Excuse me?'

'The movie.'

'Never seen it.'

'Anyway, I then looked at the numbers again trying to figure out what I was missing and then it hit me. It was staring me in the face,'

'What was?'

'The circles. Around each number, there was a circle and that was the missing piece. I searched again using the words: 'Seven, Circle and Satan,' and the answer appeared.'

'Wow this is exciting.'

'Dante's Inferno,' revealed the detective.

'Not that exciting then.'

'Inferno is a fourteenth century epic poem that tells the story of Dante as he travels into hell to save his beloved Beatrice from eternal damnation. The hell in this poem is made up of nine circles and each circle represents a sin and the punishment.'

'Actually quite exciting; so what are circles four and

seven?'
Deepak gave the young man a venomous look before he continued.
'Circle four, the number painted on the wall of the accountant, represents greed and is punished by the sinners having to carry heavy loads around on their chests. This represents their selfish drive for fortune and material goods.'
'Grim.'
'Circle seven, the number carved on the chest of Karen's dad, represents those who have committed acts of brutality. The souls in this circle are submerged in a river of boiling blood and if they rise too high out of the river, they are shot at by centaurs.'
'Wow, this Dante fellow had quite an imagination. So, what we have is a satanical gang of killers who pose as a self-help group and then somehow convince people to kill and torture their victims.'
'Correct,' said Deepak.
Just the thought of a satanical group torturing and killing their victims sent pleasure signals all through Deepak's body and he felt his usual feeling of arousal which he needed to satisfy. He grabbed his coat and without saying a word to Mark, left the station and jumped into his car.
Deepak parked up on Hartswood Road outside Wendall Park and lit a cigarette. Although bitterly cold, he turned off the engine and peered into the darkness of the park. He felt euphoric at having got so close to catching the killers and his entire body tingled with energy. He had to wait until evening to gate crash the group's meeting in the church so he needed to get a fix some other way. He opened the door to the car and climbed out. He threw his cigarette onto the ground and walked into the darkness of the park. He walked halfway into the park and then

stopped by a bench, lit up another cigarette and waited. After a few minutes, a woman emerged from the darkness and walked towards him. From afar in the dark, she looked like a glamour model dressed in a short coat and long black leather boots. Her hair was dyed red and her face was plastered with make-up. As she came closer to the detective, he could see that she was no glamour model but a woman in her early fifties trying to make herself a living. Deepak removed a role of twenty-pound notes from his pocket, peeled off a few and handed them to the woman. He then led her silently back to his car.

Deepak sat in the driver seat of the car and the woman in the passenger seat. From his coat pocket, he removed a small plastic bag containing white powder and from the glovebox of the car, a small mirror and a straw. He opened the bag and from it poured a small amount of coke onto the mirror. With his business card, he portioned the powder into two lines. With a small penknife he cut the straw in half and gave one piece to the woman. He then placed the end of the straw up one nostril and plugged the other nostril with his finger. He snorted a line of the coke and then passed the mirror to the woman. Deepak let the coke take effect and then felt a rush of exhilaration. He looked over at the woman in the passenger seat who was also enjoying the effect. He took out another cigarette, lit it and took a deep drag. He leaned towards the woman, grabbed her by the throat and stubbed the burning cigarette out on her cheek. Before she could scream he had covered her mouth. The woman grabbed hold of Deepak's wrist and tried to wrestle it free but he was too strong. She kicked her legs against the floor of the car and tried to struggle free but slowly she began to lose consciousness and finally she fell into darkness.

CHAPTER THIRTEEN

Vijay took a sip from his sugary Indian tea that was richly spiced with cardamoms and fennel. He hadn't slept a wink for the last twenty-four hours, since he learnt that his father may have been killed rather than dying in a car accident. What had started out as an investigation into the fire that killed Raj's family had turned into a personal epiphany. He had thought about challenging his mother about his father's death but that would cause her so much grief. He cast his mind back to his childhood and tried to think of anything that could help him, such as a memory of an overheard conversation between his and Raj's father or a strange meeting with men, who looked like gangsters. He remembered nothing extraordinary about his childhood. For now, he put all thoughts of his father's murder to the back of his mind and focused on the task at hand. Part of the mystery he had been trying to solve since arriving back home was the curious visit of Manoj's father, Mr Anand, to the police station. Kirit, the young constable who had saved him on the evening he broke into the police station had told Vijay to meet him at the café on Nakodar Road. As Vijay took another sip from his tea, he saw Kirit walking towards the café looking nervously around him. He approached the door and took one final look around and then entering quickly, he sat down at the table.

'Sorry but I have to be quick, Vijay. The inspector has forbidden me to speak to you and if I am seen with you, I will surely lose my job.'

'Don't worry my friend,' Vijay replied.

'So, every year as you know Mr Anand visits the police station and the inspector gives him an envelope full of

money.'
'Yes, you already told me that.'
'Well, the only other information I have is that the inspector collects the money from that post office over there,' said Kirit pointing to the post office opposite the café, 'So if you can find a way to get in there and you seem to be pretty good at breaking into places, then you might be able to find out who sends him the money.'
'That's useful information brother,' said Vijay sincerely shaking his friend's hand.
The young man shot out of the chair and with a nervous smile, left the café.
Vijay had visited that post office a couple of times since he had arrived back home and each time there had only been two members of staff working there. There was an older man, who appeared to be the manager or the owner and a young boy who always appeared less than enthusiastic to be working there. His only hope would be to wait until the older man left the young boy on his own in the shop. He ordered another cup of tea and a plate of samosas and settled in for a long wait but it seemed to be Vijay's lucky day because as he took a bite from his first samosa, he saw the old man walk out of the post office and head off down the road. Vijay jumped from his seat, scurried across the road and entered the shop. He pretended to be browsing the stationary on the shelves while two shoppers paid for their goods and left. He then approached the young boy and pulled out his police ID, ensuring that he covered his name with his finger.
'My name is Inspector Sharma from the Ludhiana police force,' he lied, 'I need to speak to your boss please,'
'Mr Panesar h-has just g-gone to l-lunch,' stuttered the spotty young boy.
'Where has he gone?'
'He always g-goes to Mrs. Balti's s-sari s-shop for lunch

but doesn't l-like to be d-disturbed,' he replied. The young boy slapped himself on the forehead as he remembered he wasn't meant to tell anyone.
Vijay picked up on the boy's slip-up and now felt in control of the situation – it really was his lucky day.
'Tell me where this sari shop is and I will go speak to him?'
'N-n-no, please don't, I will g-get a beating if he f-finds out that I have t-told you,' replied the boy in a panic.
'This is rather unfortunate young man and could lead you into trouble for obstructing a police investigation... unless,'
'Unl-less what?'
'You may be able to help me young man.'
'Anything p-please b-before Mr Panesar comes b-back.'
'Have you got access to the money transfer records?'
'Yes, it's all here on the c-c-computer.'
'Right then, I need to know who transferred money to a Surinder Singh Virdee this month.'
The young boy rushed over to a computer and started typing with far more confidence than he spoke. He grabbed a piece of paper and pen and jotted down a name. He folded the piece of paper and handed it to Vijay just as the door to the shop opened. Vijay looked around hoping that the manager hadn't unexpectedly returned but instead, standing in the doorway was Manoj holding a gun that was pointed straight at his head. With his free hand, Manoj locked the door to the post office.

Manoj had arrived that morning from visiting his father in Patiala. He felt so confused. He loved Radhika and Navjot and had to keep them safe, but how could he live with killing his childhood friend? As he stepped from the train, he decided not to seek Vijay out that evening, but instead to book into a hotel and think for a few hours. He set off to find a hotel and on his way, he passed the café and saw Vijay. He hid from view until Vijay left the café and then followed him into the post office. He was driven to protect Radhika and Navjot at any cost but he was under no illusion that he would come out of this situation alive. He had two bullets in his gun, one for Vijay and one for himself.

The young shop assistant ducked under the counter and started reciting a prayer to the Gods. Vijay stared in bewilderment at his friend, who stood there silently gun in hand.

'Manoj, you're not still upset about me going to boarding school?' said Vijay trying to lighten the mood, 'Tell me, brother, what this is all about and we can sort it out.'

'I'm sorry, Vijay, but I have to finish what I started, to protect my family,' replied Manoj.

'Finish what you started…, I don't understand.'

Manoj pointed the gun at Vijay's leg, 'It was me who shot you.'

Vijay looked at Manoj in horror and thought back to the shooting all those months ago. Why the shooter hadn't killed him had been bothering him since it happened, but now he knew why.

'Thank you, Manoj.'

'Why are you thanking me for shooting you, Vijay? You always knew how to annoy me.'

'Thank you for not killing me that day. I sensed the hesitation when you had the gun pointed at my head that day and then you moved the gun down. You knew exactly where to shoot me without causing a fatal injury. Don't you see, it was fate or karma, or whatever you want to call it. If it had been the other guy with the gun, I would be dead. Why do you need to kill me, Manoj?'

'He will kill my family if I don't. Believe me, if I had another choice, I would take it in a heartbeat.'

'Who will kill your family?'

'I got myself mixed up with this gangster, Vijay, and he found out that I let you live, so I need to finish the job. Otherwise my wife and child will die. They are all I have, Vijay.'

'There is always another way, Manoj. Let's talk and we can work it out.'

'No, this Rahul guy doesn't listen to reason!' shouted Manoj as he shifted from foot to foot and gripped the gun with both hands.

'Did you say, Rahul?' asked Vijay.

'Yes, he's the biggest gangster in Mumbai.'

'I know,' replied Vijay.

Manoj's finger was on the trigger but he pulled it away and lowered the gun slightly.

'How do you know, Rahul?' he asked.

'It's a long story, Manoj, but if you put the gun down, we can talk about it. Like I said, there's always another way. I will help you and I think you might be able to help me.'

Manoj released one hand from the gun and rubbed at his forehead. He thought frantically about what to do. He didn't know which path to take.

'Listen to me, Manoj, did you tell this Rahul guy when you would carry out…' Vijay hesitated as he looked for the right words, 'this, this task to finish the job.'

'I have another three days.'

'Well then. We have three days to find another solution,' said Vijay.

Manoj closed his eyes and took a deep breath. He slowly lowered the gun to his side. He backed up against a wall, slid down it and sat on the floor letting tears fall from his eyes. He placed the gun on the floor and put his head in his hands.

Vijay called out to the young boy who was cowering behind the counter. The boy nervously stood up with his

hands in the air.
'Put your hands down boy. Now listen, this is official police business so you must not tell anyone what you have seen or heard here today, understood.' instructed Vijay sternly.
The boy nodded dumbly and slowly put his hands down.
Vijay walked over to Manoj and lifted the gun from the floor and lifting his shirt tucked it into his trousers. He then offered his distraught friend a hand and pulled him up from the floor. He placed an arm around Manoj and pulled him into his shoulder.
'We need to get out of here before the Manager gets back and finds the door locked.'
Vijay led Manoj out of the door and then across the road back into the café. They sat in silence for a few moments while Manoj regained some of his composure.
'So, you think it was karma that I shot you?' Manoj asked, breaking the silence.
'Something like that.'
'So, my entire life was mapped out so that I, at that precise moment, could save your life?'
'I wouldn't think too deeply about it, Manoj.'
'Well as you know, I was never a deep thinker. You were the clever one.'
'You're going to start an argument with me after you tried to kill me?' protested Vijay, with a smile.
'I have no idea what I'm going to do,' said Manoj.
'Tell me how you got involved with Rahul.'
Manoj looked at Vijay and told him everything from his meeting Radhika and being thrown out by his parents to finally making his way to Mumbai and being offered work by one of Rahul's men.
'I only found out yesterday that it was my own father who set me up with the job. He has been working for Rahul for many years,' said Manoj finishing his story. 'So, you

see, that's a lot to happen to a person just so he can save the life of an arrogant police man.'
'Arrogant?'
'Yes, you were always arrogant, always thought you knew best.'
'I suppose I was.'
'So how do you know of Rahul?'
'After Rahul's little helper shot me in the leg, I came home to recuperate,' started Vijay. 'I don't know why, but I started thinking about that fire years ago, you know, the one that killed Raj's family.'
Manoj nodded.
'There were some things that just didn't add up, so I thought I'd start looking into it and there was something else that was strange.'
Vijay talked Manoj through finding out about the conspiracy behind Rahul having his father killed and Raj's family murdered and the mystery around Deepak Chopra.
'Wow, that's quite a story,' Manoj said once Vijay had finished.
'There's one more piece of the jigsaw that I haven't told you about.'
Manoj looked at him quizzically.
'I found out that your father comes to the village every year at the same time to visit the inspector at the police station.'
'What for?' asked Manoj, his curiosity peaking.
'Money, a big wad of money.'
'Why would the inspector be paying my father money?'
'The inspector is just a middleman.'
'So, who is the money from?'
'That's what I was here to find out. The name is on this piece of paper,' he said showing Manoj the folded piece of paper.

'Well bloody open it then.'
Vijay opened the folded paper and read out the name.
'Deepak Chopra.'
A waiter interrupted their moment of discovery and the two men ordered some food. They both sat silently at the table and waited for their food to arrive giving them time to digest all the information they had just received.
Manoj hadn't eaten properly since he had left Mumbai as he was trying to save what little money he had left. He sat feeling shameful taking charity from his friend, from the man he had almost killed.
'I promise I will pay you back Vijay but I spent all my money getting here.'
'Stop talking nonsense Manoj, we are brothers, we made a pact if you remember. You will stay with me tonight; Mother will be so happy to see you and then we will catch a train in the morning to Mumbai and see if we can resolve this situation.'
Manoj nodded and fell silent again.
'Remember when we stowed away on that train and we ended up in Chandigarh, a hundred miles away,' laughed Vijay.
'Yes, it was Raj's idea, as usual, and we always followed him like idiots,' replied Manoj.
'But we had some great adventures, didn't we?'
'Yes, like being lost in a strange city and almost getting kidnapped and sold to a gang.'
'We seem to remember things slightly differently. I recall seeing a beautiful city full of excitement and feeling grown up. I wanted to explore the streets instead of the same boring alleyways of the village,' said Vijay.
'I was scared and have been for a long time. I put on this front of being strong in front of Radhika but I'm just a fake.'
'Listen to me Manoj, it takes strength and courage to

stand up for love, especially when everyone is against you. You have given up everything to stand by what you believe to be right. There are many forms of courage and bravery, Manoj. I will never be as brave as you.'

'The mighty policeman who got shot and survived. I have heard stories of your heroism.'

'There's something I've never told anyone before because I am weak and lack your convictions.

'What is it?'

'I'm gay, Manoj, but have never told anyone.'

'Really, maybe I should have shot you in the balls rather than your leg,' said Manoj.

'Well, that's not a very nice thing to say.'

'I was only joking Vijay, you can't decide who you fall in love with, just take a look at me. You need to be honest with yourself and then follow the path that life leads you down.'

The two men fell silent again as the food arrived and was laid out in front of them. A large dosa, a rice pancake filled with potatoes and spices for Vijay and a lamb kharai with naan bread for Manoj. The two men tucked into the food with zeal and when finished, sat there satisfied and content. They ordered two cups of tea and some coconut sweets.

'Have you heard from Raj at all?' asked Manoj.

'I've tried searching for him but I can't find him on social media or in any phone directory. The only information I have is that he's in England. He has no family around here so no one to ask and my mother doesn't know what happened to him either. All she told me was that he would be living with relatives in London.'

'I'm sure he would want to know this theory of his family being killed by Rahul.'

'I think you're right Manoj. Before we go to Mumbai, let's go to your father's house and interrogate him about the

money. I'm sure he must know more about the murders. He was working for Rahul at the time.'
'It's incredible isn't it? You think you know someone and their entire life ends up being a lie. I always thought of my father as caring, supportive and hardworking and he turns out to be a spineless gangster puppet. If he had anything to do with the murder of your father or Raj's family, I will put a bullet through his head myself.'
'Manoj, you need to stay calm and put that anger of yours to one side. We only want to ask him some questions, that's all. Don't forget that I still work for the police so I can't have you shooting your little pistol around.'
'It's not that little,' replied Manoj smiling.
'Still, I will look after the gun for now.'
Manoj nodded reluctantly.
'So, tell me more about your little boy?'
'Navjot gives me reason to live and if anything happened to him, I don't know what I would do. He has this smile that just makes you feel warm and loved. He's just started walking. He waddles around trying not to fall on his arse. I want to give him a better life and that's why I took the job with Rahul. At first, it was just to run errands and collect stuff. I never asked what was in the packages but I had my suspicions. I was content to play ignorant because he was paying good money, well good money for someone living in the slums. But then I was asked to help out on the bank job and that's when I realised I was trapped. After this, I think I'll take Radhika and Navjot away and try to find a place where we can't be found.'
'I will help you Manoj. I have some money saved, enough for you to start somewhere new.'
'I don't want your charity,' said Manoj more aggressively than he had intended.

‘Like I said before Manoj, I owe you my life.’

CHAPTER FOURTEEN

The Karma Club was mostly empty but Raj still chose to sit in a dark corner at the back of the club. He cradled his glass of whisky in his hands as he stared desperately at the entrance. He had an hour before the next self-help group session started but he wanted to talk to Gabby before he decided whether he wanted to go along. The self-help group that Lucy ran was like no other that he had ever heard of. He was baffled that he was the only member of the group in need of help. He couldn't quite work out the roles of the other four men and they hadn't spoken a word to him so far. He took a sip from his drink and thought back to the first time he had talked to Gabby in the club. It seemed like a lifetime ago and he wished that he could relive that day forever. He could still remember the euphoria he felt when she agreed to meet him after work and the small light of hope that had flickered in his heart. After that first meeting, the light had been slowly growing but now it had been extinguished and his heart burnt to ash. He knew that there was no future with Gabby as she would never love him like he did her but he still needed to be with her. He couldn't explain the desperate longing he had to be close to her and how he felt lost and alone when she wasn't there. Lucy had become a surrogate but he felt nothing when he was with her. In fact, the feelings of dread he had always lived with intensified when he was with Lucy. He sensed that he was heading towards a closure and playing out an end game. He couldn't see a future for himself beyond the coming days and that both scared and appeased him. If these were to be his final days on Earth, then he felt a sense of anticipation that he might see his family again in the afterlife. He missed his mother so dearly and wanted her to hold him in her arms again. He wanted to feel like he did when he was a little boy. He could almost feel the warmth of her arms around his waist and that fresh cooking smell from her clothes. His thoughts turned to his father and memories of him standing like an oak tree, strong and resolute. Although he wasn't so close to him, his father had been the figurehead of the family, the one who put food on the table and clothes on their backs. Raj had always looked at him with respect and, of course, a small amount of fear. Then there was his sweet little sister, Heera, who annoyed the hell out of him by persistently following him around with her dolls. She would pester him into playing with them and then reward him with loads of cuddles. His two brothers, Danvir and Parveen, were the best younger brothers he could ever have wished for. They enjoyed endless evenings of playing cricket in the back yard. Danvir always wanted to be the wicket keeper even though he couldn't catch a ball to save his life. He spent most of the time running back and forth to the end of the yard to gather the ball. Parveen was great at sports and there was a fierce rivalry between the two of them. They competed to see who could get the most wickets. Had Parveen lived, he would have been a professional cricketer for sure; he had so much passion and talent. Raj's mood turned sombre at the thought of his loved ones and he had a desperate aching to be with them again. In that moment, he decided to let go of any doubts about Lucy and her group and leave fate to the Gods. He would go along to the session tonight and let it lead him wherever it willed. He was tired and exhausted with life and drained by the endless guilt. He drained the remaining drink from his glass and left just as Gabby emerged from the back door and into the bar.

*****

Deepak sat in the cold darkness of his living room and sucked on his cigarette. The adrenaline rush from meeting with the prostitute had already worn off and he was feeling edgy and a little nervous about his impending visit to the self-help group. He knew that a case like this had a small window of success before the suspects sensed danger and shut up shop. He had never been good at subtlety and he had to be careful not to spook the lady who seemed to be in charge. Otherwise, he could lose the case, for sure. He was so close but he was frightened that the slightest error could foil his entire plan. This case would be his crowning glory and he would leave the force with high respect and enjoy his retirement back home. He hadn't been back to India for many years and he was finally looking forward to it. He was sure that all the chaos he had left there had calmed down and that no one would be on the hunt for him now. He had worked his way up the police force to a high position but then foolishly got involved with a local gangster who had lured him in with drugs and all the prostitutes he wanted. It didn't take long for this Rahul to call in some favours and from then on, Deepak had spent more time covering cases up than solving them. He closed his eyes and thought back to the heady days of being within Rahul's inner circle. Outrageous parties filled with decadence and debauchery that would last for days on end. He would spend the entire time in a drug fuelled haze and soon his work started to suffer. He fell from grace rapidly and finally he was given an ultimatum by his superiors. The choice was simple, leave the force or get investigated for corruption and be sacked. Once in England, he was reduced to creeping around the cold streets of West London to seek out junkies, so he could steal their drugs and pick up grubby hookers like the one he'd met with the previous night. Over the last few years, he'd scrimped and saved his money so that he had more than enough to enjoy life in India. After selling his house, he imagined he would live like a king for the remainder of his days. His plan was to buy a beautiful villa in a part of the Punjab where nobody had heard of him. He was even considering changing his name to make sure Rahul would never find him. The gangster boss didn't take kindly to anyone leaving his organisation. He didn't want anyone taking their knowledge to the police. Rahul left Deepak alone in England because they had struck a deal; Deepak had promised never to return to India. Deepak blew a plume of smoke out into the darkness and looked at his phone. It was almost time to leave for the church on St. Mary's Road. The energy he was looking for started flowing through his bones.

*****

Raj looked at Lucy and wondered why he didn't have the same feelings for her that he did for Gabby. Apart from their sense of dress and the colour of their eyes, they looked identical. He followed her with his eyes and tried to understand the distinction between the two. It was the little differences that set them apart so dramatically. A warm and comforting smile on Gabby compared to a mocking laugh from Lucy. Gabby's hazel eyes were like a deep well filled with summer light and hope, whereas Lucy had eyes of blackness that seemed to want to suck in your soul. They were both mesmerising in their own unique ways. Lucy always came across as superior rather than as an equal like Gabby, but Lucy was still captivating and charming. As he pondered the question, two of the four men, who always followed a few minutes behind Lucy, appeared and sat in their seats. Lucy stopped what she was doing and looked at Raj in her usual head teacher-like stance.

'So today we want to delve a bit deeper into your past and understand the root cause of your problems so that we can come up with a plan together on the way forward,' started Lucy. 'Tell us about the last time that you were truly happy, Raj.'

Raj did not need to think too deeply about the question at all as he knew the exact moment he was last happy.

'It was just before my family died and I was hanging out with my two best friends in the school yard,' answered Raj.

'Describe to me the feelings that you had at that moment.'

'Joy at not having a care in the world. I have learnt since that having peace of mind is the most valuable emotion you can ever possess. Only having fun and playing with your friends to think about, with no concerns, is just pure joy,' he said while rubbing at his grizzly beard.

'Tell us about the emotions that you felt when you learnt about the death of your family.'

'At first, it was just a numbness that took hold of me. My brain just couldn't process what had happened. But as the days moved on and I searched within myself for answers, I came to the conclusion that it was my fault and ever since then, the overwhelming emotion I have felt is guilt.'

'Why do you blame yourself?'

'I was a disobedient child and I was always being told that if I didn't behave then something bad would happen. On the night of the fire, I crept out of the house and met my friends in the school yard so that we could smoke a cigarette that I'd stolen from my teacher. I was meant to be asleep. If I had been, then I would have died too. I was meant to die.'

'The death of your family is a horrific event but people overcome such dark events through nurturing and love. The reason for your anxiety and depression is that you ended up with an evil uncle and instead of helping you heal, the reverse happened. Your guilt intensified and he fuelled that by the way he treated you. This is the issue that we need to deal with and where we can help you. Tell us more about your uncle and the way he treated you.'

'He was a bitter and twisted man who had no intention of looking after me so I have no idea why he agreed to it. To be honest, I am not even sure to this day if he is my uncle. He has no family resemblance. I remember him picking me up from the airport and not speaking to me at all. We drove to his house in silence and once we got there, I heard him tell my aunt that she had better keep me out of his way. The only good thing was that he worked long hours, so the times he wasn't there weren't too bad, but I was living in constant fear of him coming home. He looked for any excuse to get angry and lash out at either me or my aunt.'

'Are you able to tell us what he did to you?' asked Lucy.

Raj looked round nervously at the men sitting in the room with him and then at Lucy. He didn't like talking about the pain that his uncle inflicted on him. It brought back all the awful memories that he was trying to push to the back of his mind.

'It gave him pleasure to inflict pain on people and watch their suffering; you could see it in his eyes. Most of the time he was drunk but looking back now, I'm sure he was high on drugs sometimes too.'

'What was the worst thing that he ever did?'

'I don't really want to talk about that,' replied Raj.

Lucy walked forward, knelt down in front of him and took

hold of his hands in hers.
'You can't start the healing until you accept what has happened to you. The first step is to admit what happened and then we can move onto the next step,' assured Lucy.
Raj looked into the blackness of her eyes and their power sent him into an almost hypnotic state.
'He especially took pleasure in the smell of burning flesh,' explained Raj, with a shaky voice.
'Your flesh?'
'I think anybody's.'
'And how did he burn the flesh?'
'With a cigarette.'

*****

Deepak walked into the entrance of the church and looked around for the stairs to the loft. He found a door that led upstairs and ascended them with his excitement growing. As he climbed the second set of stairs, he could hear the voice of a man which he thought he recognized. He couldn't quite remember where he had heard it before, but he decided it wasn't important and continued to climb until he stood outside the slightly ajar door. He listened for a few seconds to the voice of the man he thought he recognized telling the woman about a dream. He was just about to enter, when the woman replied, telling the man that his dream was a reflection of another scene from Dante's Inferno. Deepak knew he had the right people, that his crowning glory was not far off. Without knocking, he entered. At first, he couldn't see the man who had been talking because he was obscured by a woman in a red dress and a tartan scarf. As the woman turned slowly round to see who had entered the room, the detective saw the man sitting in the chair and realised who it was. Raj was also dumbstruck as he looked at the man who had made his life a misery for so many years. Seeing the monster standing in front of him sent a chill down his spine.

'What is it Raj?' asked Lucy, using his real name.

'That's him,' he said, his voice betraying his fear.

'That's who?'

'That's my uncle.'

Lucy looked at the man standing by the door and then turned back to Raj and smiled.

'Well, that's perfect then.'

'What do you mean?'

'This means that we don't have to go looking for him.'

Lucy turned back to the detective and smiled at him also.

'Welcome Deepak,' she said politely.

The detective was caught off guard with the sudden change in circumstances. The sequence he'd played out in his mind didn't include this scenario and he was confused and unsure what to do.

'I've no interest in that pathetic wretch of a boy,' he spat. 'I need to talk to whoever is in charge of this group.'

'Oh, I know what you've come for Deepak and I must say you've done rather well solving this case. I applaud you. Karen has told me all about you,' said Lucy giving the detective an elaborate bow.

Deepak was more confused than ever and instinctively sensed that he was now in danger and that he had to make his escape.

'I will need you to come down to the station to answer some questions,' said Deepak to Lucy while backing up towards the door.

'I'm afraid that we won't be going to the station, Deepak, you included.'

Deepak backed up to the door and turned to leave but came face to face with two men wearing Captain Kirk and Chekov masks. Kirk, in a lightening move, punched the detective full in the face and then Chekov followed up with a kick in the groin. Deepak fell to the floor and before he could let out a cry for help, the other two men, who were sat with Raj shot up out of their chairs. One of them had produced a piece of cloth from somewhere and proceeded to gag the detective. The other man with another piece of cloth turned the man around and tied his hands up behind his back. The four men, along with Lucy, stood around the detective looking down at him while he struggled to wriggle free from the constraints. Raj sat in his seat, shocked and unable to comprehend what had just happened. The entire evening had just turned surreal and he didn't know whether to run away or take the chance to give his tormentor a good kicking. McCoy went to a bag in the corner of the room and produced a syringe and a small bottle of clear liquid from it. He filled the syringe with liquid from the bottle and then, kneeling down, injected the detective in the arm. Deepak struggled for another minute and then slowly fell into a deep sleep.

'Time to let karma out of its cage,' said Lucy, looking at Raj and smiling.

CHAPTER FIFTEEN

Deepak opened his eyes gingerly and tried to focus on what was around him but everything, including his mind, was hazy. His eyes automatically closed again and he could feel drowsiness overtaking him but he used all his energy to force his eyes open. After a little while, images started to form around him and he could see that he was in the middle of what looked like a huge factory. He had been placed on a chair that had been secured to a metal pillar and his arms were tied behind his back. His feet were manacled with a metal chain but he was no longer gagged. The factory was mostly dark accept for a large cauldron at the back of the room where he could see a fire burning within. He looked around but he couldn't make out what type of place it was and he couldn't see any doors or windows. He knew it would be useless trying to shout for help because if there was any chance of anyone hearing him, he would have been gagged. He tried wrestling free from whatever was holding his hands but there was no give at all.

The last thing he remembered was turning around in the church loft and bumping into two guys wearing masks. Everything had happened so fast that he still couldn't process what had happened. He certainly hadn't expected to see Raj at the meeting. He hadn't even thought about the boy in years; that was a part of his life he was trying his best to forget. After his wife had taken her own life and their adopted daughter had been taken into care, he had decided to close that chapter of his life. He had felt no guilt over his wife committing suicide nor felt any love for Kiran. He had only agreed adopting her because they couldn't have children of their own. There were only two possible reasons why he had been kidnapped and brought to this place. Either the group had somehow discovered that he was close to solving the case or he had always been intended as their next target. The group was targeting people who had committed crimes against their clients. This time, their client appeared to be Raj. He knew how he had treated Raj and understood he would want revenge, but if he escaped alive from his current predicament, he would find that boy and kill him. As he tried to free his restraints again, the lights to the factory suddenly sprang to life and the loud sounds of machinery could be heard echoing around the large space. Deepak squinted as the bright lights pierced his eyes and the machinery noise vibrated his already throbbing head.

He could see the blurred images of people walking towards him in a single line and then all spreading out as they came closer to him. As his eyes adjusted to the light, he could see that four of them wore masks but the woman and Raj didn't. The woman approached and stood staring at him with hands on her hips.

'I'm Lucy,' she said.

'Well nice to meet you Lucy and how can I be of assistance to you?' asked the detective.

'Do you believe in karma?' asked Lucy.

'I believe that you and your motley crew will be brought to justice for what you've done,' answered the detective.

'Karma is the cycle of cause and effect. What happens to a person, happens because they caused it with their own actions,' she said ignoring his comment. 'What is happening to you and what is about to happen to you is because of your own actions.'

'So surely at some point, the same will happen to you for what you are doing to me?' replied the detective.

'What if I told you that I had been sent by the Lord to

Earth to lay my vengeance upon evil men?'
'I'd say that you have been watching too much Pulp Fiction,' replied Deepak.
Lucy turned around and shrugged her shoulders, 'What's he talking about,' she asked.
'Samuel L Jackson makes this speech in the film, Pulp Fiction, about laying his vengeance upon people, he basically recites Ezekiel 25:17 from the Bible,' explained Kirk.
'Oh ok, remind me to watch that,' said Lucy as she turned back to the detective.
'Would you like to say anything to Raj before we get started?' asked Lucy.
'Yes, I wish I'd beaten the little fucker to death,' snarled Deepak.
'No repentance then?'
Deepak sat there silently in defiance even though he knew that his life could very well soon be over.
'Scotty, check on the furnace,' asked Lucy. 'Raj, come over here.'
Raj stayed where he was, unbelieving the events unfolding in front of him. He had never deliberately hurt anybody in his life before. He hated the man more than anything in this world, but he didn't know if he could inflict any pain on him. Lucy beckoned him again but still he did not move. Finally, Lucy walked over to him and taking him by the arm, led him away from the others.
'Raj, don't you see that this is the right thing to do. Why do you think he appeared at the church when we were talking about him? He can't be left to get away with the pain he inflicted on you and countless others. If we let him go, he will be free to destroy other lives. Is that what you want?'
Raj put his hands on his head and closed his eyes and wondered how it had come to this. All he was looking for

was peace of mind and here he was about to take a man's life. He knew it was not the right thing to do but Lucy had persuaded him that this would make everything better. He opened his eyes and decided to believe in her and trust her judgement. He took hold of her outstretched hand and walked back to where his uncle had been restrained.

As they walked towards the detective, Raj could see that a large cauldron with molten metal inside had started to bubble and turn red. The four men all stood waiting for Lucy's instruction and each of them held a weapon. As they approached Deepak, Lucy nodded. Slowly Kirk walked towards Deepak yielding a hammer and took a swing at the man's left hand. Deepak let out a harrowing scream as the bones in his hand were crushed by the blow. Raj closed his eyes and felt bile rising in his stomach and his head started to spin. Next, McCoy approached the detective with a large, serrated blade. First, he cut open Deepak's jumper and vest to reveal his bare chest. Then, he took the tip of the blade and placed it at the top of the detective's chest.

'You can make this a lot easier if you just repent,' said Lucy.

Deepak spat towards Lucy, who shook her head in disappointment and then nodded to McCoy.

McCoy dug the blade deep into the detective's flesh and then worked it diagonally down his chest until it reached just above the stomach. Deepak let out an inhuman scream as blood poured from the open wound and dripped to the already red stained floor. His head sagged onto his chest and his breathing became ragged and hoarse. Scotty swapped places with McCoy and, taking hold of Deepak's head, pushed it back up. From his back pocket, he removed a large pair of pliers and forced open the detective's mouth. Deepak realising what was about to happen, furiously shook his head from side to side in an attempt to thwart the man's effort, but it was in vain. Scotty placed Deepak in a head lock, forced the pliers into his mouth and grabbed hold of his front tooth. He worked the pliers back and forth until the tooth came loose and with a final tug, yanked it out from its socket. As Scotty let go of his head, Deepak leaned forwards and vomited.

Lucy gave Kirk a signal and he disappeared for a few seconds and returned with a bucket of water. He approached the detective and threw the entire contents of the bucket over him. Deepak took in huge gasps of air as the unexpected soaking made him loose his breath. He spat out a mixture of water and blood from his mouth and looked up at the people standing in front of him.

'Fuck you all!' he shouted as blood dripped from his chest and mouth.

Chekov moved forward holding a long cylindrical rod that was connected to a battery that he dragged along the ground. When close to the detective, he flicked a switch on the battery and prodded the detective in the chest with the rod. Deepak's entire body jerked forward as fifty thousand volts shot through him. Chekov moved in for another prod, but Lucy instructed him to stop.

Lucy walked forward and looked at the pathetic man sitting in the chair soaked in water, blood and vomit.

'Why don't you just say sorry to Raj and I will make sure that you die cleanly with no more pain. This could go on for days and nobody wants that. We all have busy lives.'

Deepak lifted his head and looked into the dark eyes of the woman in front of him. He realised that she was enjoying inflicting pain on people as much as he did. He knew that at some point, they would leave him alone. They would continue their torture later because they wouldn't want him to slip into unconsciousness. He just

had to take the pain until then and then find a way to escape. He wondered, though, how much more pain he could take.
'I'll take that as a no then,' Lucy said and motioned to the men to continue.
The four men continued their onslaught one by one. This time the hammer smashed the old man's right kneecap and the blade tore through the detective's left thigh pouring blood onto the already stained floor. The man with the pliers pulled three fingernails from the shattered man's right hand. Then, another fifty thousand volts were sent through Deepak's broken body by the man holding the electrocution rod.
Deepak sat in his seat delirious with pain and could sense himself floating in and out of consciousness. He couldn't take any more and was close to pleading for them to end his life. His ears were ringing with pain and he could barely hear the woman in the red dress and tartan scarf talking to him. He spat another mouthful of blood onto the floor and then managed to strain his neck upwards to look at the woman. He could see her lips moving but couldn't make out the words.
'I said, I hear you like the smell of burning flesh?' she said as she summoned Scotty, 'Get the metal rod and give it to Raj.'
Scotty walked over to the cauldron that had been burning hot for the last hour and removed a long square metal rod that was burning hot at its end. He gave Raj a pair of heat proof gloves and handed him the metal rod. Raj walked hesitantly towards where Lucy was standing in front of the old man and looked upon the horror of what they had done to his uncle.
'Raj, take the rod and stick it in his eye,' instructed Lucy.
'I can't do it,' replied Raj, his hand shaking.
'Think about all those times he held that burning

cigarette to your chest while you screamed for him to stop. Raj, you were only a little boy, so helpless and alone and he destroyed you. The only way you will free your aunt from that hell where she has been trapped is by avenging her. Send him there instead.'

Raj walked forward with the rod in his hand and slowly moved the burning end towards his uncle's eye. As it got closer, Deepak screamed out and shook his head violently. Lucy motioned for Kirk to come forward and hold down the detective's head. Once he could no longer move his head, Raj moved the rod closer until the tip was millimetres from the man's eye.

'Stop!' shouted the detective, 'If you kill me, you will never know where your family is!'

Raj pulled the rod away from the man's eye and looked at him in bewilderment.

'What are you talking about?'

'Your family is alive!' he shouted.

'That's impossible; I've seen their dead bodies with my own eyes,' shouted Raj back.

'Promise to let me go and I'll tell you the truth,' he pleaded as he spat out another mouthful of blood.

'Don't believe him Raj; he's trying to trick you,' said Lucy.

Raj lifted the rod, stepped forward and held the burning end to the detective's chest.

Deepak screamed as the smell of burning flesh filled the air.

'You're a liar!' shouted Raj as he pulled back the rod from the man's chest.

Deepak's head flopped to his chest and he fell silent. Raj grabbed the empty bucket from the floor and ran over to the tap to re-fill it. He rushed back to the detective and threw the water over his head. Deepak took in deep breaths and shook the water from his face. Raj, consumed with rage, grabbed the detective by the throat

and slapped him full in the face.
'Wake up you son of a bitch!' he screamed and slapped him again.
Deepak opened his eyes and, seeing the madness in Raj's eyes, he laughed and spat blood in his face. Raj fell back, wiped the blood away with his sleeve and retrieved the metal rod.
'Tell me what you're talking about or swear to God I will burn out both your fucking eyes,' said Raj losing all control.
'Promise... to let me... go,' replied Deepak through rasping breaths.
'If what you tell me is the truth, then I promise to let you go,' assured Raj.
'Raj, you will regret it if you let him go,' shouted Lucy, 'this is madness!'
'It's my life Lucy and I need to know what he's talking about.'
'Fine,' replied Lucy 'but if he isn't telling the truth, promise me you will finish him off!'
'Agreed,' replied Raj, 'Better start talking old man before our lady friend changes her mind.'
'Your father owed money to a gangster called Rahul... but he didn't have it. He had a week to pay it back or Rahul..... was going to kill him and the rest of your..... family. I helped him to fake his and his family's death and get new.... identities.' Deepak stopped as he tried to catch his breath.
'How do I know you're telling the truth,' Raj shouted.
'You already know. That's why there were six burnt corpses dragged out of the house. We placed them... there to look like all six of you had died. But, of course, you... disappeared that night so there was an extra body.' The detective fell silent as his head flopped again to his chest.

Raj dropped the steel rod on the floor and looked at the man in front of him blankly. All this time he had thought his family were dead but they were alive and well. This evil man had known all these years and never told him. Instead, his uncle had repeated over and over that it was his fault his family were dead. Years of blaming himself and guilt had tortured his soul for nothing.

Raj walked towards the man. He lifted his head and felt more hatred than he had ever felt. He wanted so much to kill him but he had made a promise. He refused to lower himself to the standards of his uncle. As he looked into the face of the man who had tormented him for years, his uncle opened his eyes again.

'Where are they?' asked Raj.

'I don't know,' replied Deepak.

'I don't believe you. If it was you who helped my father arrange it, you must know where they moved to.'

'Yes, but since then, they have moved again and I lost contact with them,' he replied.

'Tell me the first address and I will find them.'

'They moved to the town of Bhiwandi just outside Mumbai.'

'What did my father change his name to?'

'All the family kept their first names but the surname was changed to Nagra.'

'Let him go,' instructed Raj turning around to face Lucy.

'You're making a big mistake, Raj,' replied Lucy.

'A promise is a promise.'

'Ok boys, untie him and dump him outside the police station,' instructed Lucy, shaking her head in disappointment. 'What's your plan, Raj?'

'I will go to India and find my family.'

*****

The two friends stood outside Manoj's parents' house in the town of Ajit Nagar in Patiala. They had discussed the plan over and over again on the train journey but they were still nervous about the coming confrontation. Manoj grabbed hold of Vijay's arm and pulled him to the side of the road out of view from the house.

'Let's go through it one more time,' said Manoj.

'Seriously?'

'You know it feels like just the other day I was here,' said Manoj nervously.

'You were here just the other day.'

'I know, but the last time I was here, I punched him in the face. I thought you should know.'

'Now you tell me?' said Vijay.

'Sorry.'

'It doesn't matter. The plan remains the same. You tell him that you have changed your mind and that you are willing to leave Radhika if he takes you back. Once he lowers his guard, we can ask him about Rahul and Deepak and the money. We get out of there and never come back, got it?'

'Yes.'

'And don't forget to keep your cool. We don't want any theatrics. No punching anyone in the face.'

'Got it.'

The two men shook hands and hugged.

'Did you just touch my arse?' asked Manoj.

'Oh God, I wish I'd never told you.'

Manoj laughed as they headed towards the house.

Manoj buzzed the intercom on the gate and waited.

'Yes,' said an electronic sounding voice.

'Father, it's Manoj. I need to talk to you.'

There was a pause and then the gate started to roll open. The two men walked into the garden and approached the front door. Mr Anand opened the door

and stood, blocking the way into the house.
'If you have come here to fight with me again, Manoj, it's best you leave. We have nothing to discuss unless you have changed your mind about that girl.'
'You were right all along Father. She is no good. She has left me and taken my child back to her family. I have been a fool and deserve everything that has happened to me. I betrayed the family that raised and loved me and all I want is to be back with you. I don't ever want to see her again.' Manoj spoke with tears running down his face. 'Vijay here has made me see sense. He has helped me come to terms with what I must do,' he cried.
His father looked at the two men and then stepped aside and motioned for them to come into the house.
'Don't overplay the part,' whispered Vijay.
Manoj looked at Vijay and strained his eyes shut to produce more tears.
Vijay shook his head in despair as they followed Mr Anand into the house and then into the kitchen.
'It was tea with no sugar?' he said to Manoj.
'Yes, that's right.'
'How about you, Vijay?'
'Coffee, black please, Sir.'
'How is your mother, Vijay?'
'She suffers from her arthritis, especially in the knees but apart from that she keeps herself busy with her cooking, cleaning and temple work. How is Aunty Anand? Is she not here today? I would love to meet her again after all these years.'
'She is away but will be pleased that you visited, Vijay. She was pleased you went to boarding school and studied hard,' he said looking at Manoj. 'I hear you work for the Delhi Police now.'
Vijay had hoped that the old man wouldn't know about him working in the police force. The entire plan was in

jeopardy now, as it was unlikely he would answer any questions about Rahul.
'Yes Sir. I was with the force but I decided to leave and return home. I've discovered that I enjoy cooking far better and I have my eye on that café for sale on the main street.'
Mr Anand finished making the drinks and then sat at one of the breakfast stools opposite the other two. He sipped his tea and looked at them silently. No one appeared to want to re-start the conversation. Vijay realised quickly that Mr Anand was playing a game of chess; he wanted them to make the next move.
'So, what made you move to Patiala Sir?' asked Vijay, wanting to place the spotlight back on the wily old man.
'I wanted to get out of the village, you know, the dust and all that cow shit everywhere didn't really suit me; the asthma you understand. You've seen how clean the streets are here and we have good security around, so your aunty feels nice and safe.'
'Must be really expensive to live here. You've obviously done alright for yourself?' replied Vijay, going into police interrogation mode.
'You reap what you sow.'
'Well, whatever you've sown has come up smelling of roses but even roses wither and die once they've been exposed to the elements.'
The two men glared at each other, while Manoj sat chewing at his fingernails aware of the tension building in the room. It was not going to plan already and they had only been in the house for ten minutes. He decided to intervene and put the focus back on himself.
'So, I was hoping to see Gopal today.'
'Gopal is out with his friends and won't be back until later. So, Manoj tell me more about your plans for the future now that you have decided to ditch that low caste

tramp,' said the father, intentionally trying to provoke his son.

Manoj clenched his fists and tried to control his breathing and forced a smile to form on his lips. 'I want to come and live with you, dear father. I miss Mother so much. I will do anything to make it up to you.'

'What about that half-breed son of yours?'

Manoj felt the anger rise within him but he had promised Vijay that he would stay calm and not let his temper overtake him. They were only words; he had suffered much worse over the last few years. He looked over at Vijay and saw his contorted face and watched him reach behind his back and grab the gun he had tucked into the back of his trousers. Within a couple of heartbeats, Vijay had stood up, pushed the stool back with his leg and was now pointing a gun at Manoj's father.

'You miserable old bastard. How dare you insult another human being that way. I should shoot you in the head right now,' Vijay spat.

The old man smiled and looked past the two men to the other side of the room. Vijay heard the click of another gun being cocked. He turned around and saw Manoj's mother standing in the doorway with a rifle in her hand. Vijay could feel sweat droplets start to form on his forehead. The situation had escalated quickly. There was a strong chance that they were never going to get out of the house alive. He had to think fast and swing the initiative back towards them. He looked over at Manoj, who surprisingly looked calm under the sudden pressure.

'Well, we seem to be in a bit of a dilemma,' started Vijay, 'Tell the old woman to put down the gun or I will blow your brains out.'

'Not if she shoots you in the arse first,' replied Mr Anand.

Manoj climbed off from his stool and walked slowly to

stand between his mother and Vijay.
'You'll have to shoot me first, Mother.'
'I have no problem with that, Manoj,' croaked the old woman.
'I didn't think you would but that's Father's crappy old single shot rifle and once you've shot me, Vijay can still blow your head off.'
'Put your hands on the counter,' instructed Vijay to Manoj's father.
Mr Anand did as he was told and nodded to his wife, indicating for her to keep the gun pointed at their son.
'You two idiots thought you could come here and treat me like a fool. I work for Rahul. Don't you think I know that Manoj was instructed to kill you, Vijay. You show up here like a pair of clowns putting on an act.'
'Listen, this doesn't need to end badly. We just want answers to a couple of questions and then we will be on our way,' explained Vijay.
'Depends on the questions,' replied Mr Anand.
Vijay looked to Manoj and then the old woman holding the rifle. Sweat was now dripping into his eyes. He quickly wiped his forehead with his sleeve. He could feel his heart rate increase and his throat drying as he licked his lips to try and create some saliva. The palms of his hands were also beginning to sweat and the gun felt heavy in his tight grip.
'We want to know the truth about my father's death and also the truth behind the fire at Raj's family home.'
Mr Anand furrowed his brow and started tapping his fingers on the kitchen worktop. Vijay quickly interpreted his body language as a sign that he hadn't expected the question. The shift also told him that he knew the truth and it made him feel uncomfortable.
'For you to ask this question, you must already know that your father, Bhavesh and Raj's father owed Rahul a lot

of money. Rahul wanted your father killed but I persuaded him to only scare him. Unfortunately, the hoodlum that he sent to do the job was incompetent.'

'What happened?'

'The guy was supposed to run your father off the road into a field, to send him a message, but instead he ran him off a bridge and into the river. Believe me, I was as distraught as anyone when I learnt of his death.'

Vijay felt the emotion rise within his belly. He felt as if he would explode but he pushed back the feelings of anger, pain and hate to focus on the current situation.

'What about Raj's family?'

'I must admit that was a good plan,' said Mr Anand calmly.

Both Vijay and Manoj looked at the old man in horror. Vijay gripped the gun tighter, his finger still on the trigger.

'Your explanation for this one better be good or you can say goodbye to your wife, Sir,' said Vijay.

'After your father died, Raj's father, Param knew that he would be next, so he hatched a plan with the detective in charge of the investigation into Bhavesh's death.'

'Deepak Chopra,' said Manoj.

Again, a tremor of shock ran across Mr Anand's face.

'You boys have done your homework. I'm impressed.'

'Anyway, they were old friends so they arranged to fake the family's death and I must say it worked perfectly. Deepak was in charge of that investigation too, so he could cover up any holes and no one ever knew any different. Ingenious.'

Vijay and Manoj looked at each other in confusion and Mr Anand noticed the look on both of their faces. He rubbed at his chin, realising that he had just fallen for the oldest trick in the book and disclosed more than they already knew.

'I must say that you two are not as thick as I thought you were. I should have known that being in the police force would have taught you a trick or two.'
'So, Raj's family are still alive?'
'Yes,'
'Where are they?'
Mr Anand hesitated and then reached inside his trouser pocket. Vijay stepped forward and held his gun closer to the man's head.
'I just need to get my phone from my pocket,' he said holding his hands in the air.
'Slowly,' Vijay instructed.
Mr Anand removed his phone and scrolled through his address book. He grabbed a pen and paper, wrote down an address and handed it to Vijay.
'I don't suppose it matters now,' he said as he handed the paper over. 'Any more questions or can you fuck off now and leave us alone?'
'Why is Deepak Chopra paying you all that money every year?'
Mr Anand smiled and shook his head. 'You could be a good asset for Rahul if you'd like to jump the fence Vijay.'
'Just answer the question.'
'Param didn't trust Deepak fully so he told me about the plan. Ever since, I've been blackmailing Deepak. He was working for Rahul at the time and double crossed him. They had a deal that Deepak could leave his service providing he stayed in England and never came back. But if Rahul ever found out that Deepak had helped Param get away without paying back all that money, then it would be all over for him. He would die a horrible death.'
Vijay processed this information. He couldn't believe all the conceit and lies that had been told over the years for

money. Lives had been destroyed and loved ones murdered just so that some gangsters could have their fun.

'I think we should go now,' said Manoj, leaning back and touching Vijay on the shoulder.

Vijay stood still and kept the gun aimed at the old man. He wanted so badly to pull the trigger to get some sort of revenge for his father's death. Killing Thakur Anand wouldn't bring his father back or give Vijay any true closure, but he so badly wanted someone to pay for the murder. He contemplated pulling the trigger but another idea formed in his mind.

'Deepak sends you five hundred thousand Rupees a year, right?'

Mr Anand nodded.

'I think that money should go to your son, to keep his mouth shut about your knowing Raj's family didn't die. After all, Manoj works for Rahul as well and it might slip out. I would say for the last ten years that amounts to five million Rupees.'

'Five million Rupees, are you insane!' shouted Mr Anand.

'Well, like you said, you reap what you sow.'

The old man looked angrily at Vijay and then across to his wife who still had the rifle aimed at Manoj.

'If I agree to this then I never want to see either of you two again and this conversation never happened.'

Both Manoj and Vijay nodded their heads.

'Give me your account details,' instructed Manoj's father.

Manoj gave his father his bank card and then logged into his bank account on his own phone. Once the transaction was complete, he gave Vijay a nod. The old man passed the card back to his son and the two men slowly backed away towards the door of the kitchen keeping a wary eye on the old woman.

'If I ever see either one of you again, I will kill you,' shouted Thakur Anand as the two friends left through the front door.

They hurriedly walked down the road, constantly looking over their shoulders until they were at least a couple of miles away. They hailed the first taxi they saw and then sitting in the back, both took a deep breath and looked each other in the eye and smiled.

'I'm glad that you took your own advice in there,' said Manoj.

'What advice?'

'To stay cool.'

The two men laughed.

'What's the plan now?' asked Manoj.

'Now we go to Mumbai and seek out Rahul and make sure your family are safe.'

CHAPTER SIXTEEN

Raj stood in a street as the sun darkened and the stars appeared as if they were weeping. Dishevelled women ran past full of tears and other women stood weeping with extreme sadness. Dead birds fell from the sky and the earth trembled as a man appeared pale and hoarse. He told Raj that the lady that was so lovely had died. Raj looked up to the sky and saw angels returning to the sky singing glorious hymns. His heart, heavy with loss, carried him to the dead body where he could see other ladies covering her with a white veil and she had the look of true humility and peace. Grief stricken Raj called upon death to come to him as well but as death approached, he awoke. Sitting up in his bed, he felt immense grief and anguish at the dream that had felt so real. He thought back to when he dreamt of his aunt and the truth from his dream. He had a desperate longing to seek Gabby and gaze upon her with his own eyes. As the beautiful face of Gabby floated in his mind, the alarm on his mobile phone started to buzz. He leaned over and switched it off. He picked up his packet of cigarettes and lighter, placed them on the bed in front of him and waited for the usual time. He closed his eyes and slowed down his breathing as Gabby had taught him and felt his mind clearing. The deep sorrow he was feeling after the dream lay heavy on his heart but he couldn't allow himself to drown in emotions; he needed to stay focused on the days ahead. He had booked himself a ticket to Mumbai and would leave that night. He had no idea how he was going to find his family in such a large city and there was a good possibility that they may not even be there. He opened his eyes and checked the time again and then removed one cigarette from the packet and picked up the lighter.

Just as he was about to touch the flame to the cigarette, he stopped and put the lighter and cigarette back down on the bed. There was no need to follow the nightly ritual anymore. It meant nothing. So many years of his life had been wasted to overwhelming guilt. None of it was his fault and there were souls out there in the world who knew the truth and could have changed his life in a heartbeat but chose not to. His own family had betrayed him and cast him aside to be abused and mentally tortured all because of money. He was still trying to understand and get to grips with the enormity of what his uncle had told him. Years of grieving for his family and longing to be with them again and they were reachable in this world. He could have walked up to them and touched them, hugged them, cried to them and he could have been loved.

Over the past fourteen years, he had only felt the touch of love twice: the first was from his aunt and the second was when Gabby had smiled at him across the dimly lit bar. His aunt's love was frail whereas the love that emanated from Gabby was pure and unwavering like the brightest of lights from a shining star. The warmth of her light touched him so that he felt no more pain and even the creatures that lurked in the corners of his mind hid in the shadows. His heart ached to see her but he didn't want to disturb her in the middle of the night. It was a Sunday, so he would wait until morning and then go to find her at the church.

For the next few hours, Raj lay awake in his bed staring into the darkness and fantasised about a life different from the one that he had lived. He imagined himself playing with his friends, Vijay and Manoj, in the fields close to their village home. He was sitting at home, cross legged on the floor, while his mother cooked him his favourite paratha stuffed with potatoes. Playing cricket with his brothers in the dusty alleyways until the sun hid itself beyond the horizon. He imagined himself growing up in a big city that wasn't too far from his village and working as a professional, who commuted to his office every day. He would meet his friends after work for a beer at the local bar and then head to his apartment, one that overlooked a beautiful park. Then he would marry the girl of his dreams and gorgeous children would follow.

This entire alternate reality could have been his life, if it wasn't for the selfishness of his father. He was trying his hardest to suppress the feelings that were rising from within him but he was finding it difficult. He felt bitterness and hatred for the treacherous father who had put all his family in danger and then run away from his responsibility like a coward. He had no idea what he would say to him, if he finally met with him after everything he had learnt. His emotions felt as though they were wading through quicksand and slowly sinking. As his thoughts meandered from his fantasies of a better life to the impossible reasons for what his father had done, he drifted in and out of sleep. His dreams were even stranger than his waking thoughts. He saw his friends, Vijay and Manoj, standing next to him with shining swords as he travelled through visions of hell. All around them were frozen lakes with sinners, who were trapped below the ice. In the distance, they could see the devil with half his body trapped in the ice and huge wings that flapped, sending a freezing wind across the lakes. He had three faces that each held a sinner, their screams filling the hellish place. The three friends came across a shadow of a man who was frozen in the lake up to his neck and asked him what this place was.

'This is the ninth circle of hell where those who have been treacherous reside. People who betray others lack love so they are trapped in this cold place, which has no warmth.'

As the shadow lifted from the man, Raj gasped and fell backwards. It was the face of his father. He ran from that place on slippery ice until he could run no longer and then came to a sudden stop as he came face to face with the devil. His friends joined him and together they battled the demon and eventually defeated him and imprisoned him below the ice. Raj looked into the distance and saw a light floating towards him and he yearned to go to it but his friends held him back.

'Raj, it is not your time yet brother,' said Manoj.

'The light will return soon and then you shall embrace it and know peace,' said Vijay.

*****

Raj stood at the back of the church as the congregation sang 'Hosanna in the Highest.' The stirring words and music filled the entire church and he could see the pure joy on the devoted faces. He looked over the sparsely filled pews for Gabby but he couldn't see her anywhere. Worry touched the back of his mind and he started to get a tightening feeling in his stomach. He knew that she rarely missed the Sunday service so he imagined that something terrible must have happened to her. The dream of her death floated hauntingly in his mind and he tried to push it away but the intrusive thought was too overwhelming. He felt the rise of panic and was about to turn around and flee when he felt the light touch of a hand on his shoulder and all feelings of dread vanished in a heartbeat. He turned around and was met by a radiant smile. As he looked into those soft eyes, he knew

only love.
'Come let's sit down,' she said as she placed her arm in his and walked into the hall.
They found an empty pew and sat close together enjoying the peacefulness of the service and hymns. As usual when he was with Gabby, all doubts and bitterness fled and were replaced with contentment and joy. The service was almost over and the priest was saying his final words before communion. Gabby, as always, was fully engaged with the ceremony and took communion with both delight and humbleness. After it was over, they both stood and made their way from the church back out into the world. They walked silently arm in arm towards town and felt comfortable in the silence. The chill air was being mellowed by the bright sun in a cloudless sky as they walked. They decided to grab a sandwich and enjoy the pleasant winter's morning in the park. They strolled down St Mary's Road into Walpole Park and found a bench that was bathed in sunlight.
'Do you want to share?' asked Gabby.
'Sure,' replied Raj.
Gabby removed half of her cheese and onion sandwich from the packet and passed it to Raj and accepted half of his ploughman's in return.
'So how come you were late to church today?' asked Raj in between bites of his sandwich.
'Lucy,' replied Gabby.
Raj felt a knot in his stomach as soon as she mentioned her sister's name.
'Lucy?' asked Raj.
'She told me about your family still being alive.'
Raj stopped eating and looked over at Gabby.
'She told you?'
'Yes' replied Gabby.
'Did she tell you how I found out?'

'I don't need to know the details, Raj,' she said putting her sandwich down and turning to face Raj.
'It's wonderful news, Raj and you need to take this chance to heal the intolerable grief that you have suffered. Forgiveness is the key to unlocking a better future. Don't forget that everything that happens to us is an experience, whether good or bad. We are connected and there is a bigger and higher plan for all of us. Do not give in to hatred and bitterness; try to be the best person that you can be.'
'Gabby, come with me to India?'
'This is a journey that you will have to make by yourself, Raj although don't be afraid because there will always be help when you need it most,' replied Gabby.
'I won't need to be scared or afraid if you come with me, Gabby. I always feel stronger when I'm with you.'
'I must stay here. I have my own path to follow and I can't leave Lucy alone. Father would not be best pleased. I'm meant to be looking out for her.'
'I think she can take care of herself.'
Gabby laughed and took hold of Raj's hand and held it to her cheek.
'You are such a gentle soul, Raj.'
Raj looked away in embarrassment but then turned back towards her and smiled.
'I love you, Gabby,' he confessed, finding the words easy to say.
Gabby smiled towards Raj and took hold of his other hand as well.
'My love for you transcends the physical; it is not earthly and has no concept of time and space. I have loved you before we met and will love you still when the flowers stop growing and the earth turns into ash.'
'I understand that now,' he replied. 'I understand why I can't look into your eyes too long before I have to gaze

to the floor and surely it was God's intent to make something rare when he created you.'

'You flatter me with your kind words.'

They both sat in reflective silence and thought about the separate paths that they would now take. Raj hoped that all his questions would be answered in India and that he would finally find the peace he so longed for.

'How do you think you will find them?' asked Gabby.

'I have a name and a last address so I will start there. I searched the internet and social media for them but didn't find anything, which I expected, as they don't want to be found. I'll try the relevant government departments and registers to trace the name they are going under now. Although they may have changed their name again, so it could be a challenge.'

'Have you been to Mumbai before?'

'Once on a family holiday. It was such a fantastic trip. Both my best friends at the time came as well with their families. We spent a week in a hotel by the sea and the three of us explored the city during the day, free from our parents. At night, we strolled through the street markets and food stalls trying all the strange foods we had never seen before. Wandering in the dark when all the market lights glimmered and sparkled and the aromas filled your senses was fantastic. I remember trying pani puri for the first time and thinking wow!'

'What's that?'

'It's a small, crispy ball made from a pancake-like recipe. A hole is made in one end of the ball and filled with chickpeas and potato and tamarind-flavoured water. The fun part is trying to fit the whole thing in your mouth at once.'

'Sounds fun. I'd love to try them,' said Gabby.

'I'll take you for some when I get back,' replied Raj.

Gabby smiled.

'What was your favourite place there?'
'About a mile up the beach from our hotel, there was this little fair that had rides and we used to go there first thing in the morning before it got too busy or too hot. We spent a couple of hours going on the rides and playing some of the games and then right next to the fair was a beach café selling snacks. With whatever money we had left, we would buy a plate of food and sit there sharing it. Sitting there enjoying a plate of food with your friends and looking out to sea was such a joy. I didn't know it then but thinking back to the memory makes me appreciate how special it was.'
'Make me a promise, Raj.'
'Anything.'
'When you get to Mumbai, make sure you visit this place first, before you do anything else.'
'Why?'
'Do you trust me?'
'Yes.'
'Then do this for me.'
Raj nodded his head, looked away into the distant sky and saw dark clouds beginning to form on the horizon. His mood became gloomy as his thoughts turned to his impending flight and his time away from Gabby. Leaving her to travel hundreds of miles away made his heart tremble and he felt as though his soul would depart from his pulse.
'Will I see you again when I come back?' he asked.
Gabby also looked in the distance and her eyes seemed to be filled with a heavy sorrow. She did not reply straight away but let the question hang in the air while she searched for the least painful response. Finally, she turned to him and taking hold of both his hands spoke softly.
'I promise that one day we will see each other again but

please promise me not to grieve for the past and to only look to the future. Remember, forgive and you shall be forgiven.'

Raj nodded.

'Now, go and get ready for your flight and may the angels protect you on your journey,' she said as she leaned forward and kissed him on the cheek.

'I like the new look by the way,' she said.

'Thought I'd better shave it off; otherwise my family might not recognise me,' he replied, rubbing his chin.

Gabby gave him a final smile and then gathered her things from the bench. Raj closed his eyes; he could not bear to see her leave. When he opened his eyes seconds later, she was gone.

CHAPTER SEVENTEEN

As the taxi slalomed its way through the midday chaos of Mumbai's main roads, Raj sat in the back seat and let the sights and sounds wash over him. He had experienced a flood of emotion as he stepped out of the airport terminal and into the street. The crowds of people and the oppressive heat gave him immediate flashbacks of being a child and only seeing the legs of hundreds of people. The smell of nostalgia also hit him like a slap on the face: that unique mixture of smells only found in India, burning incense, masala chai, jasmine flowers all mixed together with the undoubtable whiff of cow dung. He looked out of the window and took in all the hustle and bustle of everyday life. The vibrant colours of women's saris, the exotic fruits and vegetables adorning the stalls by the roadside, spice sellers with buckets full of turmeric, coriander, paprika and hundreds more. Everywhere there were people moving to and fro, children, men, women each on their separate journeys through the streets of Mumbai. The taxi took a right turn and to his left he could see the beautiful beach and the sea disappearing into the horizon. He felt as though the emotion of being back in India after fourteen years would overwhelm him but he fought to stay in control. The taxi slowed down and came to a halt outside a hotel. Raj climbed out of the taxi and handed the driver three hundred Rupees for the fare and an extra fifty as a tip. Throwing his rucksack over one shoulder, he walked up the steps into the Atlantic Sea Hotel. He was hoping for some relief from the intense heat when he walked into the foyer, but the small rotating ceiling fan barely whispered a breeze towards him. Raj dropped his rucksack to the floor and taking off his coat, unzipped his bag and took out a bottle of water. He downed what was left in the bottle and then wiped the sweat from his forehead with his shirt sleeve. He looked around the small foyer for a receptionist but the place was empty. Noticing a small bell on a desk in the corner of the room, he walked over to ring it a couple of times. From a door behind the desk appeared a young woman with a half-eaten samosa in her hand. Ignoring Raj, she sat at the table and once she had finished her snack, she shuffled around a few papers and then looked up.

'Yes,' she said nonchalantly.

'I have a room booked.'

'Name?'

'Raj Khatri.'

After more shuffling of paper, the woman handed Raj a piece of paper.

'Sign.'

Raj looked around for a pen.

'Do you have a pen?' he asked.

The woman sighed heavily and from a drawer found a pen and handed it to Raj, who signed the paper and handed it back to the woman. Raj looked at the woman and shrugged his shoulders and shook his head in despair.

'Room number please?'

'Thirty-three.'

'Wow, you can say more than one word,' Raj said as he turned away from the woman and picked up his belongings.

He followed the room number signs up to the third floor and into room thirty-three. The room was small with barely enough space for the double bed but the view from the window was at least decent. He stared out towards the Arabian Sea and imagined finding his family and maybe visiting the beach with them. He wondered if his brothers and sister would recognise him after all these years and would they be pleased to see him. It wasn't long after they had visited Mumbai that the fire had happened and his life had been turned upside down. Every time he thought about the incident now, he could feel the anger and bitterness well up within him, replacing the feelings of guilt he had lived with for so many years. He checked the bathroom, which was no more than it needed to be and looking inside the mini fridge, he wasn't surprised to see it was empty. He took off his shoes, lay on the bed and stared at the yellow-stained ceiling. He felt exhausted, as he hadn't had any sleep during the nine-hour flight. It was only the second time he had ever flown after arriving in England all those years ago. He felt like a child again going through the airport and climbing aboard the plane. He spent the entire flight fighting his nerves both about the flight itself and the possibility of meeting his family. He looked at the time on his mobile and worked out that it was just past nine o'clock in the morning in London; he thought about messaging Gabby. The last meeting with her in the park had left him unsure. It had felt like a final goodbye but he so desperately wanted to have some sort of relationship with her. His stomach rumbled but he fought back the hunger as he wanted to get some rest before venturing out into the city. The temperature difference between London and Mumbai was incredible; he had left London on a bitterly cold day with a chilling breeze cutting through him only to arrive to thirty degrees which caused sweat patches all over his shirt. The room had no air-conditioning and felt like an oven but he didn't have the energy to even open a window. He closed his eyes and drifted off into a deep sleep. He dreamt that he was a child again, running through the alleyways of his village.

His sandal slipped off and he almost fell face first into the dirt but gained his composure and slipped his sandal back on and continued his journey. He ran until his lungs burned and his face was drenched with sweat and then came to a sudden stop as he reached his destination. A few seconds behind him came Manoj, who was so out of breath that he collapsed onto the floor and took in big gasps of air. Raj helped his friend up from the floor and half carried him to the main bus stop of the village. Sitting at the bus stop with his father, was a forlorn looking Vijay all dressed up in a new school uniform with a suitcase by his side. As his friends approached him, Vijay tried to smile but couldn't. There was no need for words. The three friends hugged each other and tried not to shed tears. They renewed their pledge to stay friends forever and grow old together. That had been one of the last times that all three friends had been together before their lives sent them separate ways. As Raj fell deeper and deeper into sleep, his dreams deserted him and all around him was darkness and silence. For the rest of the day and night he slept peacefully and when he awoke, the sun had just started to rise over the Arabian Sea and a bright new day had begun.

Raj stood on Juhu Road outside the hotel enjoying the warmth of the sun after a taking cold shower. He needed a good breakfast but didn't fancy risking the grubby looking buffet on offer at the hotel. He looked both ways down the main road and decided to go right as he could see more shops in that direction. There were mainly fashion stores dotted along the road but eventually he came across a smart looking café and as he entered, he was handed a menu and shown a table by the window. Raj didn't need long to decide what he wanted as he

knew what he was craving.
'Two aloo parathas and a cup of tea please,' he told the waiter who smiled and walked off towards the kitchen. He didn't have a definitive plan to try and find his family but there was one thing he needed to do before he went on the search and that was to keep the promise he had made to Gabby. As he sat looking out of the café window, he thought back to the events of the last few days. The memory of what Lucy and her four henchmen had done to his uncle had become almost surreal, as if it had been a dream. The image of his uncle sitting shackled in that chair with his body and face battered and broken made him feel like throwing up. He had no love for his uncle and agreed with Lucy that he deserved to pay for his sins but the torture was brutal and had made Raj extremely uncomfortable. Lucy was very different to Gabby.
As the smiling face of Gabby floated into his mind, the waiter returned and placed in front of him two aloo parathas, a bowl of yogurt with masala spice sprinkled on top, with a generous knob of butter and mango chutney. The waiter disappeared for a brief moment and then returned with a glass of water and the masala chai. Raj devoured the food as if it was his last supper and then sipped his tea lovingly with both hands wrapped around the mug. He paid the waiter and left him a tip before leaving the café and strolling down the road. On his way down to the beach, he stopped off at a bank that he saw along the way and exchanged another two hundred pounds into Rupees. While there, he asked if anyone knew about the fair that used to be situated along the beach but none of the young twenty-somethings knew what he was talking about. The bank manager who had been eavesdropping in an office behind the tellers came out and told him that the fair was

no longer there.
'What about the café that was next to it?' asked Raj.
'Oh yes, that's still there. They do a lovely Akuri on toast,' he said rubbing at his round well-fed belly.
Raj accepted directions and then thanking the salivating man, he walked on towards the beach. Strolling along the promenade, he looked towards the sea and felt the salty warm breeze flow over him. In the distance, he could see the small hut that was the café, with round plastic tables and chairs set outside. He saw again the three young boys running towards the café from the fair in their sandals and clutching onto their small coins. They were sitting on one of the round tables, each sucking through a straw from the same glass of milkshake. The image slowly blurred and vanished as he came closer and from inside the café, he saw two men emerge and sit at one of the tables. A spark of familiarity touched his mind and a feeling of déjà vu coursed through his veins. His skin tingled with anticipation as his brain leapt ahead of him and decided who the two men were. He quickened his pace and felt his breathing becoming more intense as he approached them. When he was only a few yards away, he stopped and felt the palms of his hands start to sweat and his head start to spin. Surely he had let his imagination run away and they couldn't really be his friends. He licked at his dry lips and thought of turning around and fleeing rather than risk disappointment. He took a deep breath, wiped his palms onto the sides of his trousers and stepped forwards. As he cast a shadow over the table in front of him, the two men turned towards Raj and looked at him with bemusement. Raj looked at the faces of the two strangers and slowly backed away apologising. He turned away from the table and cursed himself for being so stupid and thinking that in a vast country with over a

billion people that two of his best friends would coincidently appear in the same place as him. Why had Gabby told him to come to this place? He was angry with himself for having built up some hope. He walked over to the café and ordered himself a sweet lassi and sat at one of the tables outside. He took a sip through the straw and looked towards the distant horizon as the sun blazed onto his back. Moments later that sun lost its power as a shadow fell over him. He turned to see two men standing behind him. He used his hand as a sun visor to see who they were, but the sunlight was too bright.

'Where's our straws?' asked Manoj.

Raj instantly recognised the voice and leapt up to grab hold of Manoj's shoulders and turn him away from the sun, so that he could see his face more clearly. He did the same to Vijay and together they hugged each other tightly. For Raj the years of pain and suffering since he had last seen his friends was overwhelming and he broke down and cried. His friends held him close until his tears dried up and they sat together around the table looking at each other dumbly.

'You can't believe how good it is to see you both,' said Raj.

'Well, it's a bloody miracle that's what it is,' replied Vijay.

'It feels like it,' said Raj.

'We've been trying to get hold of you Raj, without any joy and here you are,' said Vijay.

'How are you both?' asked Raj.

'We are fine, Raj, and we have lots to catch up on,' said Manoj.

'Wow, it's so good to see you guys; how long has it been?' asked Raj.

'Must be about fourteen years or so,' replied Vijay.

They all sat back and silently thought about all that had

happened to them over the past fourteen years.
'What will you have to drink?' asked Raj.
'I will get the drinks,' said Manoj jumping out of his chair.
'No let me,' protested Raj, also jumping up.
'No, I have come into some money recently, so it's my treat,' replied Manoj.
'It's true,' confirmed Vijay.
'How about some snacks?' asked Manoj.
'I had a huge breakfast so nothing for me thank you,' said Raj.
'Just get a thali Manoj but make sure you get some veggie bits,' said Vijay.
'You don't eat meat now?' asked Raj.
'He doesn't eat meat, drink or smoke,' laughed Manoj.
'That's not a bad thing,' replied Raj.
'He doesn't even have sex with women,' added Manoj.
'Manoj!' protested Vijay.
'Or men,' laughed Manoj out loud.
Vijay just shook his head.
'I obviously have a lot of catching up to do,' said Raj, laughing too and slapping Vijay on the back.
Over the next few hours, the friends caught up on each other's lives and how they came to this point, sitting around the same table. Manoj retold his story of finding love but then how society and his family rejected him as an outcast. He told of how he joined Rahul's gang that led to him shooting Vijay and then their confrontation with his father. Raj sat in astonishment as Vijay explained how he had discovered his father had been murdered and that Deepak was behind much of what had happened. Raj listened to it all and then it was his turn to tell his friends how he had suffered at the hands of his uncle and how he had felt that he was to blame for his family's death. He told them the truth about how he had discovered his family were alive and also his

relationship with Gabby, and how it was she who had told him to come here.
When all had been shared, the three friends leant back in their seats and looked at each other. They saw for the first time the emotional scars imprinted on each other's faces. It had not been easy for any of them and each of them had suffered their own fate.
'It seems that this Rahul has affected each of our lives in different ways,' stated Raj sombrely.
'He still has a hit out on Vijay and when he finds out that I didn't do it then I'll be on the list too,' said Manoj.
'Looks like our next step is to see Rahul and bargain with him,' replied Raj.
'He doesn't do bargaining,' replied Manoj.
'Well, we need to find a way,' said Vijay.
'We could kidnap his son,' suggested Manoj.
'I still work for the police, Manoj, so I think not,' replied Vijay.
'Let's come up with a plan today and see him tomorrow. Then I need to find my family,' said Raj.
'Oh yes, that was the other thing we were meant to tell you,' said Vijay as he removed a piece of paper from his pocket and handed it to Raj. 'We know where your family is now.'

CHAPTER EIGHTEEN

The three friends spent the day reminiscing about their younger years and walking through the streets of Mumbai, recalling the adventures from when they were last there. Manoj and Vijay helped Raj pick out some gifts for his family. He bought a beautiful sari for his sister in her favourite colour, for his two brothers he bought replica India cricket tops and for his mother a gold necklace. Raj's two friends tried to persuade him to buy his father a gift too, but he flatly refused. He blamed everything that had happened to him on his father's greed. Getting involved with criminals and then running away from his problems like a coward had ruined Raj's life. He would never forgive him, no matter what excuses he tried to sell him when they met.

Later in the day, Manoj took his two friends into his humble home in Dharavi, where they met Radhika and Navjot. Radhika made them tea and freshly fried pakoras and they sat on the floor and talked until the sun went down. The three friends then headed back to Juhu beach to finalise their plans for the next day.

They caught a rickshaw to the beach and stepped onto the sand amongst thousands of other people. The beach was beautifully lit with streetlamps and children ran up and down to the water with their glow sticks. The three men walked for a while in silence enjoying the warm evening in each other's company. They made their way to the street food market area of Juhu beach and walked around the brightly lit bustling stalls and were tempted by many of the dishes. They stopped off to share a plate of chilli paneer, a cottage cheese with a Chinese sauce, spring onions and peppers. They watched the man

behind the next stall make pav bhaji; he took a handful of boiled potatoes, mashed them on a large steel pan with tomatoes, onions and peas. He then spread lashings of butter on some soft buns and handed the plate to the three friends. Vijay immediately took hold of one of the buns and tore off a chunk. He dipped it into the sauce and shoved the huge piece in his mouth. Manoj and Raj followed suit and they all stood there moaning in delight at the wonderful flavours. Manoj and Raj then insisted on hunting for some non-veg food which they found at a stall cooking fresh chicken tikka. They stood next to cages of live chickens while the cook performed his magic. They followed that with street kachori, mutton roll and dahi puri and then stood groaning like children, having eaten way too much food.
'Where are you staying, Raj?' asked Vijay as he loosened his trouser belt.
'At the Atlantic Sea Hotel,' replied Raj.
'Seriously, even the rats refuse to stay in that place. Let's get your things and you will stay with me and Manoj at the Marriot,' said Vijay.
'No really, it's fine,' protested Raj, half-heartedly.
'Raj please, I've got a bottle Jameson's in my bag,' said Manoj trying to tempt his friend.
'It really is a dump,' smiled Raj, 'and I could do with a drink,' he added.
'Good, settled,' finalised Vijay, as he hobbled ahead with his walking stick.
The three friends walked casually to Raj's hotel, where he collected his belongings, paid his bill and checked out. They walked back along the beach to the Marriot and went straight up to Vijay's room, which was ten times the size of Raj's with panoramic views over the beach and beautifully decorated with soft cream shades and lighting on both the walls and ceiling. Two king size

beds created the centre piece of the room with a desk and armchairs by the windows. In the corner, was a door to a bathroom, large enough to hold a party, with an elegant bathtub and shower cubicle. Leading from the bedroom was a balcony that held a round table and four chairs with spectacular views along the beach.
'Tell me again how you came into all this money?' joked Raj.
'Vijay has paid for this room my friend, not me,' replied Manoj.
'I like luxury,' said Vijay shrugging his shoulder, 'besides, like Manoj mentioned, I don't drink or smoke, or gamble for that matter, so what else am I going to spend my money on?'
'Fine by me,' replied Manoj as he walked out onto the balcony and placed a bottle of Jameson on the table. 'Vijay, get me some ice please,' he shouted.
Raj and Vijay joined Manoj on the balcony bringing a bowl of ice and three crystal glasses. Vijay disappeared back into the room and returned with a can of coke. He opened the bottle of Jameson's and poured two doubles; he then poured himself a coke. He dropped three cubes of ice into each glass and then picking up his own glass, he held it up high. The other two men also lifted their glasses aloft.
'A toast to friends and a pact they once made,' said Vijay.
The three friends brought their glasses together with a clink and took a sip. They sat round the table looking out towards the sea, enjoying the silence, which was wrapped in the warm humid air of a beautiful Indian evening. Each man had their own reason for being there but they were all overjoyed at having the chance to share the burden. Vijay wanted closure for the death of his father, Manoj was seeking an escape from criminal

life and Raj needed to see his family and stop living in the past.

'So, let's go over the plan one more time,' said Vijay.

'Hey, who put you in charge,' protested Manoj.

'Wow, one sip of your drink and already you become disagreeable. I was hoping that lovely wife of yours would have cooled your hot blood,' replied Vijay.

Manoj laughed and downed the rest of his glass. He looked at Raj, encouraging him to down his as well. Raj obliged and they poured another round.

'Go ahead boss, but I say we still kidnap the boy,' said Manoj cheekily.

'Manoj, first thing in the morning you call Rahul and tell him that I have held you hostage and that I have evidence that he killed my father. You tell him to meet us in the Ramada Hotel restaurant. That way he won't know where we are staying and we will be in a public place.'

'What if he wants to see the evidence?' asked Raj.

'I love that accent. It's like half English, half Indian and half Russian,' said Manoj.

'I see your maths hasn't improved and how do you hear Russian?' queried Raj.

'Well, that's what I hear,' replied Manoj. 'I'm hungry, can we get room service?'

'Seriously, we ate a week's worth of food at the market,' chided Vijay. 'Menu's by the phone,' he added.

Manoj emptied his glass and wandered off to order some food while the other two men continued discussing the plan.

'We can only hope that he falls for the bluff,' Vijay answered Raj's question.

'It might be more convincing if I say I found his case notes while living with Deepak in London,' Raj said.

'That's good. We tell him that I have scanned the files and sent them to a friend at the Delhi Police Force and that if anything happens to me, he will open them. It might just work.'

Manoj came back to the table and poured himself and Raj another drink.

'What did you order?' asked Vijay.

'Chicken Tikka pizza,' replied Manoj.

'Disgusting,' said Vijay

'And chips,' added Manoj.

'Right.'

'And barbecue chicken wings.'

Vijay paused.

'Is that it?' asked Raj.

'Of course; I'm not a pig.'

All three men laughed heartily and raised their glasses to clink them together. With all the chat and reminiscing they had done that day, Raj was feeling more relaxed than when he had arrived in India. Meeting his friends had been a God send and he wondered if Gabby somehow knew that his friends would be there or whether it was simply another coincidence of life. Manoj slapped Raj on the thigh and told him to hurry up and finish his drink. The two men drained their glasses and then Manoj poured another round.

'Guys slow down! Don't forget we have a very important engagement tomorrow,' said Vijay.

'Oh, stop being such an uncle, Vijay. I think you must have been born old. Even as kids you were telling us not to do this and not to do that,' chided Manoj.

'Well, I had to be the sense of reason. Otherwise you would have followed Raj into every crazy venture he thought of.'

'I must admit, looking back now, some of those ideas were stupid,' laughed Raj.

'Like when you tried to persuade us to grow weed in the school greenhouse so we could sell it to the teachers,'

said Manoj.
'That would have made us some good money,' replied Raj.
Manoj lifted his glass and was about to empty it down his throat, when there was a knock at the door.
'Wow that was quick,' said Manoj. He jumped from his chair to answer the door.
'So, tell me more about these twin friends of yours, they sound very intriguing?' Vijay asked Raj.
'That's a good word for them. I still know very little about them except that they are total opposites when it comes to how they view life,' said Raj. His thoughts travelled back to London and the twins.
'It sounds like you really like this Gabby girl.'
Raj was just about to answer when he heard a glass smashing from inside the room. The two men jumped out of their seats and ran inside. Manoj was lying on the floor with broken glass around him. His face was bleeding from various cuts and he was writhing on the floor holding onto his right arm where a piece of glass was impaled into his flesh. Standing over Manoj were Sanjeev and Toni holding guns and behind them was Rahul.
Vijay instinctively went to check on Manoj, but Sanjeev pushed him back and stood blocking his path. Rahul walked past Vijay and Raj and out onto the balcony. He picked up the half-finished bottle of Jameson and carried it back into the room. He unscrewed the top and standing above the bleeding Manoj, he poured the remaining liquid over his face. Manoj screamed in agony as his skin burned from the alcohol spilt over his cuts. Raj and Vijay could do nothing but watch the man inflict pain on their friend as the two heavies aimed their guns towards them. When the bottle was empty, Rahul placed it on a nearby table and then sat down on one of the

armchairs staring at Raj and Vijay.
'I am Rahul, but you already know that,' he said as he brushed down his suit trousers and adjusted his tie. 'You have five minutes to give me a reason not to kill all three of you, starting from now.'
Vijay wiped the sweat from his brow and looked over at Raj and then back towards Rahul.
'We have evidence that you ordered the hit on my father,' said Vijay. 'Let us go and I will make sure that the evidence never surfaces.'
'Really, go on!'
'I got the case file from Deepak Chopra and I have emailed it to a colleague of mine at Delhi Police station. If anything happens to me, the evidence will go straight to the chief.'
'Vijay, you think this Deepak fellow is the only bent officer that works for me. Half the Delhi Police Force is in my pocket. I'm afraid that just isn't good enough. Get that arsehole up from the floor,' he instructed his men.
The two men walked over to Manoj and grabbing hold of him by the arms, dragged him up from the floor and pushed him against the wall. Manoj screamed in agony as the glass in his arm dug in deeper. He wiped the blood from his eyes and looked at Rahul with venom.
'Manoj you really are an idiot. What makes you think you can defy my instructions and then stroll around my city with your two equally stupid friends and get away with It?'
Rahul shook his head in disappointment, stood up from the chair and pulled a gun out from the inside of his jacket.
'Walking around, eating chilli paneer with the guy you were supposed to shoot. For fuck sake Manoj, I can't believe it, you're even staying in my hotel, you idiot!'
'Rahul, I'm sorry, but he's my friend and I couldn't do it. I

was going to come and see you tomorrow and try to work things out,' pleaded Manoj.
'Vijay, what leg was it that Manoj shot you in?' asked Rahul.
'The left one,' Vijay replied looking confused.
Rahul lifted his gun and shot Vijay in the right thigh.
Vijay screamed and collapsed onto the floor holding his leg as it bled. Vijay desperately tried to put pressure on the wound to prevent blood loss.
Manoj and Raj looked at Rahul in horror. The guy meant business and if they didn't think fast on their feet, they would all be dead.
'Here's what we're going to do,' started Rahul, as he removed the cartridge from his gun and removed all but one bullet from it. He pushed the cartridge back into place and then handed the gun to Manoj.
'Manoj, you are going to shoot Vijay in the head or Toni here shoots your friend dead.'
Manoj looked at Raj, licked his lips and swallowed hard.
'This guy is a nobody Rahul. We only met him at the beach today and invited him for a drink. Just let him go and we can talk about this.'
'You mean this guy?' he pointed towards Raj. 'You started to pick up strange men on the beach, Manoj?'
Manoj looked at Rahul and thought for a second about shooting him with the gun in his hand but he looked towards the two heavies; if he lifted the gun, they would kill him.
'What annoys me is when an idiot treats me like an idiot. I know who Raj is, so stop the delaying tactics and shoot the fucker!'
Manoj stumbled forwards with the gun in his hand and stood over Vijay who was starting to tremble as the blood flowed freely from his wound. Manoj lifted the gun and pointed it towards Vijay's head.

‘I’m sorry, Vijay,’ said Manoj.
‘It’s ok, Manoj.’
‘Look after my family,’ said Manoj preparing to shoot himself in the head.
‘No! wait!’ shouted Raj.
Manoj stood still with the gun pointed at Vijay’s head and looked over at Raj. Sanjeev had his gun pointed at Manoj and Toni had his pointed at Raj.
‘Rahul, I have a deal for you,’ said Raj.

CHAPTER NINETEEN

Raj stood outside a gated house in the city of Bhiwandi, twenty kilometres from Mumbai. The sun was beating its midday heat over him and he wiped the sweat from his forehead with his sleeve. He checked the address on the piece of paper that Vijay had given him and looked again at the building. The house was set in a beautiful street, with plenty of space between each home. The neighbouring houses were immaculate, with white-washed exteriors and greenery lining the front gardens and polished ornate metal gates for security. In contrast, the house he stood before was overgrown with weeds and the exterior of the house was mouldy with crumbling plaster. He crossed the road, walked up to the rusty gate and pushed it gently with his hand. It creaked loudly but gave no resistance so Raj pushed it harder and walked into the front garden. The path towards the front door was just about visible under moss and weeds. An old Maruti Jeep sat forgotten, rusty and coated in dirt in one corner of the front garden and he could barely see the downstairs windows, where Devil's Ivy climbed up the walls and smothered them. He walked up the steps to the front door and rang the doorbell but he heard no ringing. He waited a few heartbeats and then knocked loudly on the door. There was still no answer. Raj's heart began to sink as the possibility that his family had moved again swept across his mind. Despair crept towards him like a cloaked assassin and all he wanted to do was return to the comfort of self-pity and loathing. He closed his eyes and breathed slowly and let his mind clear. There was so much hanging on him finding his family; failure was not an option. He needed to get inside.

Maybe there he could find some clue of where they had moved to. He retreated down the front steps back to the gate and turned to view the house. Over the weeds he could see a side gate to the right although the path was blocked with tall weeds and stinging nettles. He looked around for anything he could use to create a path and noticed a large flat wooden sheet lying next to the jeep. He lifted the piece of wood and threw it onto the weeds, flattening them. He walked on top of the wood and then repeated the same process three more times to reach the gate. As with the front gate, it wasn't locked, so he opened it and walked down the side of the house. Here also were overgrown weeds but the path was accessible and led him into a large back garden. Grass a metre high swayed gently in the warm breeze and fruit trees lined one side of the grass. Rotten oranges and apples lay strewn under the trees and fruit flies swarmed around them, filling their tiny bellies with sweet juice. He turned towards the back of the house where the back door was wide open. He entered and saw only misery and decay. The kitchen and living room area were mostly dark except for tiny beams of light that peered in between the ivy outside. The kitchen was grimy with grease-covered worktops and dishes piled high in the sink. Crumbs of food were scattered all over the worktops and floor, mixed with mouse droppings and dirt. What once must have been a beautifully furnished living room lay in disrepair, with broken furniture and peeling paint. No pictures hung on the walls or sat on mantelpieces to give the home warmth or belonging. A crumpled, yellow-stained blanket lay on one of the sofas, with only a black-stained pillow for company. Propped up against one of the walls was a once elegant chest of drawers, whose only job now was to house a thousand spider webs. Raj walked up to the chest of drawers and wiped away some webs to prize open the top drawer. In amongst the clutter of keys, remote controls and menus was a photo album. He carefully lifted the album from the drawer and carried it over to the kitchen, where there was a little more light. He placed it gently on the kitchen worktop and opened the cover. A feeling of both joy and immense grief overtook him. There, on the first page was a photo of the entire family from their trip to Mumbai. The photo had been taken on the beach on the day before they were to return home. His father was standing at the back carrying little Heera and his two brothers were standing either side of him. He was sitting on the sand with his arms wrapped around his mother's neck and giving her a kiss on the cheek. He remembered the day vividly and he could even smell the perfume his mother was wearing and hear the sound of the sea behind him. He turned through the pages of the album and forgotten memory after memory hit him like a tidal wave. He had repressed all those memories over the years. He had no one to share them with and didn't ever expect to see those family photos again. For years he had believed that all his family's personal belongings had perished in the fire. Of course that was also untrue. He closed the album and headed back outside into the garden for some fresh air. About to head back into the house and search upstairs, he heard a raspy cough from somewhere in the garden. He turned towards the noise, noticing a narrow path leading through the grass, possibly made by wheel tracks. He followed the tracks and in a small clearing under a banyan tree sat an old man in a wheelchair. He had his back to Raj, but great plumes of smoke rose into the air from a cigar he smoked. After each puff of the cigar, the old man coughed as though his lungs were on fire and his body jerked back and forth. Raj walked slowly around the old man to stand in front of him.

The gaunt figure looked up and stared at the young man in front of him and at first did not recognise him. As the young man's features became more familiar to him, his expression changed from confusion to utter grief. Raj saw the old man's lips begin to tremble and his eyes fill with reservoirs of tears. He dropped his cigar onto the grass and held a shaking bony hand up to his mouth, as the tears started flooding his face. Raj stood staring at the pathetic man in front of him. This was his father. The once strong and resolute man was now frail and broken. A white plastic garden chair was lying on its side forgotten in the tall grass near where they stood. Raj lifted it and brushed the dirt from the seat; he removed his rucksack from his back and sat down opposite his father. He looked at the wrinkled, weathered face of the man, who was not even sixty years old yet. His white stubble and wispy hair made him look haunted. The old man dried his eyes with the back of his hand and with a cloth wiped the drool from his mouth.

'Is it really you, Raj?' the old man asked, his voice breaking into a cough.

'It is Father,' replied Raj, uncertain what else to say.

'But he told us that you had died,' replied the old man, tears beginning to form at the corners of his eyes again.

'Who told you that?' asked Raj rather more forcefully than he had intended.

'Deepak,' answered his father.

Raj sat there cold and numb with this new information. It was definitely the kind of depraved and inhuman thing that his uncle would do, but why?

'Why would he say that?' asked Raj.

'Deepak isn't your uncle, Raj. He was just a family friend who helped us.' The old man stopped to clear the catarrh from his throat. He wiped the mucus on a cloth and then blew his nose into it. 'We needed to make sure that you were safe so we asked him to keep you in London until we settled down somewhere new and then we were going to send for you to come home.'

'Why would he tell you that I had died?' asked Raj.

'I don't know Raj, but the day he did, it destroyed our lives,' cried his father.

Raj felt anger building inside of him and tried his best to remain calm.

'The day that you took money from a gangster was the day that you ruined all of our lives,' said Raj. 'It doesn't make sense for a man like Deepak to help you out of the goodness of his heart.'

'He didn't do it out of kindness; he did it for money, a lot of money,' replied his father.

'But I thought you were in loads of debt and that was why you faked the fire?' asked Raj confused.

Raj's father averted his eyes from his son's. Raj's mind whirled with the question of how his father had afforded to pay Deepak.

'I get it now,' Raj said as realisation struck him, 'You never paid your debt to the bank and kept the money you took from Rahul. You conned him. Did you have insurance for the house and your lives too? Who got that money?'

Raj's father looked at his son with shame written across his face and raising both his hands, he held the palms of them together.

'Please forgive me son,' he said his voice breaking, 'I did what I had to, to protect my family. You must believe me.'

'How is stealing money from a gangster protecting your family?' asked Raj angrily.

'I wanted to give you all more than we had, a bigger house, better toys and a better education,' he replied as

another coughing fit stole his words.
'We were happy; we didn't need anything else!' shouted Raj, 'Was Vijay's father involved in this scam as well?'
'I was in charge of the money, so he didn't know anything about it.'
Raj clenched his fists. He wanted to scream and shout in his father's face but he restrained himself. Vijay's father had died because of his own father's greed. He placed his head in his hands and rocked back and forth in his chair trying to calm himself down. He took deep breaths for a couple of minutes and then looked back at his father.
'Where is Mother?' he asked.
The old man again averted his eyes from his son's and his face became paler.
'She never forgave me for what I did, especially when she heard of your death. She died soon after from heart failure, a broken heart I was told by your brother.' The old man broke into another coughing fit and slumped in his chair. 'I'm so tired of this life, Raj that I pray every day that death comes for me but he never does.'
Raj sat silently taking in the death of his mother. He looked down at the rucksack on the ground next to him and wanted to hurl it at the old man and hurt him. This wouldn't bring his mother back though. He felt cold and empty inside as the tiny glimpse of hope from when he discovered his family were alive was now all but destroyed.
'What about my brothers and sister?'
'As soon as they were old enough, they left. I haven't heard from them since. Your mother made sure that they knew what a monster I was and they hated me for it. I don't blame them but if Deepak had sent you home everything would have been fine,' he said solemnly. 'Instead, I lost everything and I just sit here alone waiting

for the cancer to eat me from the inside.'
'The cancer started a long time ago, Father. Once you became dishonest, karma pricked up its ears and came looking for you and one day it will catch you and make you pay for your sins.'
'I am already paying son,' replied his father.
The two men fell silent and reflected on everything that had been said. Each man felt sorrow burning in their hearts. One fateful decision many years ago had led to so much misery and pain for so many people. Lives had been destroyed and loved ones had died from a simple exchange of money between arrogant men.
'How have you been, Raj?'
Raj felt bile rise up in his stomach as he digested the question and thought of his life in London. He tried every day to forget the years of torture and humiliation that he suffered at home and school, with suicide always lurking at the back of his mind like some vile companion.
'Every day of my life since the fire has been filled with guilt and self-loathing. I wake up in the morning with a fear in my chest that never leaves me. Every night, I lie awake in the darkness wondering what I did wrong that my family had to die as my punishment. I have been beaten and tortured by a sadistic man, who I thought was my uncle but now I learnt isn't. The only person to show me any love killed herself and abandoned her adopted child to escape him. I smoke drugs and drink excessively to try and forget who I am and wish that I had never been born, but apart from that, I'm fine.' Raj clenched his fists and felt his entire body tensing.
'I am sorry, Raj,' said his father.
'Save it for when you meet God!' shouted Raj standing up from his chair.
'Raj, please sit down. let's talk.'
'What did I die from?'

'What?'
'What did Deepak tell you?'
'He said you had a high fever as it was so cold in London and you died from a chest infection,'
'And you didn't bother checking?' shouted Raj feeling himself lose control of his emotions.
'We couldn't Raj. We were in hiding from Rahul. I couldn't just get on an aeroplane and come over to London. I had changed my name and my passport had a different name.' His father's voice was pleading and he broke out into another coughing fit.
'You are hiding from Rahul in a city just a few miles away from his empire. That sounds really fucking clever.'
'Maybe I am tired of running, Raj,' replied his father.
'Just as well you are in that wheelchair, then,' Raj said, as he turned away from his father to leave.
'Raj, please! I beg for your forgiveness.'
Raj paused and stood statue still for a few seconds. He recalled what Gabby had said to him about forgiveness. He turned back to his father and saw the torment in his eyes and the crippled state of his body.
'I can never forgive you for faking that fire and destroying so many lives, but I can forgive you for not coming back for me. I can see that it was not your intention to leave me. I hope that is enough to feed your guilty conscience.'
The father looked at his son with teary eyes and wept like a child. As he cried, he coughed violently and his body shook with pain. He wiped the tears from his eyes and phlegm from his mouth with his cloth and smiled at his son.
'That is more than I deserve and gives my soul comfort enough to face the next life. Thank you, my son.'
Raj took one final look at the broken old man and made his way through the side alley of the house, collecting

the photo album along the way and then into the front garden. He walked back out of the rusty gate where three men were waiting outside leaning on a black Land Rover. He nodded to them and then taking a right, he started moving down the road towards the bus station. Behind him, Rahul and his two men entered the house and made their way to the back garden.

CHAPTER TWENTY

The nurse checked the dial on the blood pressure machine, looked at her watch and then back at the dial. She released the pressure and removed the cuff from the man's arm and noted the reading down on the form pinned to the clipboard. She hung the clipboard back onto the end of the bed and walked off without a single word to the recuperating man on the bed. Vijay leaned his head back onto the pillow and groaned heavily as the pain in his leg shot through his body. He closed his eyes and clenched his fists tight to fight the pain and slowly, the intensity eased and the pain became more tolerable. He lay there staring up at the hospital ceiling and thanked God that he was still alive. He was facing another few weeks of rehabilitation but he didn't care. Only two days earlier, he thought he was dead for sure when Manoj pointed the gun at his head. He had said his last prayers and was prepared to sacrifice himself for his friends. Instead, Raj had agreed to tell Rahul where his father was to save their lives, but only if Rahul promised to leave the rest of his family alone. Raj understood how Rahul's mind worked and that at his stage of life he valued respect and honour above money. Getting revenge on Raj's father would send a message to everyone in his organisation and that of his enemies. There was an intense five minutes, while Rahul took in the new information and eventually agreed with the plan. Once Rahul had left, Raj called for an ambulance and they explained to the police that Vijay had tried to stop a burglar that he had walked in on in the hotel room. Rahul had any CCTV footage from the hotel deleted and spoke to his police contacts.

Manoj was discharged in the morning but Vijay's wound was more severe so he would be spending a few more days in the hospital. Over the last couple of days, he had thought about everything that had happened, which prompted him to think over his future. He had been hiding his true feelings from his family and that was one thing he had to change. He should be honest, even if it meant opening himself up to insult and pain. Manoj was an example of someone being true and standing up for their beliefs. He would leave hospital and then have an honest conversation with his mother. As he lay there thinking about how he would approach the topic, Raj arrived and grabbing hold of Vijay's hand, he sat down on a chair next to him.

'How did it go?' asked Vijay.

'Not so great,' Raj replied honestly. 'How are you?'

'Don't worry about me. I'm used to getting shot,' Vijay laughed.

They both turned their heads towards a sound at the door as Manoj arrived, holding a big bunch of flowers and a box of chocolates. His face wore three plasters and there were stitches on his chin covering a red and angry scar. His left eye was swollen and black from where one of Rahul's goons had punched him. Around the top of his arm was a tightly wound bandage hiding the deep gash. He walked up to the bed and dropped the box of chocolates onto the injured man's leg. Vijay winced in pain and let out a curse towards his friend.

'Sorry brother,' apologised Manoj, as he gently lifted the box off the bed.

After placing the flowers on a side cabinet, Manoj sat and opened the box of chocolates. He dropped the wrapper on the floor, opened the lid and picked out a small, round caramel flavoured chocolate, which he shoved into his mouth.

'Caramel, my favourite,' he said as he closed his eyes and groaned with delight.
'Do you ever stop eating, Manoj,' laughed Raj.
'Constant hunger gives you appreciation for even the smallest of things,' replied Manoj as he popped another chocolate into his mouth. He offered the box to Vijay, who shook his head, so he passed it on to Raj.
'How's the arm?' asked Raj as he fished out a Turkish delight from the box.
'Very sore but looking at poor Vijay, here I think I got the better deal. How did it go with your family, Raj?'
Both Vijay and Manoj looked at Raj in anticipation. They hoped that he would have some good news for them.
Raj fell silent, took another chocolate from the box and bit it in half. He took in the warming taste of coffee and thought about the question. He had travelled back by bus that morning, feeling nervous and frightened about what he had done. He had sacrificed his father to save his friends. His loyalties had been torn. On the one hand, his father deserved his fate and should pay for what he'd done, but he was still his father and that meant something. But knowing how his father's deeds had affected his family, Raj no longer felt any guilt; karma had to be served. He turned towards his friends. They listened intently as Raj told them that he had found his father all alone and close to death. He told them how his father's plan to fake their deaths had led to heartbreak and suffering and caused the death of his mother. He told them that he had lost hope of ever seeing his siblings and that he was truly alone now. He then told Vijay about how his father had conned Rahul, but that Vijay's father had known nothing of his plans.
Vijay gazed away as Raj told him the truth. He then turned to Raj and held out his hand which Raj grabbed hold of.

'It's all in the past now, so no use dwelling on it. You have paid your father's debt by saving our lives, Raj.' Manoj stood up, walked round to where Raj sat and wrapped an arm around his shoulder.

'As long as I live, you will not be alone Raj,' he said, 'I am your brother, Radhika is your sister in-law and Navjot is your nephew.'

'You have two brothers, whether you like it or not, Raj,' said Vijay squeezing Raj's hand. 'Remember when my mother used to always call you "son" when we were little. She used to call you my brothers when she asked after you both. She liked to imagine she had more than one boy, a typical Indian mother, I guess,' laughed Vijay.

Raj squeezed Vijay's hand tight and gave Manoj a hug. He felt a lump in his throat; a sense of belonging flowed within him once again.

'For so long I have felt alone and abandoned but I have hope by the words you have just spoken. You will never know how much that means to me,' Raj replied.

'We will help you search for your brothers and sister, so don't worry,' comforted Vijay.

Raj smiled at his two friends and lifting the chocolate box, handed it back to an eager Manoj.

'So, what are your plans Manoj?' asked Raj.

'With the money I have, I can buy a nice little house back home in Punjab,' he replied. 'Radhika wants me to set up a clothes shop where she can work as a tailor so I will look into that. I just hope that people will accept us now,' he said with a frown.

'If they don't, I will arrest them and they can spend some time in the cell,' said Vijay with his policeman's voice.

'Arrest them all the way from Delhi? That will be tough even for the hero who got shot by a gangster, twice,' laughed Manoj.

'I'm not going back to Delhi,' replied Vijay.

'You are leaving the police force?' asked Raj.
'I've had enough of living away from home and I miss my mother's cooking too much, so I too am moving back home. I have been offered a senior role at Nakodar police station by Inspector Cheema. He says that he is close to retiring and wants someone competent to take over when he goes.'
'That's great, Vijay,' said Raj, taking his hand again and giving it a gentle squeeze.
'I can't believe after all these years that we will be living in the same village again, Vijay,' said Manoj, elation showing clearly on his face.
'Oh damn! I forgot. You will be there too. Maybe I will go back to Delhi.'
'Oh shut up, you old grandad!' replied Manoj. 'Raj, you should buy yourself a house in the village too and then we will all be together again. We will find you a nice Indian bride and you can forget about that Gabby girl.'
'That does sound tempting,' replied Raj. 'I might take you up on that, one day.'
'So, what will you do now?' asked Vijay.
'There are a few things that I need to do back in London, before I can think about the future,' Raj responded. His mood became darker thinking of the cold streets of London and the confusion he had left behind. 'I need to resolve my feelings for Gabby and draw a line under my relationship with Lucy. Most of all, I need to find that so-called uncle of mine.'
'Why would you want to do that, Raj?' asked Vijay, showing his concern.
'For forgiveness,' replied Raj.
Manoj and Vijay both looked at him in surprise.
'I realise that I have been wallowing in self-pity for the last few years and that I really need to forget the past and focus on the future. To do that, I need to forgive

Deepak for everything he has done. I also need forgiveness from him for the pain Lucy and I inflicted on him. When I forgave my father, not for everything but in part, I felt a heavy weight lift from me. I want to feel free and move on. Gabby tried to teach me that forgiveness lets you move forwards with your life and sets you free. You no longer allow someone else to have authority over your mind and heart. I didn't understand or believe that before, but I do now so as soon as I get back to London, I will seek him out and ask for his forgiveness.'

'I thought you didn't know whether he was alive or dead,' said Vijay.

'This may sound crazy, but for the last few days I've had this recurring dream, in which my uncle and I are alone in a room and we are talking. After a while, he disappears and I am all by myself. Then the room turns into a ball of light and I feel this immense joy and happiness that I've never felt before. Gabby has described that feeling to me before. She said it only comes from forgiveness. It's heart-breaking when I wake up and that feeling of pure joy slowly fades away. I want to hold onto that feeling forever so if forgiving Deepak is the way to do it, then that's what I'll do.'

Vijay and Manoj both looked at Raj and smiled, but in their hearts they felt a touch of fear and foreboding.

*****

The heart monitor bleeped as the syringe injected another dose of antibiotics and morphine into the patient's body through the catheter in a vein in his neck. The cuff over the man's arm inflated automatically and recorded his blood pressure on another screen. The heart monitor bleeped again as the pulse oximeter hooked to his finger measured the amount of oxygen in the man's body. Apart from the sound of machinery, the room was silent and relatively dark. For ten days, the man had been unconscious and unaware of where he was and in what condition he lay. His wounds had been slowly healing but his broken body was far from mended. The crushed bones of his left hand would render it useless for the rest of his life and the three fingertips that no longer bore nails had turned yellow and infected. The swelling in his mouth caused by the tooth extraction had just started to reduce, but the deep cut now stitched in his chest still oozed puss that needed to be cleaned regularly. His right knee was all but ruined and the cut in his thigh still sore and angry. The electric shock he had endured had left burn marks across his body and had also caused scarring to his kidneys. As the clock struck two o'clock in the morning, the man's finger twitched and he took in a deep breath, as if he had just emerged from under water. His eyes opened reluctantly and although the lights were dim, he squinted like a new-born baby. Deepak tried lifting his left arm a little but couldn't feel any sensation in his hand. He lay in the darkness adjusting his eyes to the surroundings. His mind felt drowsy and numb and he was having trouble remembering where he was or how he had got there. He searched the depths of his mind for an answer but only silence met his questions. He turned his head to the left an inch and pain shot across his jaw causing him to wince with agony. He took deep breaths and then prepared himself for more pain as he turned his head further left. He gazed at the monitors that showed his vital signs and the row of syringes that were pumping him full of drugs. Once he realised he was in a hospital, he felt a tiny spark in his memory and the image of a woman in a red dress and tartan scarf flashed across his mind. He closed his eyes and focused on that image and

with intense effort brought the woman back into his memory. He started to paint a picture around the woman. A scene started to unfold and he found himself looking at a huge warehouse with hot molten metal burning all around him and characters from Star Trek stood in a semi-circle like cowboys ready for a gunfight. The picture panned to the right and a man he recognised stood there holding a metal rod, but he couldn't see who he was pointing it towards. He focused on the man as he tried to recall who it was but the face became blurred and distorted. He kept moving to the right until he came across another man, but this one was sitting in a chair with his head lowered to his chest. He walked towards him slowly and as he approached him, the man looked up and Deepak screamed in horror. At the sight of himself, beaten and broken, all the memories came flooding back and anger pervaded his mind. He had been tortured and humiliated by the boy who was once his belonging and for that he would have his revenge. To his right, there was a table with an assortment of pens and his mobile phone. He moved the fingers of his right hand and felt something attached to it so he lifted his arm towards his mouth and using his teeth pulled it off. Intense pain shot through his jaw but he ignored it and moved his hand towards his neck. He felt for the tube that was inserted into his neck and slowly pulled it out, splattering blood over the white bedsheets. He leaned towards the table and stretched out his arm to reach the phone. He switched it on. The battery was on red and he only had two percent charge left. He scrolled through his contacts, found Mark's name and rang his number. Deepak's anger flared as the tone rang endlessly; after a minute, Mark finally picked up the call.
'Is that you, Detective?' asked the trainee groggily.
'Come to the hospital now and take me home,'

demanded Deepak through raspy breaths.
'I'm not sure you can be discharged yet, Sir. You looked pretty bad earlier on, when I visited.'
'I don't give a fuck what you think. Just get here now!' he said as the phone battery died and everything went silent.
Deepak closed his eyes and hoped that the young constable would be frightened enough to obey him. He was relieved to hear that Mark had already visited, as he wouldn't have been able to tell him where he was.
Deepak continued to remove all the equipment from his body in the hope that Mark would come to his salvation. He tried moving his left hand but the crushed bones had destroyed all feeling in his fingers. He used his teeth again to remove the blood pressure cuff from his arm and then fell back on the bed exhausted. Pain racked his body and his breathing had become ragged but hatred and thoughts of revenge consumed him. With great effort, he swung his legs from the bed and sat on its edge. He touched his right thigh and followed the deep scar with his fingertip down to his knee which burned like fire. His entire right leg felt numb and useless and he knew that he would not be able to put any pressure on it. He would have to rely on his left leg to move. He sat in the darkness while his monitors flashed silent redundant warnings for a sleeping duty nurse. He waited for what seemed hours, replaying the torture scene in his mind, allowing the memories to fuel his hatred towards Raj and Lucy. As he replayed the scene in his head for the hundredth time, he heard a noise behind him and he turned to see Mark.
'Help me get off this bed and then get me out of here,' the detective whispered.
Mark walked over to stand in front of Deepak and looked at him with concern.

'You look like shit, Sir. I don't think you are going anywhere. Let me go get the nurse.'
In his weakened state, Deepak could no longer threaten the young man with violence. He grabbed hold of the constable's arm and pulled him closer towards him.
'I can give you money, Mark, lots of it. Just get me out of here!'
'I don't want your money,' replied Mark.
'Buy yourself a new car or treat your girlfriend,' pleaded the detective.
'I don't have a girlfriend.'
'That's because you have a shitty car and no money you idiot,' said Deepak raising his voice.
'Look, keep your money. I can see how much you want to get out of here, so I'll help you, but it's at your own risk.'
'Fine, help me get down from the bed and then you'll have to support my right side.'
Mark placed both of his arms around Deepak and slowly lifted his upper body up from the bed until his feet were touching the floor. The detective winced as his damaged leg touched the floor. He could only balance on his other leg by holding onto Mark.
'Where are your clothes?' asked Mark.
'No idea. We'll have to go like this.'
Mark shook his head and removed his own coat. He wrapped it around the old man and slowly and painfully hobbled the detective out of the room and along the corridor. They crept past the sleeping nurse and as they passed one of the wards, Deepak saw a wheelchair tucked in a corner.
'Put me in the wheelchair,' he instructed the young man.
Once in the wheelchair, they made better progress out of the hospital and to Mark's car. They passed a couple of nurses along the way but they didn't seem bothered that

a patient was roaming around the hospital at three o'clock in the morning with a stranger. Mark assisted the old man into the car and abandoning the wheelchair in the car park, drove out of Ealing Hospital and towards Acton.

'How did I get to the hospital?' asked Deepak.

'A passer-by found you outside the station and ran in to tell us. We called the ambulance. What happened to you?'

'A bunch of yobs outside a pub decided to beat up on the brown guy,' lied the detective, as he felt himself drifting off to sleep with the soothing humming of the engine.

Mark fell silent. He could tell that the old man was lying but he didn't want to challenge him in his current state. Deepak forced his eyes open and stared out into the darkness of the streets that he was so familiar with but looked so different. He was no longer the powerful detective that ruled the streets with fear and terror. He had never been scared to walk the dark and threatening alleyways of his hometown. Looking out into the darkness now, he felt fear for the first time and knew that a thousand petty criminals would celebrate his downfall. The word would already be out that the detective had been given a beating. The only silver lining was that he was about to retire anyway, so there was now even more reason for him to move away from the area. He felt his anger rise further as he thought about what they had done to him and how that had jeopardised his plans to move to India. He squirmed in his seat as pain shot through his body and he felt bile rise from his stomach to his throat. He fought the desire to throw up. He closed his eyes again and allowed himself to drift off to sleep until they reached the outside of his house. Mark helped him out of the car and supported him to the front door,

where the detective showed him where he kept his spare key. They entered the house and together made it to the living room, where Mark gently lowered him into an armchair. Mark walked over to the light switch and flicked it on.
'Turn that fucking thing off!' Deepak shouted.
Mark turned the light back off and then looked around the shadowy darkness of the Deepak's house. The place reeked of cigarette smoke and mould and what little furniture there was looked old and worn. The sofa was threadbare and the walls stained and yellow.
'Go get me some clothes from upstairs, first room on the right,' Deepak instructed.
Mark walked up the stairs and was aghast at the squalor that the old man was living in. The upstairs not only smelt of smoke and mould but also of urine and sweat. Mark covered his mouth and nose and quickly grabbed some clothes from the floor and returned downstairs. With great difficulty and much swearing and yelling from the detective, Mark helped him dress.
'Right. Is there anything else you need before I go?' asked Mark, keen to leave.
'From the kitchen, get me a box of paracetamol, a bottle of whisky and pass that packet of cigarettes and lighter,' he said pointing at the small coffee table.
Mark fetched him the things he wanted and placed the items with an empty glass on the coffee table, which he pushed closer to the old man.
'Now you can go but come back at seven thirty tonight,' he instructed.
'But I start work at seven.'
'You still work for me so just do this last thing for me and then I'm done,' he replied feeling the pain and exhaustion starting to take over him.
Mark nodded and returned to his car. Inside the house,

Deepak sat on the sofa, drank his whisky, smoked his cigarettes and swallowed pain killers until Mark's return. All the while, his fury swirled in his stomach until it had taken over his mind. All he could think about was revenge. He felt pity for himself as he sat there, crippled and weak, like a frail old pensioner. He would ensure that those responsible rued the day that they let him live.

CHAPTER TWENTY-ONE

The night was bitterly cold but the cloudless sky gave the moon permission to spread its light across the graveyard and over Gabby as she sat on a small bench a few yards away from a gravestone. She looked at the large stone cross that stood proudly over the grave and admired its strength and purpose. Whenever she felt her faith wavering, she would come and sit by the cross and let its spirit exorcise her bleak thoughts. For the past few days, she had felt deep sadness and loneliness. She was no stranger to being alone but whenever she got close to someone, it made isolation unbearable. She felt sorrow for not having helped Raj enough to battle the demons that were destroying his life. She hoped that he had found some comfort in India and that any revelations there didn't make matters worse. There was nothing more that she could do for him now. His life had taken on its own momentum and would lead him to his final destiny. Karma had been awoken and would finish what she and Lucy had started. As she sat staring at the cross and wishing she was back home with her father, she heard soft footsteps approaching from behind. Lucy gently sidled down next to her and put an arm around her sister.

'Why do you always sit here staring at that cross?' Lucy asked.

'It brings me comfort,' replied Gabby.

'Do you even know who this Seth Megane is?' asked Lucy reading the name on the gravestone.

'No, but he must have been loved dearly. The flowers around the grave are beautiful and always fresh like a wonderful winter garden.'

'Are you feeling sad that your boyfriend left you here alone?' asked Lucy as she played with Gabby's hair.
'I'm alone even when there are a hundred people around me, Lucy. There is only one thing that would make me happy but that cannot happen because I have to look after you and make sure you don't get up to mischief.'
'Well, you made a bit of a hash out of that!'
'That makes things immensely worse. Father won't be happy with me for not restraining you better.'
'Father doesn't care about you Gabby.'
'Don't say that.'
'If he cared about you, why would he send you to West London of all places? There are a thousand better places on this rotten Earth that he could have sent us. Although it's an improvement on the last place we went to. I mean Brisbane has got be the most boring city in the world.'
'I liked it,' replied Gabby.
'Well, you would.'
Both girls fell silent, lost in their own thoughts about the coming days and where life would lead them next. They never stayed too long in one place and their time in West London had almost come to an end.
'What are you doing here anyway, Lucy?' asked Gabby breaking the silence.
'I told the church that last week was my last session, so I have a free night tonight. Raj was my last client before wrapping up here,' replied Lucy.
'You should have left him alone; I was getting through to him.'
'Gabby, how many times have you made the same mistake? These people you try to help fall in love with you and their problems get worse because you can't love them back, well not in the way they want you to. Trust me! My way works far better. Didn't he find out

about his family?'
'Not sure that will help him.'
'Salvation comes in many forms,' said Lucy. 'You did your best, so let it be. Anyway, what are we eating tonight? I'm famished.'
'I was just about to walk down to the fish and chip shop. What would you like?'
'Have you ever eaten anything else apart from fish on a Friday?' asked Lucy rhetorically. 'I'm going to cook a steak so just get me some chips please.'
Gabby headed towards the gate of the graveyard that led to the street, but Lucy called after her.
'It's freezing Gabby and you're walking around with that thin jumper. Here take my coat and scarf,' said Lucy, unravelling her tartan scarf from around her neck.
'I'm fine, Lucy. I don't like wearing coats,' replied Gabby.
'At least take the scarf,' insisted Lucy.
Lucy gently wrapped the scarf around Gabby's neck and then leaning forwards, she placed a kiss on her sister's cheek.
'There that's better. You're all set now.'
Gaby smiled at her sister and started walking back toward the gate.
'Oh, one more thing Gabby,' called out Lucy. 'I left my handbag at the church earlier, could you please pick it up for me. It's upstairs in the attic.'
Gabby nodded and smiled to her sister and then headed towards the church.

*****

Deepak poured the last drops from his bottle of whisky into his glass and lit another cigarette. His body and head felt numb from the cocktail of alcohol and painkillers he had been consuming all day. The pain all over his body had been reduced to a dull throbbing, which allowed him to walk unaided small distances. The house telephone had been ringing every hour and he knew that it would be the hospital looking for him. The police had also been ringing the doorbell and trying to sneak a peek through the windows. All through this, he had only got up twice to piss in the kitchen sink. He didn't want to waste energy climbing the stairs.

He had drifted in and out of sleep in his armchair and his dreams were filled with strange images and fleeting glimpses of his past. Disturbing mangled creatures prowled around him with their teeth gnashing and blood dripping from their jaws. He ran from them through a bleak wood where the trees seemed to be alive and from one of the trunks emerged the face of his wife. Her eyes were sorrowful and her branch like arms reached towards him but he ran on through a clearing in the trees. He ran until he thought his heart would explode and suddenly came to a halt at the edge of a mountainside. He looked downwards and there below him he could see a river of boiling blood and within it a thousand screaming souls. He backed away hoping to feel the trees behind him but instead he fell backwards down another mountainside and landed on sand. At first, he was relieved that the sand had softened his fall but then he lifted his hands and saw that they were burnt with tiny flames that danced across them. He screamed as he started sinking down into the burning sand and deathly fireballs hailed from the sky. The creatures had returned with bows and rained arrows down at him from atop the mountain. As he shielded himself from the arrows, he was transported back in time to when he was a young boy shielding himself from the belt of his father. He felt himself being dragged across the yard by his arm and thrown into the outdoor toilet that reeked of faeces and urine. He sat there scared and crying in the dark for hours until his father fell asleep drunk. His sister opened the door and pulled him out and gave him a piece of bread that she had saved from her own measly supper. He followed his sister to bed and they both lay there in the dark holding hands, wishing that their mother was still alive. The dream shifted again and this time he found himself tied to a chair with a hammer cracking open his knee cap. He screamed at the top of his voice and cried for his mother to come save him but she stood silently at the back of the room. He knew that she would not save him. She hadn't even been able to save herself from her husband. As a knife cut through his chest, he felt his mother's presence next to him and when he looked up, he saw that she held the blade dripping in his blood. That last dream had left him enraged as the memories of his childhood came flooding back. He read the time from his phone, picked up his glass and drained the remaining whisky. He took another drag of a cigarette and then as he put it out in the empty glass, the front door opened and in walked Mark.

'You are five minutes late,' groaned the old man as he strained to get out of his armchair.

Mark ignored the comment and walked over to help, but Deepak shrugged him off.

'I'm not a child!' he screamed.

Mark backed off and walked to the front door.

'I'll wait for you in the car then,' he said. 'You fucking old arsehole,' he added under his breath.

Deepak stumbled forward a few steps with his back bent and then slowly he straightened up and tried his best to walk normally. He lifted his coat from a hook by the door and with great difficulty swung it on and plodded into the kitchen. He opened the drawer next to the rusty old cooker and took out a large carving knife, which he

carefully tucked into the inside pocket of his coat. He slowly made it to the front door, walked down the garden path and crawled into the passenger seat of Mark's car.
'Where are we going?' asked Mark.
'To the church on St. Mary's Road,' replied the detective.

*****

Raj looked at the clock in the bar of the Marriot hotel, just as it struck midnight. He was feeling melancholy that he had to spend his last night in Mumbai on his own. Vijay was still in hospital and Manoj had returned to Dharavi to be with his wife and child, who was ill. He took a sip from his glass of Jack Daniels and thought of his bittersweet time in India. Meeting his friends after all those years had been a joyous occasion and one that he would cherish for the rest of his life. He finally felt that he had a family, even though they were not of his own blood. Vijay and Manoj had treated him like a brother and he would make sure that he kept in touch with them and visited them often. He even had plans at the back of his mind to move to India one day and buy a house in his childhood village. The bitter side to his time in India had been seeing what had become of his real family. His father had become a twisted and tortured soul who had destroyed the lives of all his family with greed and stupidity. The truth had driven his father almost insane and had eaten away at him until he begged for death to take him. Learning that his mother had died had felt like losing her twice in one lifetime. The hope of seeing her again had given him something to live for and faith to believe once more. Knowing that his two brothers and sister were still alive had also given him some comfort and as soon as he was back in London, he would start the search for them, with help from Vijay and Manoj. He looked at the clock again; it would be around seven thirty in the evening back in London. He smiled to himself; he knew exactly what Gabby would be doing right now. She would be on her way to buy fish and chips for her Friday night treat, which she rarely missed. They had spent a couple of wondrous evenings sitting in the cold on a street bench, eating fish and chips out of the paper with passers-by giving them strange looks.

'Another top-up?' asked the barman, noticing Raj's empty glass.

Raj looked up from his thoughts and nodded to the barman.

The barman picked up the glass and poured Raj a double and threw in some ice. He placed the glass back in front Raj, who was sitting on the barstool in a near empty bar.

Raj removed his wallet from his pocket and was about to pull out some money, when the barman stopped him.

'On the house, if you answer the following question.'

'Question?'

'Pleasure or business?' asked the barman.

'Neither,' replied Raj.

'Intriguing.'

'Intriguing no, tragic yes,' replied Raj with a smile, as he took a sip from the glass.

'Right. So there is no way you can say that and not tell; I won't allow it.'

'It's complicated.'

'Give me the edited version.'

'Well, I'll try,' said Raj, taking another sip from his glass. He would normally never indulge anything about his personal life to a stranger, but several glasses of whisky had softened his inhibitions.

'There's this girl…'

'I knew it.'

'There's this girl that I love, who has a twin sister who is evil and together they led me to discover that my family, who I thought had died when I was thirteen, were still alive. I came to India to find them but instead found a dying father and that my mother had already died. My brothers and sister are alive somewhere but no one knows where. I learnt from my dying father that my abusive uncle wasn't really my uncle and he was the reason why I thought my family were dead in the first place.'

'Wow, that's tragic. Tell me about this girl that you love?'

'I have this constant aching to be with this girl, because when I'm close to her, I feel at peace and calmness comes over me. It's like all the bad things in the world at that moment just don't matter anymore and I have a feeling of pure love.'

'Does she know?'

'I think so.'

'Does she have the same feelings?'

'I don't think so.'

'Your life is tragic my friend. Here, have another drink on the house. I think you need it,' said the barman topping up Raj's glass.

'So, what's your next move?'

'I go back home tomorrow.'

'What are you going to do when you get back home?'

'I will tell this girl that I can't live without her and it doesn't matter that she doesn't love me back.'

'What if she wants to move on, my friend?'

'Then life won't be worth living.'

*****

Deepak looked up at the stairs and grimaced as he rubbed at the excruciating pain coursing through his knee and leg. His breath was ragged as the effects of the pain killers and alcohol started to wear off. The burn marks on his chest were stinging and itchy but he resisted the urge to scratch at the blackened skin. He climbed up one step at a time, holding on to the banister. One agonising step after another, he climbed the stairs until he reached midway and then stopped to catch his breath. His head had started to spin and he felt nauseous as bile climbed up his throat, threatening to explode from his mouth. Searing acid burned the inside of his oesophagus as he threw up a little into his mouth. He gasped for air as he swallowed back the vomit and started coughing. He punched the wall next to him and cursed those that had created the pathetic creature he had become. With a renewed determination, he carried on up the stairs until he had reached the top and then stood just outside the door, taking deep breaths. He closed his eyes, controlled his breathing and waited until the spinning in his head had reduced to a slight sway. He grabbed hold of the door handle and pushing the door open, stepped inside the attic. He looked around the empty room and slammed the door shut in frustration. All that wasted effort and agony for nothing. He was exhausted and couldn't face climbing back down the stairs without a rest, so he stumbled towards a chair and sat down.

'Fuuuucckkk!' he screamed to the empty room, clenching his good fist into a ball and punching himself in the thigh. He closed his eyes as the pain shot through his body and the nauseous feeling returned. He dropped to his knees on the floor and threw up violently. He then wretched a couple of times before the sickness abated. He forced himself up from the floor, wiped the tears from his eyes and wiped his mouth with the back of his sleeve. He started to walk back towards the door, when he noticed something from the corner of his eye. He turned towards the object and walking towards it, lifted it up onto a chair. He unzipped the handbag and took out a passport. The image was of the girl who had led his torture. As he looked in hatred at the pretty face, he heard footsteps coming up the stairs. He quickly removed the knife from his coat and hid it behind his back. He positioned himself behind the door, so whoever it was wouldn't see him as they entered.

The handle moved downwards and the door swung slowly open. In came Gabby, who walked straight up to where Deepak had been sick and stared at the vomit on the floor. Deepak slammed the door shut and stood in front of it blocking her exit.

'Hi Lucy James,' said Deepak still holding the knife behind his back.

Gabby turned and looked at the old man, who stood with his back against the door and with pain written all over his face.

'I'm not Lucy,' replied Gabby calmly.

'The tartan scarf and that pretty face say otherwise,' he replied.

'You don't look very well,' said Gabby.

'No shit!' he shouted, 'What did you think I would look like after you left me for dead, you bitch.'

'You're Deepak, Raj's uncle,' stated Gabby.

Deepak let out a snigger and stepped forwards towards Gabby, who took a couple of steps back, being careful to avoid the soiled floor.

'I am not that bastard's uncle,' the old man said, as he moved closer to Gabby.

'Why don't you sit down and we can talk about whatever has happened?' suggested Gabby.

Deepak seemed to relax for a moment, as he listened to Gabby's soft voice and looked into her deep wondrous eyes. He saw no hatred there, only pure love. For an instant, he felt he was a little child again feeling the warm hug of his mother, days before she was suffocated to death by his drunken father. He could feel his mother's soft hands stroking his hair and the smell of the oils she used on her skin. Jasmine and sandalwood filled his senses as he dug his face deeper into his mother's breast. He was a child again experiencing the unconditional love of a blessed soul. He closed his eyes and tried hard to hold onto the image but his mother slowly faded away and he was left alone in the darkness of his bedroom and all he could hear was wild ramblings of his drunken father. He opened his eyes and anger grew inside him once again. He walked towards the young woman. Gabby backed away further, until she was pressed up against the back wall of the attic. Her head touched the round stained-glass window showing the image of Jesus in His mother's arms and the light from the street lamp bathed her in its ethereal radiance creating a halo around her face. Deepak walked up to Gabby and looked deep into her eyes and doubt touched him again, but hate had so consumed him that he was powerless to fight it. Deepak drew the knife from behind his back and placed the sharp tip against Gabby's stomach. He pushed the blade so it just pierced her skin, wanting to see the fear in her eyes. He searched deep in her eyes for signs of panic or anguish, but he found only peace. He trembled with uncertainty as the blood began to drip from the cut and he found himself unable to avert his eyes from hers. His lips began to quiver and tears flowed from his eyes uncontrollably. He lifted the knife away from Gabby's side and for an instant thought of turning round and walking away but at the last moment he caught sight of her tartan scarf and remembered the terrible torture. He thrust the blade deep into her flesh and felt a gush of blood pour from her wound. Gabby's eyes widened as the blade entered her body and she lifted her arm to grab hold of the old man's hand. As she touched his hand, Deepak felt a wave of inconceivable love and as he pulled out the blade, he grabbed hold of the girl and cursed himself.

'What have I done?' he screamed.

He gently lowered her to the floor and pressed the wound with his hand trying in vain to stop the blood from flowing. He held her face with the other hand and wept like a child who was looking upon the dying body of his mother. Gabby looked at the old man as her life ebbed away and she smiled at him.

'I forgive you,' she whispered.

The old man's heart broke and weeping still, he placed the blade on the girl's chest and then stumbled from the room leaving the girl alone and dying.

CHAPTER TWENTY-TWO

Raj looked down at Gabby's face and felt nothing but numbness. He had become paralysed by the lifeless body that lay on the cold steel table in front of him. There were no tears and no grief. A ghostly white sheet shrouded her naked body up to her neck. With a faint smile on her lips, she looked as though she was only sleeping. Just as in the dream, she appeared more beautiful and content in death than in life. He took hold of her cold, pale hand and gently stroked it in the faint hope it might awake her. The fateful message from Lucy had flashed up on his phone along with what seemed like a thousand missed calls, just as his plane touched down. A clear crisp Sunday morning that had been filled with hope and dreams had been shattered by a single sentence. He had broken out in a cold sweat and started hyperventilating as the words sunk into his consciousness. The lady sitting next to him had called the steward over, who had led Raj from the plane first. The next couple of hours were a blur as he cleared customs, collected his luggage and caught a taxi straight to the hospital. All the things he wanted to tell her and all the plans he wanted to make had blown away into the wind like spirits. He leaned forward and placed a tender kiss on her light blue lips.

'This is all your fault,' said a voice from behind Raj.

Raj turned to see Lucy standing with a tissue in her hand and a tear in her eye.

'I am in no mood for your mind games Lucy, please leave me alone.'

'That's my sister lying there cold and lifeless, so don't you accuse me of playing mind games,' she

remonstrated.
Raj turned away from her and took hold of Gabby's hand again, while Lucy walked round the steel bed and stood opposite Raj. She stroked her sister's hair and lightly brushed her face with her hand. Then she leaned forward and kissed her on the forehead.
'What happened?' asked Raj.
'Deepak happened,' she answered.
Raj looked at her in anguish.
'You should have killed him when you had the chance,' accused Lucy.
'I didn't know he would do this,' pleaded Raj.
'What did you think he was going to do, give you flowers and a box of chocolates?' shouted Lucy.
'How?' asked Raj, his eyes transfixed on Gabby's face, as anger started to rise up from the depths of his belly.
'I found her at the church, bleeding from a stab wound to her side. If only I had found her sooner, I may have been able to save her,' sobbed Lucy. 'It should be me lying there, not her.'
'What do you mean?'
'That old bastard thought Gabby was me and wouldn't believe her when she told him otherwise. I held her in my arms trying to stop the blood and watched the light disappear from her eyes. They tried their best to bring her back, but it was too late. The last thing she told me was that she forgave him.'
'Forgiveness!' sneered Raj. 'Look at her Lucy, where did forgiveness get her!' he shouted turning away from the lifeless body. He grabbed the first thing he could get his hands on and hurled it across the room. The metal bowl clattered against the wall and fell to the floor. Raj dropped to the floor and sat against a cabinet. With his face in his hands, he wept. The tears that would not come before now flowed freely from his eyes. Lucy

walked over and kneeling in front of him, pulled him close and held him in a hug.
'This is what happens when you interfere with the natural order of things. Deepak was meant to die that day in the foundry, but you changed the path that karma was taking, so it took Gabby's life in exchange. As long as Deepak lives, the order of things is disturbed and nothing will be right.'
'This karma you talk of is bullshit,' said Raj as he removed his hands from his face and wiped the tears away. 'I went in search of my family and found more pain and misery. What have I done to deserve that? I forgave my father just before I let a maniac take his cancer-ridden life. What does that even mean?'
'Nothing is ever straight forward, Raj. You think you sentenced your father to death but what if you freed him? He would have suffered with his cancer for many more months, maybe years. His body and mind were slowly decaying, while he had no one to care for him. When you forgave him, it freed him and his suffering ended. You were his salvation, Raj, even though you think you did a terrible thing. Karma is just using you as the effect and there is nothing you can do. You must obey the rules or this is what happens,' she said pointing at Gabby.
'I don't know what to do anymore, Lucy,' he cried.
'End it, Raj. It must end today.'

*****

Raj sat in his usual darkened corner of the Karma Club sipping on his Jack Daniels and staring towards the bar where he had first seen Gabby. He imagined her still alive and floating gracefully between the customers, who were always captivated by her warm and joyous charm.

In his mind, he saw her walking towards him and replayed in his head the scene when she first spoke to him. She had agreed to meet him after work and he had felt elated. For the first time in many years, he had felt hopeful of the future. Everything that had happened since was like a dream, like an out of body experience with him watching the events unfold from above. His trip to India seemed like a distant memory, although only a couple of days earlier. He had left London with Gabby still alive. Guilt began to consume his mind. If he hadn't gone to India or if he had insisted that she went with him, she might still be alive. Images from the last few weeks kept infesting his mind: his father sitting in a wheelchair, cancer-ridden and coughing up mucus, a hammer shattering the knee of an old man tied to a chair, Manoj standing over Vijay with a gun pointed at his head, Lucy demanding that he sear out Deepak's eye, the smiling face of Gabby telling him not to grieve for the past, as if somehow she knew her own fate. He drained the remainder of his drink and made his way back to the entrance, where he handed in a token and was given his rucksack. He strapped the bag to his back and checked the time on his phone. It was approaching one o'clock in the morning. He walked the short distance to the E3 bus stop and waited the two minutes for the bus and then climbed on board. The bus was empty, except for a guy sleeping on the back seat with a piss stain around his crotch and an empty can of special brew in his hand. Twenty-two minutes later, Raj jumped off from the bus and walked a further ten minutes until he reached his destination. He stood outside a house that held so many bad memories and one that he hadn't gazed upon for many years. It looked the same, but also different as he surveyed it with older eyes. He saw his younger self as he walked from school in his ragged undersized uniform with his head down looking at his feet, dreading what suffering he would endure that evening. That little boy, helpless and vulnerable, had no chance of growing into a confident adult. He mourned that little boy who had been so emotionally tortured and given no hope of a future. He looked at the time on his phone again, walked across the road and entered the front garden. It all looked the same as he remembered; the rusty gate and the concrete footpath seemed cold to him as a child and cold to him now. He found the spare key, where it had always been, and opened the front door. The house was in complete darkness. He gently closed the door and stood in the blackness. As his eyes adjusted to the dark, he saw that nothing had changed since he had lived there, except everything looked more decayed. The change that hit him the most was the smell of the house. When his aunt was alive, it always smelt of fresh cooking, but now his senses were overcome by the smell of deviancy and sin. He walked down the hallway, into the large open plan living room and in the centre, he saw the shadowy figure of a man sitting in an armchair. He crept forward and stopped in front of the sleeping man. Even in the darkness, the sight of him instilled fear as memories of cruelty touched Raj's mind. He gazed upon the man's blood-soaked shirt and anger grew inside him, knowing it was Gabby's blood. An empty bottle of whisky sat on a table next to the armchair and a packet of cigarettes on his lap. Raj slowly backed away from the old man and returned to the hallway. He stood at the bottom of the stairs looking up. He felt his legs start to tremble as he began to climb the stairs. Sweat coated the palm of his hands. He dried his hands on his jeans and continued the climb until he stood on the landing. He suddenly felt hot as he approached what used to be his bedroom. He walked into his old room and switched on the light. Nothing had changed since he was there last. The same broken bed with a thin threadbare mattress lay in one corner, the closet where he used to hide from his uncle still sat lonely and pathetic against a tattered papered wall, the carpet stained and disgusting was still sticky under his feet. He walked over to the closet and opened the door. He saw the thirteen-year-old boy crouched in the corner, shivering with fear and cold. He looked under the bed and saw again the meagre bits of food that his aunt would dare place there for him. He took one last look around the room and then switched the light off. He made his way back down the stairs and into the darkness of the living room. He walked over to the curtains and opened them, allowing light from a streetlamp to banish some of the darkness. He removed the rucksack from his back and unzipped it. He then removed a large petrol jerry can and unscrewed the lid. He walked up to the old man and splashed the petrol onto his sleeping face and all over his body. Deepak awoke with a scream and gasped for air, as the liquid entered his mouth and his eyes. He raised his arms in vain to stop the liquid as Raj threw more and more at him.

'Please stop!' spluttered the old man, as he coughed out petrol from his lungs. 'What do you want from me?'

Raj emptied the last drops from the jerry can onto the pleading man and then placed it on to the floor next to him. He took out a packet of cigarettes and a lighter from his rucksack and approached Deepak. He checked the time on his phone and when it was exactly one fifty-two, he lit the cigarette and stared at the old man.

'I have this ritual that I performed every night for many years,' said Raj as he took a drag from the cigarette. 'At precisely one fifty-two in the morning, I would light up a cigarette and after smoking it, only then could I sleep. Do you know why?' he asked as he looked at Deepak's contorted face. 'I will tell you why,' he continued, not waiting for an answer, 'Because one fifty-two in the morning was the exact time that my house was set on fire, when I was only thirteen years old. It was the exact time that I thought all my family had died. It was the exact time that I had been smoking a cigarette with my friends and for many years I thought that was the reason why I was being punished. It turns out that was all bullshit. Funny story, don't you think?'

'Stop wallowing in your self-pity Raj. You're not the only person in this world to have had a tough childhood. When I was a little boy, my father would lock me up for hours in our outside toilet just because he was angry at the world for something. Scared and feeling nauseous from the smell, I would sit there trembling, trying to keep away from the rats that fed on the filth. Hungry and exhausted from the heat, I would finally be released by my sister, when my father eventually drank himself to sleep. It's no excuse, I know, but I need you to understand why I became this person. I didn't realise what I'd become until…,' he trailed off, as he looked at the blood on his shirt.

Raj was taken aback by the man's words and for a moment a spark of sympathy flamed within him, but just as quickly as it had appeared, it was gone and he saw again the cruel vile person he was.

'…Until you stabbed that innocent girl to death,' said Raj, finishing Deepak's sentence for him.

'I saw God in her eyes, Raj,' said Deepak.

'Was that just before you stabbed her or as she lay bleeding to death!' screamed Raj.

'Who was she?' asked Deepak.

Raj turned away from Deepak and paced up and down

the room, unable to fathom what was happening. He had expected an unrepentant sinner, cursing and swearing profanities towards him. He had expected Deepak to hurl abuse towards him and taunt him about the killing of Gabby, so that when he set him alight and watched him burn, he would feel no remorse. Repentance was not the way he had planned it.

'She was Lucy's twin sister and the purest soul you can ever imagine. She was kind, generous, humble, compassionate, loving, but her greatest gift was that she was forgiving,' Raj cried.

'As I pushed the blade deep into her, she forgave me. I've sat here for two days and thought of nothing else.'

'She shouldn't have forgiven you,' replied Raj, despondently.

'I forgive you for what you did to me, Raj, but I ask for your forgiveness in return,' pleaded Deepak.

Raj looked at the man in horror. Was this some kind of mind game or did Deepak genuinely want redemption. Raj stared at him, unable to read the expression on his face. The man he had hated for so many years and who had been orchestrating all the evil events in Raj's life was repenting.

'Tell me first why you told my family that I was dead!'

'Others suffering gave me pleasure. I wanted your family to suffer. I wanted you to suffer. As simple as that.'

Raj walked away from the old man and looked through the window into the darkness outside. He wanted so much to drop the cigarette into the petrol and set the place alight but Gabby's words were ringing in his ears. She had said that forgiveness was the key to salvation and if he wanted any hope for the future, he would need to forget about his past and move on. Deepak was part of a past that he could not change. The only thing he could do was to forgive and move on. He put out his

cigarette on the windowsill and walked back over to the old man.
'I forgive you,' he said.
Deepak looked at Raj and smiled. He then reached into the space between the arm and the seat of the armchair and pulled out a lighter. He looked at Raj and rolled his thumb over the spark wheel and let the flame dance in the air.
'No!' shouted Raj as he leapt forward to take the lighter from the old man.
As Deepak moved the flame towards his shirt, it caught the petrol and a huge fireball enveloped the old man. The flames quickly set light to the armchair and surrounding carpet, where the petrol had splashed. Raj searched around the room and grabbed a small blanket from a sofa and ran into the kitchen, where he soaked it under the tap. He returned as close as he could to the burning man and just as he was about to throw the wet blanket over him, a blistered and burning arm reached out towards him and grabbed hold of him. He tried to pull away but already his own arm had caught fire and as he struggled to get free, the flames started to spread across his body. With a scream, he yanked his arm clear and looked for the blanket but that too was now burning wildly. The entire room had become engulfed with flames. He slapped with his hands at the flames on his body, but the petrol had also splashed over him causing the flames to accelerate. Instinctively, he stumbled from the room and into the hallway and out through the door. The flames had taken hold of his legs and were rising towards his face. He ran into the street and fell to his knees as the intense heat started to scorch his skin. He felt a burning sensation on his head as the fire caught his hair and spread to his face. He screamed in agony and cried out for help.

Through the flames, Raj saw a bare footed woman appear in front of the burning house. She was dressed all in red with a tartan scarf around her neck. He could not tell if it was a trick of the shimmering heat, but from within her, there appeared another woman all dressed in white and as she walked closer towards him, great majestic white wings spread out behind her and she seemed to float in the air with grace and purpose. Behind her, he could see the woman in red turn around and head into the burning house. As Lucifer stepped lightly through the burning flames, great red feathered wings spread out behind her and a red tail swayed in the breeze.

The Angel Gabriel floated to Raj and wrapped her soft wings around him in a warm embrace and then there was no more pain. He felt himself being lifted upwards and as they climbed higher and higher, the sadness within his heart started to ebb away and all he felt was pure joy. Higher and higher they floated until his heart was so full of happiness that he passed into a dreamlike state, where he was between consciousness and ecstasy. He opened his eyes and looked at the angelic face of Gabby and then knew peace. She smiled at him and his heart leapt. His eyes slowly closed and all thoughts and memory of his mortal life faded. He gently fell into a deep and longing sleep that would last an eternity.

EPILOGUE

Vijay and Manoj carried their friend's body across the cremation ground and placed it on the funeral pyre with his feet facing south. His big toes had been tied together with string and his body wrapped in a white cloth and the pyre adorned with flowers. The two men walked over to the river and bathed themselves as the midday sun beat its heat over them. They walked back to the pyre, passing Radhika and Vijay's mother along the way; the women stood silently holding their palms together in prayer. The friends walked around the wooden pyre and then placed rice in Raj's mouth. They took a clay pot containing ghee and sprinkled it over his body and the pyre. A priest handed them a burning torch while muttering a hymn to scare away evil spirits. The two friends held the torch together and offered it to the dry wood and watched with mournful eyes as the pyre caught fire. The flames crackled and danced along the wooden sticks and then jumped excitedly onto the white cloth and then all over Raj's already scarred body. The four mourners and the priest watched as the fire raged and the flames rose up into the air, as if reaching for the sky.

High up on a hill, two Indian sisters sat huddled together holding hands and watching the ceremony unfold below. Lucia, bare foot and dressed in a red sari, placed an arm around Gabhasti.

'It's only his body,' said Lucia.

'I know, but that doesn't lessen the pain,' replied Gabhasti.

'After all these centuries, you still don't know how to let go. You need to stop getting attached to these mortals.'

'They need love.'
'That's your problem.'
'Why is love a problem?'
'Have you forgotten about poor old lovelorn Dante, who you drove insane?'
'Oh, and you didn't drive him mad with those visions of hell.'
'Well, at least he became famous for writing great poetry. I still think he should have given me co-author credit for those inferno mutterings.'
'We have a duty to ensure that justice is served.'
Lucia looked over at her twin and kissed her on the forehead.
'Where to next, dear sister?' asked Lucia.
'There was this woman in the village we just passed through, who was sat on the roadside crying for her daughter.'
'Why was she crying for her?'
'Her daughter has been taken by some bad men,' replied Gabhasti.
'Well serving justice to bad men is my business,' replied Lucia, as she stood up and pulled her sister to her feet. Lucia placed an arm around Gabhasti as they took one last look at the blazing fire in the distance and then hand in hand walked off towards a village, where a woman mourned for her lost child.

‘Angels exist because devils do’

‘The devils are always going to exist

If not in reality

then for sure in our minds

but to fight it

there will always

be an angel

and all you need to do

is follow that lil’ angel’

Saloni Verma
Find Saloni on Instagram : @salzwrites

By Harbinder Mathadu

The Stolen Soul of Somita

Reader's Digest Review

★★★★

'The Stolen Soul of Somita is an engaging and quick read. It combines the emotion and character development of a family story with the fast pace and intrigue of a thriller or detective genre novel. The contrast of Western and Eastern cultures is portrayed thoughtfully and used well to heighten the tension and explore character. The settings are fresh and well-rendered, with great details that feel lived-in and relatable across cultures.
The Stolen Soul of Somita is a well-written novel by an author who takes great care with settings, character and plot development. This novel will appeal to a wide audience, pleasing readers across multiple genres.'

Read on for a sneak preview

Prologue
A village in the Punjab, India

Shankar Lal awoke with a start and shot out of bed shaking his left leg furiously in an attempt to rid himself of the scorpion that was scurrying up it. Luckily for him the scorpion was only part of the weird dream he was having but unfortunately the screaming woman was not. He stood in the darkness and listened intently to the distant sound and realised the screaming was coming from somewhere in the village. He was normally a deep sleeper and would have slept through a marching brass band but the agonising screams of the woman had unnerved him and had chased away his sleep.

He walked across the hard clay floor of his room and wiped the sweat from his forehead with the back of his hand. Lighting a kerosene lantern he slipped into his sandals and loosely wrapped his white turban around his bald head. Throwing a shawl around his bare shoulders he walked over to the front door of his small humble home and swung it open. The monsoon rain lashed into his house drenching the now fully awake Shankar Lal. He slammed the door closed to both the darkness and the rain and crept back into his bedroom fetching an umbrella from atop of a rickety closet.

Wrapping himself tighter with his shawl and now armed with his umbrella he once again opened the front door. The full force of the rain hit him like a tidal wave but this time he took a deep breath and leapt into the alley holding the umbrella as close as possible to his turban. He could still hear the screams of the woman but now her miserable cry was joined by other muffled voices. Shankar Lal could not see ten yards in front of him so instead followed his ears and darted through the familiar narrow alleys of his village until he reached an open space. There on a grassy square in front of the baker's store and by the light of a partially visible moon he saw a large crowd of people gathered.

The villagers were all in vain trying to placate the screaming woman who was sat on the muddy ground slapping her hands against her chest whilst continually shrieking. Shankar Lal ran towards the crowd and on reaching the first villager he tapped him on the shoulder.
'Sangu, what's happened?' he asked.
The woman continued to shriek and was now pulling at her long and rain-soaked ebony hair.
'Shankar Lal, it is terrible my friend, Saravati's baby has disappeared and she has lost all her senses. She refuses to go inside and tell us what has happened,' replied Sangu, taking refuge under Shankar Lal's umbrella.
Shankar Lal looked towards the stricken woman sitting pathetically on the sodden mud pulling at her hair as if possessed by the devil himself.
'We have to get her out of this rain, come Sangu,' said Shankar Lal.
Shankar Lal followed by Sangu forced his way through the crowd who were all stood silently staring at the distraught woman. The two men knelt onto the muddy ground next to the grief-stricken woman.
'Saravati, it is Shankar Lal, do not worry we will find your baby but first you must come inside and tell us what has happened.'
Shankar Lal handed his umbrella to an elderly woman who was standing behind him and then with the help of Sangu took Saravati by the arms and heaved her up. Saravati continued to wail and tried to resist the two men but they were far too strong for her and lifting her from the ground they led her the short distance to her home.

Kamal one of the village elders had prepared a hot mug of milk and was now sitting cross legged next to Saravati on her bed. Kamal tried to force her to drink the milk but was rebuffed by huge sobs.
Shankar Lal and Sangu stood by the bed while the rest of the villagers had returned to their homes.

'Saravati please tell us what happened, we must contact the police.' pleaded Shankar Lal, drying his face with a towel.
Saravati looked up at Shankar Lal, and spoke through her tears, 'I have already been to Mr Mukhaji's house to use the phone but nobody opened the door and you know there is no other phone in the village,' she cried. 'The main road into the village has been flooded so there is no way of getting a message out until morning.'
Saravati breathed a huge sigh and tried hard to control her sobs. Kamal put an arm around her shoulders and again put the mug of milk to her lips.
'Drink, it will make you feel better,' assured Kamal.
This time Saravati grabbed the mug and took a small sip.
'Where is your husband and kids?' asked Sangu.
'He and the girls have gone to visit relatives in town and will not be back until tomorrow. I cannot contact them and they would not be able to return because of the flooded road.'
'Please tell us what happened so we can begin a search party,' pleaded Shankar Lal.
Saravati's expression was one of utter grief as she told of the events earlier that night.
'I had just put Somita into my bed after feeding her milk and gone back to the tap to wash her bottle when I heard a noise coming from my room but thought that it must be the rain pattering against the shutters. After I had washed up I went back into check on Somita…'
Saravati's sobs again grew louder. 'I noticed the shutters were open and went to close them thinking the wind may have pushed them open, that's when I noticed that Somita wasn't in the bed any longer.'
Saravati broke down and cried uncontrollably onto Kamal's shoulder. Sangu took a step towards Saravati wanting to comfort her but stopped as a young woman rushed into the room.
'Sister-in law what has happened, is it true what they are saying?' asked the newcomer.

Saravati looked up and suddenly her expression of grief was replaced by a look of pure venom. She wiped the tears from her eyes with her head scarf and standing up slowly walked up to the young woman and launched a slap with her right hand towards her, striking her full on the face. Manjula let out a shriek and stumbled backwards towards the open doorway. Sangu leapt forward and grabbed her just as she headed towards the hard stone floor. Saravati took a stride forward and launched another attack but Shankar Lal stood in her way and held her back.

'What have you done with my baby?' Saravati screamed.

Manjula, nursing her throbbing cheek stood next to Sangu with utter disbelief written on her face.

'Saravati, why would Manjula take your baby, you are delusional, you need to rest and let us try to find Somita,' said Shankar Lal sternly.

'No!' Saravati screamed, 'she has always hated me and has taken Somita to make me suffer. I can see her laughing at me behind that fake look of concern.'

Saravati again lunged for Manjula but Shankar Lal held her back.

'You best go Manjula,' said Shankar Lal, 'we will handle this.'

Manjula's eyes filled with tears as she held her palms together as if to pray. 'I know we have had our problems but I would never do anything to hurt you Saravati, I promise you,' she cried.

Saravati turned her face away from the anguished woman and walked back towards the bed. Manjula wiping away her tears left the room.

'Kamal keep Saravati here and try to keep her calm,' instructed Shankar Lal.

He then turned to Saravati and in the most reassuring voice he could muster, softly spoke.

'I promise we will do all that we can to find Somita, I am sure we will find her, do not worry.'

As he spoke the words Shankar Lal knew in his heart of hearts that Saravati would never again see her baby.

Printed in Great Britain
by Amazon

68911306R00175